What Reviewers Say

"With each new book Kim ⸻ ⸻ her storytelling. *Flight Risk*, he⸻ ⸻ction and vibrant depictions that ma⸻ ⸻ she was right in the middle of the story…⸻ moving with crisp dialogue, and effective use of the characters' thoughts and emotions…this reviewer could not put the book down. Baldwin outdid herself with *Flight Risk*…her best storytelling to date. I highly recommend this thrilling story." —*The Independent Gay Writer*

"A hallmark of great writing is consummate characterization, and *Whitewater Rendezvous* does not disappoint…Captures the reader from the very first page…totally immerses and envelopes the reader in the Arctic experience. Superior chapter endings, stylishly and tightly written sentences, precise pacing, and exquisite narrative all coalesce to produce a novel of first-rate quality, both in concept and expression." —*Midwest Book Review*

"Nature's fury has nothing on the fire of desire and passion that burns in Kim Baldwin's *Force of Nature*! Filled with passion, plenty of laughs, and 'yeah, I know how that feels…' moments, *Force of Nature* is a book you simply can't put down. All we have to say is, where's the sequel?!" —*Outlookpress.com*

"…filled with non-stop, fast-paced action…Tornadoes, raging fire blazes, heroic and daring rescues…Baldwin does a fine job of describing the fast-paced scenes and inspiring the reader to keep on turning the pages." —*The L Life*

"'A riveting novel of suspense' seems to be a very overworked phrase. However, it is extremely apt when discussing…*Hunter's Pursuit*. Look for this excellent novel."—*Mega-Scene* magazine

"A…fierce first novel, an action-packed thriller pitting deadly professional killers against each other. Baldwin's fast-paced plot comes…leavened, as every intelligent adventure novel's excesses ought to be, with some lovin'." —*Q Syndicate*

"Clever surprises and suspenseful drama resonate on each page, setting the wheels in motion for an exciting ride. Action sequences fire rapidly in succession leaving the reader breathless. The total effect will have you riveted to Kim Baldwin's book. Once you pick up *Hunter's Pursuit*, there is no putting it down." —*The Independent Gay Writer*

By the Author

Hunter's Pursuit

Force of Nature

Whitewater Rendezvous

Flight Risk

Visit us at www.boldstrokesbooks.com

FOCUS
OF
DESIRE

by

Kim Baldwin

2007

FOCUS OF DESIRE

ISBN 10: 1-933110-92-9
ISBN 13: 978-1-933110-92-9

THIS TRADE PAPERBACK ORIGINAL IS PUBLISHED BY
BOLD STROKES BOOKS, INC.,
NEW YORK, USA

FIRST EDITION: OCTOBER, 2007.

CREDITS
EDITORS: SHELLEY THRASHER AND STACIA SEAMAN
PRODUCTION DESIGN: STACIA SEAMAN
COVER DESIGN BY SHERI (GRAPHICARTIST2020@HOTMAIL.COM)

Acknowledgments

For M.—You've put up with an awful lot since I started to write, especially this last year. Thank you for your endless patience, for the countless sweet and selfless things you do for me, and for never complaining that I rarely cook anymore.

For my dear friend Xenia—as always, I am deeply grateful for your countless ideas and insights, unfailing enthusiasm, and most of all, for the good times. When the next book is published, I look forward to toasting it together.

Every day I say thanks for my good fortune to sign with Bold Strokes Books. My eternal gratitude to Radclyffe, publisher/author/mentor/friend, who has my deepest admiration for her talent, vision, humor, ability to inspire, and unmatched ability to find the right word at the right time, both in her prose and in everyday life.

I continue to learn and grow with each project, under the expertise of my superb editors. Shelley Thrasher, who did the lion's share getting this book in shape, my deepest thanks. Senior consulting editor Jennifer Knight, you remain the goddess. You've taught me so much, and my books are so much richer for your guidance and experience. Thanks also for Stacia Seaman's input and meticulous eye for detail. And Sheri—graphic artist extraordinaire—when I saw this awesome cover, it inspired some great new ideas for the book. I'm in your debt.

To Connie Ward, dual thanks—for your tireless efforts as BSB consulting publicist and for your wonderful insights and encouragement while beta reading for me. Also to my beta reader Sharon Lloyd, co-owner of Epilogue Books, who seems to catch every typo and other careless omission.

I have a wonderful bunch of friends who provide unwavering support for my writing endeavors. Linda and Vicki, Kat and Ed, Felicity, Marsha and Ellen, and Claudia and Esther. You are family, and near or far, I hold you always close to my heart.

And most especially, to all the readers who encourage my literary efforts by buying my books, showing up for personal appearances, and taking the time to e-mail me. Thank you so much.

Kim Baldwin 2007

Dedication

For my mother
Who always encouraged and supported
my creative efforts

CHAPTER ONE

New York City
October

Natasha Kashnikova wouldn't ordinarily have given the model a second glance. She favored blondes, and three delicious specimens were currently being made up there in her Manhattan studio for the cosmetics ad shoot, so chances were excellent she could have one or more of them later. But it was the short-haired brunette who caught her attention when she arrived wearing a sexy black minidress that looked like something a dominatrix might wear. *Well, aren't you just yummy?*

"Hello, Kash. I'm Fawn, and I am *very* happy to meet you."

Fawn squeezed the hand Kash held out, prolonging the contact. She was young—probably nineteen or twenty—and short for a model, only five-six or so, but her classically beautiful face and flawless complexion had obviously won her this opportunity. *And that smile. I bet you've practiced it in the mirror more than a few times.* Showcasing her full, rosy lips and perfect teeth, her smile oozed naughty sensuality and was guaranteed to sell a lot of lipstick.

Fawn released her finally, but maintained the smile and seriously direct eye contact as she took a deliberate step closer. "I can't tell you how thrilled and excited I am to finally get the chance to work under you."

Kash made her choice, but decided to let this one sweat a while before she acknowledged her acceptance. "Pleased to meet you, Fawn." She gestured toward the blondes, who were in the corner of her spacious loft studio. "If you'll join the others, we'll start soon."

Only a fleeting glance of disappointment passed over the brunette's face, enough for Kash to notice, but not so much as to appear unprofessional. "Of course."

The assignment was a breeze—two or three hours' work with four beautiful women. She took this kind of job almost exclusively these days because she made good money and invested little time, and also enjoyed an endless supply of beautiful sex partners.

She took the group shots first, then did the blondes individually, saving the brunette for last. Even after they were alone she remained all business, not because of any professional ethics but because the distance would enhance the moment when she let the model know she would get what she wanted.

Night fell as they finished the shoot, and the floor-to-ceiling windows that overlooked Central Park became mirrors in which Kash glimpsed herself in her low-cut black jeans and snug black T-shirt, her apparel of choice most days. She had begun to avoid her reflection lately because she could no longer ignore the small lines by her eyes and mouth and between her eyebrows. But the likeness in the window was kind, erasing the last decade of hard play and making her appear thirty again.

The layered, collar-length cut of her medium brown hair complemented her androgyny. Her face was strong, almost masculine, but full, feminine lips and long eyelashes over soft hazel eyes balanced her square jaw and chiseled features. Her enviable metabolism gave her the same lean, taut frame at nearly forty that she'd had two decades earlier.

"I think we're done." Kash wasn't surprised that Fawn didn't budge from her stool, even when she started turning off the lights that illuminated her from three sides.

"Before I leave I want to make sure that I've impressed you enough that I get to work with you again," Fawn said.

"Well, I know you can follow directions very well." Kash knelt to stow her cameras and lenses carefully in their bags. "That's very important."

"Oh, yes. You tell me what to do, and I'm there." The model slipped off the stool and approached Kash slowly, stopping only a couple of feet away.

"And I have to say your dress has made a favorable impression," Kash added as she stood and, for the first time, gave Fawn the benefit of an open, appreciative head-to-toe appraisal. "Is it meant to make a statement?"

"Let's say it was intended to get your attention," she replied, smiling that naughty bedroom smile.

"Attention or reaction?" Kash slowly circled the model to drink in the dress from every angle.

"Both."

"Then it's certainly done the trick." She let her gaze linger on the high, tight ass. The sheer, clingy fabric made it clear that Fawn wore nothing underneath. *Nice. Very nice.* She felt a sharp twitch low in her belly. "If I didn't know better, I'd say the design of this dress…" She feathered her hand over the large *X* the straps created on the silky skin of the model's back.

"Lets you know I like to play?" Fawn slowly faced her.

Kash stepped forward so that their bodies almost touched. "So, what's your game?"

Fawn didn't answer immediately. Instead she started to stroke Kash's face, but Kash intercepted her before she could and grasped her wrist firmly. Then she pinned both of the girl's hands behind her back and spoke into her ear. "Is this your game?"

Kash could feel her tremble as she nodded.

"Nothing too rough," Fawn whispered.

The spasm in Kash's belly became a steady throb. "Keep your hands right there."

She removed the long, silky scarf from Fawn's neck, tied it around her eyes, and smiled at her sharp intake of breath. Then she held Fawn's wrists behind her again while she kissed her neck, her shoulders, and the exposed skin of her back. Lightly at first, making her want more. Soon the kisses became bites. Not too hard, nothing to leave marks around that million-dollar face, but enough to elicit the first moans of excitement.

Glancing around the sparsely furnished loft, Kash dismissed the couch and half dozen comfortable chairs. The coffee table that held a tidy stack of recent magazines wouldn't do either. Her photo backdrops, lighting equipment, and a couple of sturdy stools filled the other side of the large loft, and her glass-and-chrome desk, crowded with papers and photos in neat piles, stood at the back. None of these were appropriate. She even considered the sink in the bathroom off to the left, and the other one, in her darkroom, next to it. But the last time she'd tried using a sink for something like this, it had broken off the wall right as the woman she was fucking was getting there, and both of them had gotten soaked.

No, the big off-white easy chair was the right choice today, she decided, visually gauging Fawn's height against it. She led the model over and stopped beside the waist-high, padded back. *Perfect.*

"Put your hands here. That's right."

Once Fawn had braced herself on the chair, Kash pressed down on her back until she was bent forward over it, invitingly poised.

She ran her hands down the model's sides to her hips and thighs, rewarded with more breathy moans, and when she reached the hem of the minidress and lifted it up to expose the firm, round ass, Fawn gasped and held her breath.

Kash put one of her legs between the girl's and used it to spread her thighs farther apart, opening her up. "Don't move." The model trembled again, and her hips swayed and rocked, clearly seeking some kind of direct stimulation. As Kash stepped back to admire the view, she unzipped her jeans and shoved her hand inside, quickly stroking her clit.

Whether it was her own arousal or the model's scent didn't matter. She knelt and positioned herself behind and beneath Fawn, and as she tasted the wetness, she wrapped her hands around the model's thighs, now fully controlling the amount and depth of contact.

Fawn's moans grew louder, intermingled with groans and sighs, and Kash held fast as the girl writhed.

"Fuck, that feels good," Fawn managed shakily. "Much more and you'll make me come."

Kash knew it was true; the girl was incredibly wet, and her clit was swollen and ready. She teased her with a few more strokes of her tongue, but stopped short of satisfaction. When she took her mouth away and stood, Fawn blew out a long, shaky breath of disappointment, but said nothing.

Abruptly, Kash thrust her pelvis against the model's ass and grabbed a fistful of her short hair. Fawn cried out and powered her hips back against Kash—hard, demanding.

"You want it so much." Kash wedged her hand between their bodies and pushed into her, penetrating her hard and deep, then began a hard, driving rhythm that matched the urgent pistoning of Fawn's hips.

The shrill ringing of her phone startled them both, but Kash barely paused. After three rings, the answering machine picked up, and a woman's voice came on after Kash's recorded greeting.

"I know you're there, Kash."

Fuck. Miranda. She didn't stop, but her distraction slowed her strokes.

"I'm waiting. And I'm going to keep talking until you pick up. Tell me, is she blond? Should I be jealous?"

At this remark, the model stiffened and turned her head toward Kash, but didn't take the blindfold off.

"Aw, damn. Stay there. Ignore that." Kash withdrew her hand and headed for the phone on a small table two feet away as the voice continued.

"And on our anniversary? You're screwing around while I'm waiting for you on our anniversary?"

As Kash snatched up the phone, she glanced at Fawn. She had straightened, but still hadn't removed the blindfold, though it was clear from her posture and uncertain expression that she was thinking about it.

"Damn it, Miranda. Not funny!"

The sound of laughter answered her. "You are so predictable, Kash."

"Let me call you back." Kash put her hand over the receiver and tried to head off a premature end to the evening's festivities. "Sorry, Fawn, I'll be right with you."

The model nodded, but Kash could tell from her restless fidgeting that she was ready to bolt.

"Hey, you're the one who told me this would be a good time to phone, and what I have to say will only take a couple of minutes," Miranda said. "I'm about to catch a flight to L.A., so I can't call you back."

Kash sighed. "All right. What's up?"

"I'm begging a favor. And before you say no, let me remind you that you still owe me big time for hitting on Stef. Consider this your requisite payback."

"Hey, come on with that already. I didn't know you were together," Kash argued, but she knew it was futile. It had been ten months since she had propositioned Miranda's girlfriend at a Christmas party, but her friend hadn't let her forget it.

"You would have known if you'd asked her name or whether she was available before you started describing in detail what you wanted to do to her," Miranda replied. "This is what you get for being the cad that we both know you are."

"What do I get?" Kash braced herself. Miranda had waited a long time to collect on her faux pas, so this had to be good.

"We're going to run a contest for *Sophisticated Women*, and I want you to photograph the winner for our October cover."

Miranda Claridge published *Sophisticated Women*, a glossy magazine she liked to claim showed up *Vogue* for nothing but shallow advertorial with pretty pictures. Miranda took her magazine seriously. *Sophisticated Women* covered all the usual bases—makeup, relationship, and career advice—but she also assumed chic urban women had brains and wanted in-depth articles as well. Even her international fashion spreads often included what Kash called "the conscience quota"— inserts on worthy local charities for maimed children, or whatever else had tugged Miranda's usually impervious heartstrings.

"What's the catch?" Kash cut to the chase, wanting to get back to Fawn. She knew if this was a routine cover shoot, Miranda would not be collecting the debt she owed.

"Well, you're also going to photograph her while she takes the dream vacation she wins."

"Vacation?" Kash glanced over at Fawn. She had pulled her dress back down. *Damn.* She had to wrap this conversation up quickly. "That sounds like it involves travel and time. How long, and how far?"

"Think of it as a vacation for you, too," Miranda coaxed. "Business class and four- and five-star hotels all the way, of course."

"Don't be sparse with the details, Miranda." Kash watched Fawn take the blindfold off. *Shit.* Her face said *I'm feeling pretty uncomfortable.* "Spell it out. I'm busy."

"Three weeks, late June into July. Since I'm giving you almost nine months' notice, you can't pretend your schedule is full."

"Three *weeks*?"

"The trip will really be fabulous, Kash. Four days each in Paris, Rome, and Cairo, and then a week in the Bahamas. Easy photo ops. You'll get lots of free time to explore all the nightlife. Please? Your name attached to this will be a huge plus."

Under ordinary circumstances, Kash would never have agreed to any assignment that required that kind of time commitment. But she did owe Miranda, and now Miranda would owe her back. And the itinerary *was* certainly tempting. Truth be told, she was restless for a change of scenery and a shakeup in the status quo. This constant diet of narcissistic and ambitious airheads had gotten kind of stale.

When Fawn shrugged and tentatively waved good-bye, Kash made a fast decision.

"Okay, Miranda. We'll negotiate the fine print when you get back from L.A. Now if you'll excuse me."

Kash didn't wait for a response. She slammed down the phone and caught the model as she turned for the door.

"Leaving so soon? Now you know I'll reward you with something extra special for your patience, don't you, Fawn?"

Madison, Wisconsin
Five months later

Isabel Sterling plaited her long honey blond hair into a loose braid and tucked it under her pink knit hat. She owned hats, scarves, and mittens in all colors and patterns, too many to be able to wear, so she stuck to the ones that her current crop of swimming students had given her for Christmas. Pink wasn't her favorite color, but tonight's chapeau and matching accessories had been hand made by Mrs. Eldrid, who never missed a class *or* a chance to complain about how her arthritis made knitting so much harder these days.

The community center had an Olympic-sized pool but a Little League–sized locker room, which felt cramped with her fifteen students. Nearly all were widows, the youngest fifty-five. Her Thursday senior swim class contained more of the same.

Isabel's hair was still damp but she didn't want to take time to dry it because Gillian would already be waiting outside, and temperatures this early March evening were only in the teens. After she wrapped her matching pink scarf around her neck, she stuffed her hands into pink gloves at least two sizes too large. She'd exchange them for her favorite fleece ones as soon as she got in her truck.

Nearly all the mittens and gloves her students knitted for her were too large. Though of rather average height and weight—five foot five and 118 pounds—Isabel's body was anything but average, honed by swimming laps in the closest pool for more years than she could remember. She was secretly proud of her woman's rounded curves, enhanced by the soft musculature built by her athletic endeavors.

A rotund woman wearing a bright orange one-piece, a Chicago Bulls towel, and a flowery swim cap appeared at her elbow. "Isabel, honey, aren't you the cutest thing. You coming with us to the Country Kitchen? It's all-you-can-eat cod and haddock night."

"Our treat," another of the women chimed in.

"Oh yes, Isabel, do!"

"Ordinarily, ladies, I'd love to," Isabel said agreeably. "But I'm meeting a friend, and I'm already late. Can I beg a rain check? Good night."

A chorus of good-byes and pleas to drive safely heralded her departure.

Her battered red pickup, a college graduation gift from her parents, really needed new tires, she noticed for the umpteenth time. And the driver's side door was frozen shut again, so she crawled in through the passenger side. *A little WD-40 on that when I get home.* She reached the music store where Gillian worked ten minutes after it closed. Her upstairs neighbor and best friend sat on a bench outside.

"Sorry, I got here as fast as I could," she said as Gillian got in. "You freezing?"

Gillian Menard, auburn-haired, chic, and lithely tall, was appropriately dressed for the weather in a long wool coat, hat, and gloves. But her nose was bright red and her eyes were watering. "That's safe to assume unless the calendar is somewhere between May and September," she replied, twisting the nearest vents to direct the warm air toward her face. "Want to do Chinese back at my place? We can watch a film."

"Sounds like a plan." The truck fishtailed as Isabel took a right, a slight detour from their usual route home, to stop by their favorite take-out place.

Twenty minutes later, armed with a sack of fragrant paper cartons, they were checking the mailboxes in the lobby of their apartment building. Isabel had two bills, an advertising flyer, and an envelope that proclaimed her the Grand Prize Winner of some contest.

It didn't look like the typical gaudy come-on. *They're sure making these things more convincing all the time.* High-quality envelope, and even sent priority mail, not bulk. Studying it closer, she saw that the return address was *Sophisticated Women* magazine. She'd heard of it, seen it on newsstands. She was curious enough to open it.

The notification inside appeared even more authentic than the outside. Written on embossed *Sophisticated Women* stationery, it was addressed to her personally and was purportedly from the publisher of the magazine, Miranda Claridge. It didn't seem mass-produced. In fact, she could have sworn the signature was freshly penned. It read:

> *Congratulations Ms. Isabel Sterling,*
>
> *I am pleased to inform you that you have won the grand prize in our Make Your Dreams Come True contest! Your entry was selected from more than four million, three hundred thousand submitted by mail and through our Web site. So get ready to pack your bags—you and a guest are about to embark on the adventure of a lifetime—three weeks, all expenses paid, to some of the hottest destinations on three continents. Renowned photographer Kash will accompany you to document your trip for* Sophisticated Women, *and one of her photos of you will appear on the cover of our October issue.*

The letter certainly looked authentic, but Isabel still didn't believe it was for real.

"Coming?"

Gillian was holding the elevator, so Isabel slammed the mailbox shut and hurried to join her. Once inside, she continued reading the letter.

> *And that's not all.*
>
> *You've also won ten thousand dollars in cash...a makeover by Clifton, stylist to the stars...and a new designer wardrobe selected by the fashion editors of* Sophisticated Women.

"Whatcha got?" Gillian asked, peering over her shoulder.

"I won a trip, ten thousand dollars, and a makeover," Isabel said without enthusiasm. "To go with the laptop I supposedly won last week by being the ten-millionth person to visit whatever Web site I clicked on."

"It sure seems...well, classier than most..." Gillian touched the paper, felt the weight of it between her fingers. "Let me see that, huh?"

"Oh, sure." Isabel handed it over as they reached her floor. "I was pretty well done with it anyway...just hadn't gotten to the disclaimers yet." She stepped out of the elevator. "Be right up."

After a quick change into sweats, she grabbed a couple of bags of microwave popcorn and headed up the stairs to the apartment directly above hers. She let herself in and spotted Gillian sitting statuelike on the couch, still in her coat, staring in disbelief at the contest letter clutched in her hand.

"Gill? What is it?"

"You're not going to believe this, Izzy. It's true!" Gillian sprang to her feet and waved the letter as she hurried toward her. "This is for real. You've actually won this trip. Well, I hope *we* have, 'cause you damn well better take me since I entered you in the first place. Three continents...and ten grand. Though you certainly don't have to split *that* with me—"

"Slow down." Isabel snatched the letter from her. "What the hell are you talking about? You entered me?"

Gillian nodded her head so vigorously it looked like it might fly off.

Isabel knew her friend was contest crazy, entering every sweepstakes and free offer and lottery she came across. But this was the first time she'd ever heard that Gillian had been putting *her* name on any of the forms.

"I enter us both in anything that allows only one entry per person, if the prize is a trip for two," Gillian explained. "I mean, you always say you want to travel, and I figure I'm doubling my odds of winning since I know you'll take me." She batted her eyelashes playfully at Isabel.

"It's for real? You're sure?" Isabel held the letter up to read it again.

"Absolutely," Gillian enthused as she finally shed her coat. "I remember this trip because they're keeping the destinations secret until they announce the winner."

"Golly." She dropped into the nearest chair, realization finally sinking in. *An all-expense-paid trip to three continents.* Her mind raced, considering the possible destinations. She'd be happy with most anywhere. *Somewhere in Europe, I bet. Oh, how great is this.* "And ten thousand dollars, Gill!"

"And don't forget the new wardrobe," Gillian pointed out. "Man, I hope you get some things I can fit into, because I bet you get a lot of designer clothes."

"Well, that's more your thing than mine, and where would I wear that kind of stuff?" Excitement bubbled over, and Isabel scanned the letter again for details of when she'd collect her winnings. Then she seriously noted what else she'd won.

"Okay, so the trip and the money are unbelievably cool," she said. "But the rest of this…getting a makeover and appearing on the cover of *Sophisticated Women*? I mean, come on, that is so not me. I like how I am. And I've never even picked up the magazine."

"So you get a great new haircut, which you desperately need, and your picture taken by a hot celebrity photographer. No heavy lifting there, Izzy. I'm sure you can stand it. Now come on, grab your coat. We have some serious celebrating to do."

New York
Three and a half months later

Kash was in absolutely no mood for that day's shoot, whatever it was. The miserable hangover was bad enough, but she particularly hated that she had awakened in a stranger's bed and had to face that awkward morning-after scenario with no time to go home for a proper shower and change of clothes.

When she stumbled in, yawning like a fiend, and headed straight for the espresso machine, her jack-of-all-trades assistant, Ramona Dean, was setting lights.

Ramona, a five-foot-ten skeleton with purple hair and piercings in nearly every body part, glanced up from what she was doing and studied Kash for several seconds before she spoke. "Has it ever occurred to you to keep a change of clothes here?"

It was a brilliant blue-sky day outside—bright enough in the airy studio that Kash kept her sunglasses on. She glanced down at herself and frowned. Okay, so there were a few wrinkles now in what had been a crisp white button-down, and being the neat freak she was, they displeased her no small amount. But she also knew the average person probably wouldn't have cared or noticed. "What's the problem?"

Ramona's twice-pierced lip curled upward in a smirk. "I'm trying to picture how the hell you got that stain on the back of your shirt, and exactly what it is."

"Stain?" Kash hurriedly unbuttoned the shirt and slipped it off, examining the oily patch the size of a fist in the middle of it. Sniffed. Wild cherry. The flavor of the lube that her companion for the night had produced from her bedside drawer. *Great.* She wasn't quite sure *exactly* how it had gotten there, but she knew the shirt had ended up on the bed because that's where she had discovered it this morning. And they had used a good bit of the bottle of lube while on that bed, too, so the stain was no real surprise.

"Christ. Say, I'll finish setting up. Go get me something to wear, will you? Plain black T-shirt or something." She fished a fifty-dollar bill from her wallet. "You know what I like. What the hell do we have today, anyway? I haven't seen the schedule."

"The Montrose Agency is sending models over for publicity shots this morning." Ramona glanced at her watch. "They're due any minute. The usual portfolio stuff. And then nothing after that till four, when you're shooting Ellen Degeneres for the next cover of *Animal Advocates* magazine."

"That's today?" Kash's mood brightened considerably, though her head still ached from too much vodka. "Then get going and hurry back. I want to get through the publicity stuff fast so I have time to go home for a shower and change in between."

"Okay, I'm gone." Between Kash's studio and the elevators was an exterior office and reception area that contained Ramona's desk and comfortable seating for a dozen people. Various examples of Kash's work were displayed around the walls, and her name was emblazoned over the desk as an artistic logo recognized worldwide.

As Ramona passed through the outer office, she met three women, all with the tall, thin silhouettes and practiced poses of runway wannabes. "Hello, ladies. From Montrose?" When they nodded, she gestured toward the door to the studio. "Go ahead, she's expecting you."

Four more women were getting off the elevator when it stopped to let her on. It was a safe bet they were there for the same reason, since it was Saturday and all the other tenants of the twenty-ninth floor were closed. "If you're here to see Kash, it's that way." She pointed, stepping past them. "Go right on through reception—she's in the studio."

As Ramona hit the button to the lobby and waited for the doors to close, she studied the latest group of women. Three were more of the typical runway fare, all starvation-framed and unaffected expressions. The fourth stuck out. She was at least three or four inches shorter. Nice body, but not right for a runway girl—too athletic. And obviously expecting star treatment because she wasn't even in makeup yet and was dressed way too casual for publicity photos. Hadn't the agency briefed her or what? *Kash will not be pleased.*

❖

Isabel followed the other women into the reception area and lingered to marvel at the display of Kash's work that covered every wall. Most were celebrity portraits, taken for interviews, magazine covers, book jackets, or publicity purposes. Routine photographs, usually, but Kash's stood out from others of their ilk, which was why she was in such demand. With her novel settings and precise attention to mood, light, framing, pose, and expression, not only could Kash make anyone look good, but she allowed the viewer to glimpse some aspect of her subject's life or personality.

Kash was best known for these types of photographs and had built her reputation on them, but some of her ad-campaign shots, all instantly recognizable, were also displayed. And here and there were pictures of Kash's travels: dramatic photos taken on safari in Kenya, high in the Himalayas, at a street market in Brazil.

Isabel was eager to meet the woman who could create such images. *She must be a very sensitive person. What wonderful artistry and insight she brings to her work.*

Glancing around at the other women who had paused to admire the display, Isabel realized they were all at least a half-head taller than she. They had obviously spent hours on their hair and makeup, some of them achieving garishly weird results. One's elaborate spiky hair reminded her of the Statue of Liberty. Another had applied so much eyeliner and rouge she resembled an escapee from Cirque du Soleil.

It was kind of creepy, like she'd stepped into a modern-day

Stepford Models episode and didn't belong there. She had never quite understood the allure that cosmetics held for most women. Other than some lip gloss now and then, she never touched the stuff.

They all headed into the studio, Isabel following last. The spacious rectangular loft with its polished wood floor, enormous windows, and terra-cotta brickwork walls seemed clean and organized, except for the slight disarray on the desk to her immediate right. On one side, in a casual seating area, perched three women much like those she'd come in with—lithe teenagers with vacant expressions, all with that same exaggerated devotion to developing a "look" that would get them stared at on the street.

On the other side of the studio, where a backdrop and lights had been set up for a photo shoot, a woman knelt over a large silver suitcase whose foam interior had been custom cut to accept a variety of lenses and attachments for the camera she held in her hand.

Kash. The one name was sufficient, like Madonna, or Cher, or Beyoncé, and Isabel recognized her immediately. Celebrity TV shows did stories on her all the time, and Kash's image appeared at least monthly on the cover of one of those tabloid rags at the grocery store because in addition to her talents as a photographer, she had gained widespread notoriety for her partying lifestyle and the women she purportedly bedded.

Isabel didn't believe most of the stuff that appeared in those publications had any merit. Still, she had to wonder when Kash was photographed so regularly at one trendy hot spot or another with a drink in one hand and her other around the waist or on the ass of some hot young actress or model.

The famed photographer stood and glanced toward them as they joined the other models. It was hard to see exactly where her attention was because she wore dark glasses, but when she faced Isabel, she froze briefly, apparently studying her. Her serious expression didn't change, but furrows of confusion or bewilderment appeared in her forehead.

The woman herself appeared...*different* than Isabel expected. A handsome face, yes, but even more so in person than in photos because she had a softness that pictures couldn't capture. A reflection of the artist inside, she guessed.

Kash was more diminutive than she had imagined, too, only an inch or two taller than she was. And she certainly had a nice body when viewed three-dimensionally, with narrow hips and a tight ass, small breasts and a lean frame. In other words, exactly Isabel's type physically. *No problem hanging around her for the next three weeks, that's for sure.*

Yes, indeed, she was certainly anxious to spend some time getting to know Kash. She wished she would take her sunglasses off. It was impossible to tell where her attention was focused or what she was thinking.

Isabel had arrived in New York a couple of days early to sightsee and dropped by Kash's studio on impulse, intending to introduce herself away from the glare of media attention that she feared would accompany their official meeting at the press conference at the *Sophisticated Women* offices on Monday. She saw her chance and approached Kash as she was fixing a camera to her tripod.

"Hi, Kash," she began. "I have to tell you how much I enjoy your work. It really moves me—you have such a great eye for composition, and a special talent for capturing the essence of your subjects."

"That's nice of you to say," Kash replied, a reluctant smile tugging at the corner of her mouth. But she forestalled Isabel's effort to introduce herself when she added, "but I'm on a very tight schedule today, and we need to get started. No time for chitchat."

"Oh, of course."

Kash pointed to the redhead with the spiky hairdo. "You first. Over here on the stool." As the model moved into position, Kash addressed the others. "Let's keep chatter to a minimum and pay close attention so we can get this done fast. You each get ten minutes. If you follow directions and give me something good to work with, these photos will say *star quality*. If you sit there like a stick or want to chat your time away, don't expect art. The first eight minutes are beauty shots. Face and neck only, where it's all about your eyes. Pretty eyes, soft expressions. Then you get two minutes off the stool to move, pose. Be you, and show me what you've got. Are we clear?"

Since no one had ushered her out, Isabel was content to hang around and observe Kash at work. All the better to get an idea of what might await her on her own photo shoots for the magazine. It had been relatively easy for Isabel to arrange time off. She worked as a freelance cake decorator, splitting her time among three bakeries in Madison, so she had a large measure of control over her schedule. But Gillian couldn't get more than three weeks off from her job, so she wouldn't join Isabel for two more days, right before the press conference. They would go directly from there to the airport to begin their adventure, whose itinerary was still a mystery.

That was another reason she was here. She was eager to discover where her dream vacation would take her, and she hoped Kash could give her a preview. Though Kash was obviously too busy for that at the moment, Isabel thought she might get a minute or two with her at the end of the shoot.

So she settled herself on the couch amid the Stepford models and spent the next hour watching them have their pictures taken. Initially, the only sounds in the loft were the clicks of Kash's cameras and her brief instructions—"Tilt your chin up" or "Turn your body to the right a bit." Once a model was finished, she was dismissed, and Kash would point to another, always bypassing Isabel.

When Kash began to photograph the last model, Isabel began to realize there was a lot of truth to the tabloid stories. With this one, a willowy redhead, Kash was suddenly much less businesslike. Her instructions became all flirty innuendo—"Give me something sexy," or "Hike up your dress a little and show me some thigh." And she seemed to find a multitude of reasons to touch the model—on the arm, the back, the waist—supposedly to reposition her for the next shot, but always with an unmistakable leer on her face.

The model offered Kash her phone number when she finished shooting her, and Kash pocketed it with a satisfied smile.

Such behavior shouldn't have shocked Isabel. The stories about Kash were too numerous not to have some truth. But Kash's rather blatant exploitation of her young client repulsed her a bit, and also—and this was what surprised her—she also felt a little jealous at the attention the model was getting.

Kash waited until only the two of them were left before she acknowledged the blonde who seemed like she didn't belong. The petite woman had a pretty face and a nice body, but it wasn't a typical runway physique. And her appreciation for her work was less fawning and more insightful than the typical model was capable of. *An actress, perhaps.*

However, the woman's lackluster choice of apparel for such an important shoot mystified her—blue jeans, sneakers, and a long-sleeved white T-shirt. *White, for God's sake. I'll have to change the lighting.* And the woman's complete lack of makeup and apparent disregard for how her hair would photograph puzzled her even more. *Amateur. Doesn't the agency make sure they at least understand the basics?*

Kash knew the photos would suffer as a result, and she tried to tell herself she really shouldn't care because she would get paid regardless. But she was too much the perfectionist, so the blonde's cavalier disregard for the fundamentals annoyed her. "I deliberately left you for last to give you time to get halfway presentable, but apparently for nothing. I don't know what *look* you think you're going for, but it sure doesn't work for me."

The blonde stiffened. "I don't think you understand—"

Before she could finish, Ramona burst in with shopping bags and a harried expression. "Sorry it took so long. The lines at Lord and Taylor were a bitch." She glanced over at Isabel as she crossed the loft to hand her purchases to Kash. "I got you a couple of shirts to choose from."

"I was beginning to wonder." Ignoring Isabel for the moment, Kash pulled out a black T-shirt and removed the tags before she stripped off her own shirt to change.

Isabel had certainly seen women undress before, having spent a good portion of her life in swimming-pool locker rooms. But for some reason, staring at Kash as she peeled off her button-down shirt and exposed a silk and lace bra that seemed somehow almost too feminine for her softly muscled androgyny vaguely embarrassed her.

"Like I was saying," Isabel said, getting up from her chair and crossing over to where the other two were standing, "apparently you've mistaken—"

She never got this explanation out either, because she didn't notice the extension cord that ran to one of the massive scoop lights set up for the shoot. She stumbled over it and went flying, triggering a domino effect that caught two other light stands as well and sent all three crashing to the floor in a noisy chaos. Broken glass lay everywhere.

"Christ." Kash rolled her eyes and hummed a few bars of something under her breath as Ramona hurried to make sure Isabel hadn't injured herself. "Like I really needed this. Are you deliberately trying to ruin my day?"

Isabel brushed herself off, her face warm from embarrassment, and immediately tried to help clean up the mess. "Oh, gosh, I'm so sorry…I didn't see—"

Kash waved off her apology. "Listen, you've self-destructed any chance you had of getting head shots from me today. Be glad I don't charge you for the damage and see yourself out, okay?"

Isabel frowned and got to her feet. "Sure. No problem. I…I really am sorry." She left quickly.

"Who was that?" Ramona asked as the door to the reception area banged shut.

"Who knows?" Kash replied. "Never got her name. Find her file and let the Montrose people know they'll have to reschedule her with someone else."

"It's funny, but I don't remember her…" Ramona crossed to Kash's desk and picked up the folder of photos the agency had sent over. "Hey, Kash…she's not here. She evidently wasn't from the agency."

"Not from the agency?" Kash asked as she righted the last of the light stands. "Then who the hell was she, and what did she want? She came in with the others and sat here during the whole shoot."

Ramona shrugged. "No idea."

Kash glanced over at the door Isabel had disappeared through. "Odd. Well, guess it doesn't matter, as long as she doesn't come back."

CHAPTER TWO

"So, have you met her? What's she like? Why didn't you call me?" Gillian asked without preamble when Isabel admitted her into their hotel room. She breezed by, suitcases in tow, without waiting for an answer. "And did she tell you where we're going?"

"I didn't get a chance to ask." Isabel followed her into the spacious suite that *Sophisticated Women* had booked for them. "And I'm reserving judgment on what she's like. She was working, and I didn't exactly make a stellar first impression."

Gillian dumped her bags just inside the door. "That doesn't sound good. What happened?"

"I dropped by without calling and she was busy with a shoot, so I waited around for her to finish. She was taking pictures of a bunch of models." Isabel sat on the couch.

Gillian sank into the cushions beside her. "And?"

"She obviously thought I was one of them or something, and I was trying to explain who I was, finally, when…" Isabel squirmed. "Well, there was an accident. I tripped over a cord or cable or something and knocked over some of her studio lights—the kind on stands that probably cost a small fortune."

Gillian winced. "Bet that didn't go over too well."

"That's when she told me to leave," Isabel admitted. "Frankly, I was kind of surprised she let me stay and watch, but like I said…she thought I was one of the models."

"You sure?" Gillian's tone was dubious. "I mean, no offense, Izzy, but I sure wouldn't mistake you for a New York fashion model."

"No offense taken," Isabel replied with a smile.

"You've got that homespun girl-next-door kind of appeal going on," Gillian said, tilting her head to appraise her. "Tomboy-cute, not glam-girl."

"Thanks. I think."

"Say, Iz, this trip is a great opportunity for you to loosen up and live a little."

"Not this again." Isabel rolled her eyes. "I'm not a hermit, Gill. I go out."

"Once a month, tops," Gillian said, "when I drag you to a club. And maybe you call dancing a couple of times and letting someone buy you a drink, then going home alone a good time, but I don't. When's the last time you let somebody warm your bed? Don't you miss it?"

"Honestly? Sure. I admit it's been a while, and I *am* human. But you know me. I don't do the casual-sex thing. And I probably won't meet the right kind of woman for me in a bar anyway. Believe me, when the time is right I'll meet someone and start going out again. Fate will bring us together, and I'll recognize it when it happens. At least I hope I will."

"You're *such* a romantic." Gillian patted her shoulder. "You deserve your happily-ever-after, Iz. Sylvia was such a scum to treat you like she did."

"We seemed like a good pair." Isabel shrugged. "We had so much in common."

"Only on the surface. You may like all the same things, but she's a shrewd, manipulative snake, and you're sweetness personified."

Isabel laughed. "Have I told you lately how much I cherish you?"

"I only have your best interests at heart, my friend. So I'm asking you sincerely to think about what I've said. We're about to experience what might be your best opportunity *ever* to kick back and have some *fun* with a beautiful woman or two." Gillian linked her hands behind her head and relaxed back against the couch. "Or three or four. It would do you good. I hope they send us somewhere with viable nightlife, or maybe a warm beach with some bikini-clad bodies to stare at."

"I'm hoping we get to see things like the Great Wall of China or Valley of the Kings. Maybe the Tower of London."

"I can see we're going to be hoping for different itineraries." Gillian laughed. "I wonder how much free time we'll have, and how much you'll have to spend taking photos for the magazine. You think Kash will be following us around everywhere?"

"No idea." The pained look on Kash's face when she'd overturned all the lights flashed back into Isabel's mind and she cringed. "I guess we'll find out all that at the press conference."

"So, you never said…how does she strike you in person? Does she do her pictures justice?" Gillian was watching her intently.

Isabel knew that Gillian was really hoping for a chance to spend a night with Kash. Long before this contest business, Gillian had mentioned a time or two how hot she thought the photographer was. Once they learned they'd be meeting her, they both had scoured the Internet for past stories and interviews about her and had speculated about what she might be like on the trip.

After the hour Isabel had spent watching Kash, she certainly had to agree with Gillian. The woman had obvious sex appeal. And there was a quiet intensity about her when she was working that intrigued Isabel. She had wanted very much to see exactly what Kash was capturing each time she clicked the shutter.

I bet she and Gillian will get together. Gillian has no problem at all with quick and uncomplicated, and it sure seemed as though Kash doesn't either. When they were out clubbing together, Gillian would often hook up with someone, either in the dark back hallways of the bar or at a stranger's apartment afterward, so Isabel always drove separately.

The prospect of Gillian and Kash together made her vaguely uneasy, but she didn't want to dwell too long on why. She told herself she didn't want Gillian to become one more notch on a celebrity's belt—but then, who was she to judge? *If it's what she wants, and it clearly is, why should I have a problem with it? I'm her friend, and I should support whatever makes her happy. So that's what I'll do.*

"You're going to *really* like her," Isabel answered finally. "She's definitely all *that* and more. Great body. Really nice features. Well, I didn't see her eyes—she had shades on. But definitely—like you said—probably can get any woman she wants. More subdued than I expected…and a little abrupt, even before I spoiled her day. Not a happy camper, like maybe something else was going on with her."

"Perhaps she needs something to improve her mood," Gillian suggested, her eyes narrowing as though she was already plotting what that might be.

❖

"I can't believe I let you rope me into this," Kash griped as she set down her camera bag on the floor of Miranda Claridge's impeccably fashionable office. "It's asking a lot for me to be away from everything for three weeks. Can't I just fly over to Paris for a day, and maybe Rome? Call it representative of the trip?"

"No. You know you can't. You're part of the grand prize, Kash. Your reputation helped sell it." Miranda came around from behind her desk and faced Kash, who had on low-cut jeans, boots, and a designer T-shirt. Miranda wore a navy Armani suit. It showed off her legs, still her proudest asset at forty-four. "And like I've told you, we really want you to hang with this woman some. Get more than the usual posed Eiffel Tower and pyramid shots."

Kash studied Miranda's determined expression. She knew that look, all too well. She had contributed to a half dozen charities and done several benefit shoots because Miranda had used it on her. "No chance I can get out of this, huh?"

"Come on, it'll be fun." Miranda snatched a flight folder from her desk. "Your tickets and itinerary," she said. "And the names and contact numbers for the local drivers we've hired to help you schlep your stuff and set up as needed. You have my cell. Let me know if you need anything else."

"I will," Kash promised. "So when do I get to meet the contest winner? What's her name again?"

Miranda glanced at the antique clock on her sideboard. "The press conference starts in twenty minutes. And her name is Isabel Sterling. She's a cake decorator from Madison, Wisconsin."

"Cake decorator? You're kidding. Is that a real job?"

"Of course. In New York and L.A. and a few other places you can make big money if you're good at it. Especially if you do wedding cakes."

"If you say so."

"You could appreciate it better, Kash, if you had ever set foot inside a kitchen."

They both laughed. Kash lived on take-out, restaurant fare, and the occasional dinner invitation from friends like Miranda and her partner. The women she fucked often asked her over as well, as a way to see her again, but though she loved home-cooked meals she generally discouraged such occasions. They seemed too domestic and always raised expectations for more. She wanted to keep sex simple and uncomplicated.

"So, a cake decorator from Wisconsin. Sounds like a perfect candidate for your makeover. Is she cute? Is she gay?"

Miranda chuckled. "Since when have you cared if someone's gay as long as she's cute?"

"True," Kash acknowledged, grinning back. "So?"

"Cute, yes. Blonde, so she's your type. Twenty-nine years old. And she is in *nice* shape." Miranda raised her eyebrows meaningfully at Kash. "Kind of wholesome-cute, which will be great for the makeover part. Not a lot to do to make her cover-ready. I mean, she's a great canvas to work on, but there will still be a big difference in the before-and-after pics, which we like. Before—jeans and a T-shirt, no makeup, hair needing a cut. After—well, you know what I mean."

"Yup. Sounds great," Kash said. "So she's cute. What about the gay part?"

Miranda punched her lightly on the arm. "You're incorrigible. And yes, I think she probably *is* gay, as a matter of fact. They haven't said so, but both she and the woman she brought along on the trip seem pretty obvious to me. I met them a little while ago. In fact, though she introduced her as a neighbor and friend, I wouldn't be surprised if they're really a couple. They seem close. Gillian is the friend's name."

Kash glanced at her watch. "I want to check myself in a mirror before the press conference. Meet you down there?"

"Ten minutes, Kash. Don't leave me hanging."

"No worries, Miranda. I'll be there."

True to her word, she stepped off the elevator outside the *Sophisticated Women* conference room with time to spare and came face-to-face with a dozen press and tabloid photographers, many of whom she recognized.

One of them, a paunchy, balding freelancer named Joe Dix, blinded her with a half dozen flashes before she took two steps. Dix was one of the more ruthless of the ambush paparazzi, a growing legion of photographers who spent their days stalking celebrities in hopes of catching them doing something immoral or illegal. His photos of Kash had been splashed on the covers of a number of tabloid rags in the States and abroad. "Hey, Kash. What's the word?"

"The word?" Kash squinted, trying to dispel the white spots dancing before her eyes. "How about 'irritating'? 'Intrusive'? No, wait. How about 'vermin'—that's a good one."

"Funny girl," Dix retorted as he clicked away. "Like your shit don't stink. You use your camera to get rich and get laid. What the hell do you think makes you better than me?"

"Jealousy doesn't become you, Dix. But then, nothing would. Scum is scum, any way you slice it."

She breezed by the photographers and pushed open the door to the conference room. Twenty or so reporters and a handful of cameramen and women milled around or sat in rows of chairs set up for the press conference, chatting among themselves. Miranda stood at the front, near the podium, talking to an attractive auburn-haired woman who was stylishly dressed in a dove gray silk shirt and charcoal skirt. An easel held a large poster, currently covered by a drape.

As she moved to take her place by Miranda, a few of the reporters tried to intercept her with questions, but she brushed them off with a forced smile.

"There she is." Miranda smiled approvingly at Kash and introduced her to the woman she was chatting with. "Kash, I'd like you to meet Gillian Menard, our contest winner's friend, neighbor, and travel companion."

Gillian stuck out her hand. "Hi, Kash. I can't wait to get to know you better."

Kash was a bit taken aback by the unmistakable flirtation in the redhead's eyes and tone of voice. *Gay, yes. But Miranda was either mistaken about them being a couple or it's certainly not an exclusive arrangement.* Redheads were normally not her thing, but there were always exceptions to the rule. This one was a willing piece of eye candy, and if Miranda was right about the other being a cute blonde with a nice body, then a threesome might be on the horizon.

She took Gillian's hand firmly and let her grip linger. Flashes went off, reminding her that her every move was being watched. "Nice to meet you, Gillian. Sounds like it's going to be a great trip. So..." She let go of Gillian and turned to Miranda. "Where's the big winner?"

"She got a bad case of nerves," Gillian answered, "when she saw all the photographers. Needed to collect herself. She'll be here in a minute."

Right on cue, a sudden stir of activity at the entrance to the conference room made everyone turn to see what was happening.

❖

Isabel exited the ladies' room and tried to ignore the tympanic thump thump thump of her runaway heart. When she and Gillian had stepped off the elevator into a blinding crush of photographers, all focused on *her* and all blocking their way into the conference room, the restroom had been the nearest refuge. But the news conference was supposed to be starting, and she couldn't hide out forever.

She briefly dared to hope the photographers might be kinder this time because they didn't go crazy when she rounded the final corner. There were only a few flashes until she got close, then all at once a bedlam of light hit her again.

She pushed on toward the conference room door, blinking back the stars on her eyelids. The last thing she remembered thinking was *I know the door was right there.*

But it wasn't there, because a reporter on the other side had pulled it open, so she met only thin air instead of thick oak. She crashed headfirst.

Kash glimpsed the blonde before she went down and was obscured by a crush of photographers. The ensuing barrage of flashes lit up the room.

Miranda and Gillian tied in their race to reach the grand-prize winner. Kash hung back, not anxious to be at the center of the maelstrom.

"Let's give her some air, can we, please?" Miranda's voice carried over the hubbub of reporter questions.

"Is that the winner?"

"What happened?"

"What is she, drunk or something?"

Kash's curiosity propelled her forward. She worked her way through the crush of people, horrified to find…*her. Christ. No.*

It was the blond mystery girl from the other day. *Disaster Girl,* as Kash had come to think of her.

The woman seemed a little dazed. She had her head in Gillian's lap.

"Come on, Izzy," Gillian was saying. "Please be okay. Now is not the time."

Kash glowered at Miranda. "I can't possibly owe you this big."

The comment turned all the cameras back onto Kash, and she was instantly blinded.

"What does that mean?" one of the reporters asked.

"Yeah, explain that," another chimed in. "Why do you owe her? And what does that have to do with—"

The blonde moaned, and the cameras all shifted again to photograph the action.

"What?" Isabel said groggily. "What's happening?"

"Press conference," Gillian volunteered. "I think you tripped."

Of course she did, Kash thought. *Izzy, huh? Dizzy Izzy is more like it. What the hell did I do to deserve this?* She thought of the thousands of dollars of photographic equipment she had packed for this adventure and was suddenly very glad she had insurance.

"Come on, guys, give her a break, huh?" Miranda's voice betrayed her irritation with the way her long-awaited press conference was going. She bent over her grand-prize winner. "Are you all right, Miss Sterling? Should I call an ambulance?"

It took Isabel a few more seconds to fully grasp that this was indeed her worst nightmare come to life. Yes, she was really sprawled on the floor of the *Sophisticated Women* conference room. And those actually were camera flashes preserving every single second of her total humiliation. At least, thank God, she had worn the black dress trousers with her pale lavender shell, and not the short skirt that Gillian had tried to talk her into. *Why the heck did I ever agree to this?*

Just when she thought it couldn't possibly get worse, she spotted... *her.*

Kash was staring down at her as if she had grown another head.

Oh, how she wished it was possible to disappear at will. She could feel her cheeks blaze from embarrassment. "I'm fine." She swatted away Gillian's comforting embrace and tried to get to her feet.

A strong hand took her elbow and helped her up, and she was suddenly nearly nose to nose with Kash.

Surprised by the unexpected chivalry, she stared at the photographer until Miranda took each of them by the arm and turned them toward the podium.

En route, Miranda made hurried introductions. "Kash, Isabel Sterling…Isabel, meet Kash."

"Charmed, I'm sure," Kash said, with only the tiniest measure of sarcasm.

Isabel caught it and saw Kash roll her eyes as she said it. *Oh, great.* "Sorry about the other day, Kash. I'd be happy to pay for any damages."

They were at the podium before Kash could respond, but Isabel noticed her expression soften into one of perhaps regret.

Miranda glanced from one to the other as she pulled over a chair and got Isabel settled comfortably into it. "Are you able to proceed now, or should I cancel?" Miranda asked in a low voice as the gathered media began to take seats.

"You sure you're not hurt?" Gillian asked almost simultaneously.

"I said I'm fine." *Jesus, I will never live this one down.* Isabel took a couple of deep breaths to calm herself as she brushed carpet duff off her trousers. "And yes, please," she said to Miranda. "Let's go on and get this press conference over with and maybe they'll find this more newsworthy than…well, I mean…it was an *accident*," she added. "How can anyone see where they're going with all those flashes right in their face?"

"It wasn't so bad, Izzy," Gillian tried to console her. "Maybe they won't use those photos."

"Unfortunately, they'll probably be on the front page of at least a couple of rags by the end of the week," Kash said. "And all over the Internet before that. Unconscious ranks right up there with nude, caught cheating, and drunk—in terms of popularity with the tabloids."

"Gee, thanks." Isabel sighed dejectedly. "You're a big help."

"Ladies," Miranda cut in, "should I remind you we have people with high-powered microphones behind us?"

"'Course, it's possible that someone famous will crash and burn and knock you off the front page," Kash whispered. "But I'm not volunteering."

Isabel smiled, and the change aroused the artist in Kash. She studied the young woman's face. *Perfect imbalance. That's what gives your face character.* Isabel had an almost ideal, movie-star smile, marred only by a crooked tooth left of center. The smile raised a dimple in her cheek on the same side, and the combined effect of the two gave her face an appealing asymmetry.

Miranda took the podium. She talked about the contest, the entries, the prizes, and then laid out their itinerary.

"From here, a limo will take Miss Sterling to Kash's studio, here in Manhattan, for some 'before' pictures to begin the story of her *Sophisticated Women* makeover."

Kash could tell from the sudden reddening of Isabel's face that she was remembering her previous visit two days earlier. *What a train wreck. I wonder what was she doing there?*

"Then it's off to the airport to begin their three-week dream vacation. First stop—Paris!" Miranda folded back part of the drape concealing the poster at the front of the room, revealing a montage of Parisian attractions. "After four days in the City of Lights, it's on to…Rome, the Eternal City!" Another montage was uncovered.

Isabel's shame faded as her destinations were revealed, humiliation replaced at least for now by excitement. She had yearned to travel since she was a child, but had never had the money to see much of the U.S., let alone Europe.

"Wow, Izzy. Paris and Rome!" Gillian whispered.

"Yeah," Isabel whispered back. "They're both on my top-ten list, for sure. I mean, the Eiffel Tower, Gill. The Louvre. The Vatican!"

"From Rome the lucky winner flies to Cairo, Egypt," Miranda was saying, "Land of the Pharaohs."

"Egypt!" Gillian squealed in delight.

"Oh, Gill." Isabel gasped at the photos. "How beautiful!" *This is way too cool.*

"And finally," Miranda concluded with a flourish, revealing the last of the poster, "it's westward to the Caribbean, for a full week of warm beaches and the lush nature preserves of the Grand Bahamas."

"Bikinis!" Gillian bounced up and down on her seat in delight. "Ooh. Told you. How great is this? We're going to have such a blast!"

Gillian's excitement was contagious, and for an instant, Isabel forgot all about her embarrassment with Kash and even about the photographs of her sprawled out on the floor. She was about to experience some of the cities she had long dreamed about—in style, no less—and with her best friend. *Yup. Gillian's right. We're going to have a blast.*

Her optimistic musings were tempered somewhat, however, when Miranda called Kash to the podium.

"I'm thrilled to be taking part in this adventure with the lucky contest winner," Kash began. "I know we're going to have a lot of fun together." Her pleased expression appeared to be genuine, even to Isabel, who knew better. *She sure can lie with a straight face.*

Several reporters started shouting questions at Kash at once, most of which concerned her private life instead of the contest. Isabel was astounded at the audacity of some of them. "Who you seeing these days, Kash?" "Or sleeping with?" "Care to explain that comment earlier, about you owing Ms. Claridge?" "Is it true you were pulled over in Malibu last week for drunk driving?" "Do you have a response to that online report you're being sued by some actress's husband who claims you ruined their marriage?"

Kash ignored the questions and kept a faint smile in place as she stepped back from the podium, and Miranda once again addressed the media. "Let's remember why we're here, please? And now I'd like to introduce the lucky winner of our Make Your Dreams Come True contest—from Madison, Wisconsin…Isabel Sterling."

After witnessing the media's treatment of Kash, Isabel walked to the podium on somewhat shaky legs. She had been nervous enough before she'd tripped. Now she was terrified. She generally was comfortable speaking before small groups, but she'd never faced vultures like this, who fed on personal information. That's what they struck her as. Poised and circling, waiting for any show of vulnerability.

Before she could open her mouth, they barraged her. "What happened when you came in? Did you pass out?" "Are you pregnant?" "Have you been drinking?" "What is the relationship between you and this woman you're taking on the trip? Is that her?" "Yeah. Are you gay?"

"No, I wasn't drinking…uh…well, your flashes…" Isabel stuttered badly, feeling like a bug being fried in the noonday sun under a bully's magnifying glass.

"Please." Miranda gently pulled Isabel away from the microphone and interceded. "If you don't keep to polite questions, I won't make Miss Sterling available at all."

The reporters backed off and Isabel suffered through a few basic questions. What she did for a living and how she had won. Gillian answered that one for her. Then the inevitable questions about her marital status, age, hometown.

Miranda interceded whenever a query got too personal and, after only a couple of minutes, stepped in and announced the end of the press conference. She told the reporters they would have to buy the October issue of the magazine to hear the rest of the story.

The media filed out and left them alone.

"Well, that was a rather inauspicious start to your adventure." Miranda frowned apologetically at Isabel. "They're like sharks when things don't go as planned, I'm afraid."

"Gossip sells, unfortunately," Kash agreed. "Especially photos where you lose your temper or do something foolish."

"I couldn't believe the nerve of some of those questions," Gillian said.

"Well, the worst is over now." Miranda smiled encouragingly at Isabel and Gillian. "And it's time for the fun to begin. The limo is waiting downstairs with your itinerary and tickets. You have two hours for your shoot with Kash before you all have to head for the airport."

Isabel glanced at Kash, who was watching her with a neutral expression. For the first time, she noticed Kash's hazel eyes. *God, she has the most incredibly long lashes. They could almost be fake. But she sure doesn't seem the type to wear false eyelashes.*

Isabel wasn't quite sure what to make of Kash. She had certainly just gotten a vivid idea of how reporters could invent things about someone—anything to feed the hungry tabloid gossip machine. *Maybe she doesn't deserve quite all of that racy reputation. I should keep an open mind.*

❖

Kash waited until they were alone in Miranda's office to relay the story of Isabel's visit to her studio. By the time she finished describing the aftermath of their disastrous encounter, Miranda had tears streaming down her cheeks.

"Oh, that's rich," Miranda said. "Sounds like you're in store for an interesting three weeks with this one. I wondered what was going on when I introduced you."

"I have to tell you, Miranda, I'll live up to my part of the deal." Kash picked up her camera bag and slung it over her shoulder. "I'll get you a nice variety of photos for the spread. But don't expect me to hang with Disaster Girl twenty-four/seven. Not happening."

"I'm sure you'll find plenty of time to do your own thing and still give me what I want," Miranda said as they headed for the elevators. "But be nice, huh? Granted, I only had a few minutes to chat with her, but she struck me as a really sweet woman, Kash. Might give her another chance."

"If we can get through the next hour without her destroying all my replacement lights, I'll consider it," Kash said. "But I make no guarantees."

❖

"That press conference certainly couldn't have gone much worse." Isabel took a long swallow of the champagne that had been waiting on ice in the limo.

"Oh, come on," Gillian replied, pouring her own glass. "They'll forget about you tomorrow. Where's that eternal optimist I know and love? Here we are—about to take this fabulous trip, sitting in a limo drinking champagne, you, with a check for ten grand in your pocket— and you're bitching?"

Isabel let the words sink in. "You're absolutely right." She raised her glass and waited for Gillian to do the same. "Here's to a memorably fabulous adventure, and to making sure nothing keeps us from enjoying every single solitary second."

"I will definitely drink to that."

They clinked glasses as the door to the limo opened. Kash slipped into the seat opposite them and the driver pulled away from the curb.

Kash and Isabel studied each other for several seconds, saying nothing. Kash wore an amused expression that Isabel read as cocky.

"How long do you think this will take? These pictures?" Gillian asked.

Kash chuckled. "Depends on whether my equipment survives the setting-up period. If Isabel can remain upright, no more than an hour."

Gillian started to laugh, then tried unsuccessfully to control herself with a hand to her mouth when Isabel glared at her.

"You're such a riot, Kash." Isabel took another long pull of champagne. "Are you planning to go with sarcasm the entire trip?"

Kash poured herself a glass and took a sip. "Most probably," she said finally. "But only with you."

Gillian half spewed her mouthful of champagne. "I can see I'm going to have to play referee," she said, wiping her chin. "Which is cool, I'm good with that. Whatever it takes, because we're all going to be spending a lot of time together, that's for sure."

She was positively giddy at the prospect, but Isabel and Kash both greeted the pronouncement by downing the contents of their glasses. They reached for a refill simultaneously, but Kash's hand got there first.

"Allow me," she said through gritted teeth, offering to pour for Isabel.

"*Charmed*, I'm sure," Isabel singsonged, repeating Kash's earlier greeting in the kind of mocking tone she hadn't used since elementary school. She held out her glass and allowed Kash to refill it.

As she brought it to her mouth, the limo stopped without warning and the contents of the glass soaked the front of her lavender shell, transforming it instantly into a winning wet-T-shirt contest entry. "Damn, that's cold!"

Kash positively guffawed, and Gillian was only slightly less obnoxious about delighting in her humiliation.

"Good thing your luggage is in the trunk so you can change," Kash commented. She tilted her head at Isabel's large leather purse. "Or do you routinely carry an extra shirt for such occasions?"

Gillian howled.

Isabel could feel her ears warm as she reached into the purse for a burgundy shell, similar to the one she had on. "With all due respect, screw you both."

Gillian and Kash cracked up even more and glanced at each other. Something about that unspoken interaction between them sent a chill of disquiet through Isabel, but she didn't stop to examine why.

Grateful for the tinted windows, she reached down to remove her soaked top. Ordinarily, she wouldn't have given a thought to what she was about to do. But then she realized that Kash was checking out her breasts, vividly outlined against the sheer fabric, erect nipples and all. *Could you be any more blatant about it?* She should have been appalled by Kash's overt leering, but she was surprised to find she actually kind of…liked it. Since the limo was braking in front of Kash's studio, she decided it was better to wait.

"Shall we?" Kash led them to the elevators as Isabel tried to ignore the stares of the people around them and held her purse in front of her as she crossed the lobby. They rode up without saying much, Gillian and Kash both unsuccessfully trying to keep the smiles off their faces, much to Isabel's annoyance.

"Someplace I can change?" she asked once they got inside the studio.

"Sure. There." Kash pointed to the restroom before she started setting up her lights for the shoot. Gillian stood nearby, watching her.

"Are you bringing anyone along?" Gillian asked. "Assistant or… friend, or something?"

"Nope. Only me." Kash paused to acknowledge Gillian, making no effort to disguise her slow and appreciative assessment of the tall young woman. Kash pegged her as about twenty-five or twenty-six, a bit younger than Isabel. She wore her clothes well, and her taste in fabrics and cut was superb. She was restrained in her use of makeup, and expert at what types and colors suited her complexion. *That threesome idea sure went down the tubes. But it might be amusing to spend some time with this one.* "Any particular reason you're asking?" She stared at Gillian's small but well-shaped breasts as she said this, to make her intentions clear.

Gillian waited until Kash's eyes met hers again to answer. "I thought we might have some fun together." She smiled, a little shyly.

Women who weren't famous were often like this when they came on to Kash. They probably thought they didn't stand a chance, but what the hell, why not go for it. She admired that attitude.

"No strings. Just some fun," Gillian added.

Before Kash had a chance to respond, the door to the restroom opened and Isabel stepped out.

When Isabel saw the way that Kash and Gillian were smiling at each other, once again she had that feeling of disquiet that had bothered her earlier. *Shrug it off. It's really none of your business, anyway.*

Kash directed Gillian toward the same couch that Isabel had occupied two days earlier. "You can watch from over there." Then she asked Isabel, "Ready?"

Isabel had changed her top and run a brush through her hair. She still wore no trace of makeup, however, not even lipstick. Her fair complexion would be washed out under the studio lights, Kash knew, but she was loath to ask her to apply any cosmetics she didn't ordinarily wear. Besides, the more pale and washed out Isabel appeared in the "before" makeover pictures, the more dramatic the change in the photos she would take once the professional hair, makeup, and fashion people had spent a turn with her. Miranda loved starkly contrasting before-and-afters. *I'll have to adjust my lights.*

"Yes. Where do you want me?" Isabel asked.

"Here, on the stool. Turn three-quarters face front, to start." While Isabel got into position, Kash fixed the correct lens to her Hasselblad. She fought the urge to laugh when she realized Isabel seemed to be taking exceptional care to watch where she stepped.

"Okay, Isabel, try to relax. Have fun with this. Think pleasant thoughts, and try to give me some different poses and expressions." Kash moved a couple of the lights to minimize the washout of Isabel's pale skin. "Think about how much fun you'll have on the trip. All the sights you're going to see."

It was in her viewfinder that Kash first began to appreciate the nuances of Isabel's natural beauty. It wasn't the obvious kind of head-turning presence that some Hollywood stars had onscreen. Nor the surgically enhanced, Botox-injected, or cosmetically garnered appeal that usually contributed to a model's or actress's popularity.

Most women she photographed came to her after spending hours in front of a mirror, hiding imperfections and accentuating all their desirable features until the overall effect at any distance was one of effortless near perfection.

But this one came as is. And Kash could see that she really didn't need any help to be attractive. Isabel had been blessed with a pleasing oval face, and her lightly freckled skin was flawless. She had a slightly upturned nose, high cheekbones, and naturally rosy lips over that memorably imperfect smile. The blond eyebrows and long blond eyelashes that framed her deep blue eyes might seem unremarkable from several feet away, but up close, Kash could appreciate their near-translucent purity.

No, she was nothing at all like the women Kash normally photographed and bedded. This one was comfortable in her own skin and not obsessed with how she came off on camera. Nor with how quickly she could flirt with Kash and get her attention.

When she zoomed out to take full body shots of Isabel, she could also appreciate for the first time how fit she was. And how nervous, too, though she was hiding it fairly well. Kash was used to the obvious telltale signs that so many of her subjects exhibited: fidgeting, tics, shaking hands, inane chatter. Some new models licked their lips a lot, or bit the inside of their cheeks, totally unaware they were doing it.

Isabel was trying to appear at ease. She was gripping the sides of the stool she was sitting on so tightly her knuckles appeared bony, but it kept her hands and body from shaking. Her smile was forced, though, and her breathing was shallow. And she was avoiding eye contact with the camera.

Her frail vulnerability made Kash briefly regret having given her a hard time about their first meeting. There was something very appealing about her naïveté and her thinly disguised efforts to appear more nonchalant about all of this than she really was. *But I bet this one comes with more strings attached than I want to deal with. I've been the way I am much too long to be able to give someone like her what she needs.*

"Chill, Isabel," she said. "You look like you're on trial for your life." Miranda wouldn't be pleased with "before" photos that made it seem as though the contest winner was hating every minute of this experience.

"I'm smiling," Isabel protested halfheartedly. She had always hated having her photograph taken, and this occasion was certainly no exception. She wondered how it was possible that she always seemed to be caught with her eyes closed, or mouth hanging open, or with some other pictorial defect that made her dreadfully unattractive.

"That's the smile you use with cops when you get pulled over," Gillian remarked from the peanut gallery.

"And what does she get pulled over for?" Kash asked, clicking off a half dozen shots as she moved around Isabel.

"Speeding, mostly," Gillian volunteered. "And occasional problems with her truck, usually missing headlights or taillights."

Isabel frowned and, to her annoyance, Kash rapidly took several more photos in quick succession, close in to her face.

"You drive a truck, and you have a lead foot, eh?" Kash finally paused and took her attention away from the viewfinder long enough to achieve eye contact with Isabel. "I wouldn't have guessed that. There may be hope for you yet."

That remark turned the frown into a smile long enough for her to get a few usable shots.

CHAPTER THREE

"How are we ever going to see everything in four days?"
Isabel already had written an impressive list of must-see
monuments, museums, and other attractions on the small notebook
in front of her, and she wasn't even halfway through the Paris travel
guide. "How much longer before we land?"

"Ten minutes less than the last time you asked," Gillian whispered.
Everyone around them in business class was trying to sleep. "And if
you ask me again soon, I'm going to have to drug you."

They'd bought guidebooks at an airport bookstore, and Gillian
was currently occupied with the others, busily marking pages about
lesbian clubs and bars. "By the way, don't forget you promised I can
plan what we do at night."

"Unless Kash wants to do night photo shoots," Isabel reminded
her. "I imagine she'll want pictures of the Eiffel Tower lit up and the
Champs Elysées, don't you?"

"You'd think so. Has she given you any idea how this is going
to work? I mean, is she going to follow us around and take pictures?"
Gillian laid down the Rome guidebook and flipped through the one
on Cairo. "I sure wouldn't mind that, her hanging with us. Give me a
chance to get to know her better."

That feeling of odd unease came over Isabel again. *I have no right
to object if the two of them get together. Why is this bothering me?*

"Or do you suppose it's going to be the other way around," Gillian
wondered. "We get a lot of time to ourselves and meet up with her when
and where she wants to take photos?"

Isabel shrugged. "No idea. But she probably has better things to do than stick with us when she doesn't have to." She half stood so she could see across the cabin to where Kash had moved. All the lights in that area were out. "Can't ask her now—I bet she's asleep."

"No wonder, considering you bored her during half of our flight by talking about every work of art in every museum you plan to visit in Paris. You're such a plan-every-minute, I-hate-surprises kind of person."

"Hey, I can be spontaneous."

Gillian laughed. "Since when?"

"Since always. You sound like I'm no fun at all!"

"Oh, you know that's not true," Gillian said. "If you weren't a blast to be around, I wouldn't be spending most of my free time with you. I'm only saying you plan everything way too much."

"We need some planning on this trip or we won't get to see everything we want to."

"Balance, Izzy. Balance." Gillian yawned and turned off her light. "You need to be more open to the unexpected—the cute French dyke who asks you to dance, or the hot Italian chick who catches your eye. Do you some good to let the evening take you where it wants to once in a while."

"Just because we're going overseas doesn't mean I'm suddenly going to behave like a nymphomaniac."

"I'm only saying you might be missing more than you realize." Gillian leaned her seat back and spread a blanket over herself. "There's a lot to be said for letting your body have what it wants and needs without attaching some heavy emotional baggage to it all. Think about it?"

Isabel did think about it, long after Gillian fell asleep. A part of her was indeed tempted to forgo her usual reservations about casual sex during this trip. The idea of merely having some fun and letting her body take over seemed very liberating, especially since she was in the midst of a rather long drought, sex-wise, and masturbation wasn't all that satisfying.

What's the harm, really? Other women do it all the time and don't think twice. Like Kash and Gillian. She wondered whether her long-held views on sex and intimacy were too old-fashioned and unrealistic. *You wait, you get to know them first, because you've always wanted it to be about more than mere quick physical gratification. Even though, in the end, that's about all it boils down to anyway. You always want it to be more, but it rarely is. At least not for long.*

Closing her eyes, she imagined giving in to Gillian's advice and pictured herself in a darkened nightclub in Paris, letting a stranger touch her and kiss her. Or even better, imagining Kash doing that. Her heart picked up speed, and a warm flush spread through her body. *Maybe she's right. Maybe I am missing out.*

❖

"Our driver will meet us out front," Kash told Isabel and Gillian as they waited for their luggage at Orly. The sun had barely cleared the horizon. It colored the eastern sky with an orange glow. "I thought I'd let you have today to explore. We can wait until tomorrow to take photos."

"You're not coming with us?" Gillian frowned. "Gee, it would sure be a lot more fun with someone who knows the city. I mean, you've been here a lot, right?"

Kash had to smile at Gillian's diplomacy. If she knew about her familiarity with Paris, she had learned about it from the lengthy tabloid accounts about her previous misadventures here. "Many times. Paris doesn't hold any secrets for me, and I have some work. It's better for you to do your own thing."

After they collected their bags, they made their way to customs and got in line to have their passports stamped.

"So…you told me you're going to shoot pictures tomorrow…" Isabel retrieved the list of Paris attractions she'd compiled during their flight. "Any idea how long that will take? I mean, I'd like to be able to kind of plan my time—"

"That's an understatement," Gillian volunteered, rolling her eyes.

"Hush, you." Isabel swatted her lightly on the arm.

"Well, we get four days at each location," Kash said. "The first day you can pretty much always plan to have to yourself. I'll be scouting locations. We'll do the magazine photos generally on the second or third day. But weather will be a huge factor since almost all the shoots will be outdoors, so we have to be flexible. Depending on the number of setups, it'll probably take six to eight hours in each city. Oh—and your makeover has been scheduled for your second full day in Rome. That'll take six hours at least. Hair. Makeup. Trying on clothes."

"So with your photo day...that leaves me with only two days there to myself." Isabel frowned as she dug through her bag for her must-see-in-Rome list. It was nearly as long as her Paris one.

Kash glanced over Isabel's shoulder at the lists. "That's quite a lot to cram in. You might want to trim those to the sights you want to see most, or you'll burn yourself out before this trip is half over."

"Oh, I have lots and lots of energy," Isabel said.

Usually when women volunteered that information, Kash took it as welcome news. With Isabel, however, it sounded vaguely foreboding.

"Ladies. *Next*, please." A portly customs agent waved Isabel forward impatiently.

❖

Their driver was a stubble-bearded, squat local named Alain, a serious young man currently enrolled at Speos, the Paris Photographic Institute. Kash had no idea how Miranda had selected him, but he spoke perfect English, seemed eminently capable, and fawned over her from the start. He'd be ideal. Kash hoped that Miranda had managed to do as well in their other stops.

They were barely underway before Isabel began peppering Alain with questions.

She pulled out her handwritten Paris itinerary and asked him how much time she should allow for each stop, and travel time, interrupting herself to inquire about some building they were passing. She also sought his advice on places to eat and foods to try, and penciled those in on her list.

But while Isabel talked virtually nonstop through the morning rush hour all the way to the hotel, Kash noticed that Gillian had one eye on the scenery and the other on *her*. She was obviously waiting for a reply to her sexual proposition, but wasn't going to push it.

Why shouldn't I? First off, it could be problematic if Gillian secretly harbored illusions about anything more than a one-night stand. It wasn't like she could avoid her afterward. And she still didn't know what the score was between Isabel and Gillian. If a pretty woman was making herself available, that didn't usually matter. But she was going to see a lot of Isabel, and things could get awkward if these two were involved. *No. Better to wait.*

"Voilà," Alain announced with a flourish as they pulled up in front of the historic Hotel Napoleon, a turn-of-the century building a breath away from the Champs Elysées.

"We're staying here?" Isabel took in the elegantly detailed façade with its burgundy awnings, ornate iron balconies, and window boxes filled with red geraniums. The massive glass doors at the entrance were flanked by half a dozen spruce trees, meticulously groomed into perfect cones and each in its own planter.

"Prepare to be pampered," Kash informed them. "Alain, if you'd deal with the luggage and then wait for the ladies, please? I won't need you until tomorrow."

"Yes, of course, at your service," he replied.

"You sure?" Isabel asked. "Thanks."

Once inside, Isabel tried not to seem the gawking tourist, but it was hard not to stare at the opulence of the art-deco hotel. She had seemingly stepped back in time, into some French aristocrat's mansion. The polished marble of the entry gave way to exceptional antique rugs, and the walls were decorated with Napoleonic artwork in ornate gilded frames. Directoire-style furniture—upholstered wing chairs and couches in patterns dating back two centuries—was artfully arranged into small groups throughout the expansive lobby and reception area.

"Sure beats the hell out of any place I've ever stayed," Gillian said in a low voice.

"I can't wait to see our room," Isabel agreed.

"Welcome to the Hotel Napoleon, ladies." The concierge intercepted them before they reached the front desk. Though he addressed them all, his attention was fully on Kash. "How wonderful to have you stay with us again, Miss Kashnikova."

"Nice to see you again, Claude," Kash responded.

"We've upgraded you to the Errol Flynn Suite, of course, and your friends are in the Josephine Suite. If you'll follow me?"

As they started toward the elevators, two young bellhops arrived to take charge of their hand luggage, while a third rolled a brass cart out for their larger bags.

"That's very nice of you to put me in the Flynn Suite, Claude,"

Kash said as they started the ride up. "But I'd like you to switch that, if you would, and put these ladies in there."

"My pleasure, Miss Kashnikova. As you wish."

Kash felt a hand on her shoulder. Isabel's. She half turned to acknowledge her but didn't speak.

"Nice of you to give us your room."

Shrugging, she faced forward again, a little embarrassed. She'd surprised herself with the impulsive gesture. She definitely wasn't the magnanimous type, and the Flynn had the choice view. The last time she stayed here, she had spent hours on its balcony. But she'd become jaded by such opulence, and she rather liked the awestruck expression she'd seen on Isabel's face as they walked through the lobby. She knew the luxury of the Flynn Suite would thrill Isabel in a way that had been lost to her a long time ago.

Getting soft in my old age. Kash glanced at her watch to note the date. One month and one day until she turned forty. *Forty.* She still couldn't believe it. People who hung around models thought thirty was old. To them, forty was ancient.

"I'll get you an itinerary for tomorrow by late in the day, Isabel," Kash said as the elevator slowed. "But I'd plan on leaving here at ten for the Eiffel Tower." She turned to the concierge. "Claude, I can see myself from here."

"Certainly, miss." He handed her bellboy the Josephine Suite's keycard.

"What do you want me to wear?" Isabel asked.

"Your choice on this one," Kash said. "Pick something that says *you.* That makes you feel good. See you tomorrow. Have fun."

Claude showed Isabel and Gillian into the Errol Flynn Presidential Suite, a spacious and sunny two-bedroom, two-bath suite with three televisions, a comfortable lounge area, and best of all, a private balcony with a view of both the Eiffel Tower and nearby Arc de Triomphe.

Fresh flowers awaited them, along with the usual luxury amenities. And a card welcoming Natasha Kashnikova back to the Napoleon lay in front of a sterling-silver ice bucket, within which nestled a square bottle of Jewel of Russia vodka.

"You'll not mind, I hope," Claude said, as he plucked the ice bucket off the table, "if I exchange this with the champagne that was meant to welcome you."

"Certainly not!" Isabel replied.

"Is there anything else I may do for you at present?" Claude asked.

"Answer a question, if you would." Isabel stood at the doors leading out to the balcony.

"Certainly, miss," Claude replied.

"How is this suite different from the other?"

Claude smiled. "Our Josephine Suite is a bit smaller. One bedroom instead of two, with one bath. And it has a balcony that overlooks the inner courtyard. Otherwise the appointments are very similar."

"I see. Thank you, Claude."

He gave a small bow. "I am at your service, ladies."

After he had gone, Gillian and Isabel stood on the balcony.

"God, what a view. Sure nice of Kash to switch with us." Gillian leaned over the rail to check out the people passing by on the Avenue de Friedland below.

"It sure was," Isabel agreed. *She didn't have to do that. I wonder why she did. Would I give this up for strangers?* "I want to have breakfast out here every morning."

"I bet room service here is a fortune," Gillian said. "Will the magazine pay for all that?"

"Yup. Three meals a day. It's all spelled out in those papers they gave me. There are limits on the food, entertainment, and incidental travel expenses, but they're all pretty high. I don't think we have to worry about overspending."

"Cool."

"So…you ready to go hit the streets of Paris?" Isabel was so anxious to get going she was bouncing up and down on the balls of her feet.

"Man, that list of yours is burning a hole in your pocket." Gillian laughed and put her arm around Isabel's shoulder. "Sure, Izzy. Whatever you want."

"What I really want is for time to stop. Or at least drag from here on out." She put her head on Gillian's shoulder and sighed. "I'm afraid this will all be over much too quickly."

"Like I've been saying, you gotta live in the moment." Gillian hugged her. "Don't think about the last day until it gets here, or you'll miss out on the here and now."

"Good advice." She pushed Gillian toward the door to the suite. "Come on, then. Grab your camera and let's get this party started."

❖

Since she'd given their driver to Isabel and Gillian, Kash hired a cab for the morning and had the driver take her to the places she planned to shoot Isabel the next day. She knew them well from memory, but she wanted to make sure there were no scaffolds or construction zones or the like.

By early afternoon, she was stretched out on a chaise lounge on her balcony, fresh ice chilling the vodka. Claude always remembered her brand and was compensated accordingly. *It's all in the details.* Her view was different than expected, but pleasantly serene. The inner courtyard of the Hotel Napoleon was an oasis in the heart of Paris, full of greenery and flowers. Still, she missed her old view. *I've gotten way too used to being spoiled.*

After selecting the "Chill" playlist on her MP3 player, she closed her eyes, sipping occasionally from the heavy crystal tumbler. Coltrane. *That's better.*

She usually tried to avoid thinking too hard about her life and whether it was all she wanted it to be, but lately, with the calendar pages flipping inexorably toward another decade milestone, she couldn't escape a certain amount of self-examination.

Fucking birthdays anyway. It was impossible to be facing forty. Her last birthday seemed like only yesterday, and her thirtieth not all that long ago. Time had certainly begun to speed up in recent years.

So far, her body had been pretty good to her, except for those lines materializing on her face. *Need to think about doing something about those.* Botox injections didn't appeal to her, perhaps because she'd seen so many women come out of them resembling some macabre swollen twin of themselves. *I wonder if those antiwrinkle creams and shit work.*

One of the things she dreaded most about aging was the inevitable changes to her body. *And the tabloids will chronicle every flaw.* She tried to console herself with the knowledge that she would still have all the other things that attracted women. *The money, the celebrity, the star that you can make them with your camera.* As long as she stayed on the A-list, she'd never have a problem getting laid.

But that knowledge did nothing to ease her discontent.

When she had decided to pursue photography, half her life ago, she had not been motivated by fame and money and sex. She had been into art and sharing her point of view, giving people a new way to reflect upon the world and themselves.

Somewhere along the line, though, things had changed. Not overnight, and not in a way she had recognized as harmful. The changes were insidious, masquerading as encouragement and opportunities. Increasingly, people had known her on the street and asked for her autograph. Before long, she was offered the best tables in restaurants, the plushest suites in hotels. Everyone wanted to interview her, and invitations to every important party and function started pouring in, far too many for her to accept. She had eaten it up.

Part of you wanted this. But where has it gotten you? To a place where you no longer recognize yourself and where nothing fully satisfies you. Nothing. You take whatever pictures you have to take, do what's expected of you, and then, at the end of the day, return home to an empty house and sleep alone. She remembered what Dix, the tabloid photographer, had said. "You use your camera to get rich and get laid. What the hell do you think makes you better than me?"

Though she despised the rag shooters and thought herself far above them, there was some truth to his accusation. If she didn't watch out, the line between them would be even further blurred as time went on. *How long has it been since you've taken a photo that really says something?*

What was incredibly ironic, she mused, was how different she was from the party-girl persona the tabloids had created. Not that she led a chaste life. Quite the contrary. She enjoyed sex and was often up for a quick tryst, if the woman was hot. But when she was out and captured by the tabloids she was usually fulfilling some obligation. Most evenings she spent in solitude, watching a film, reading a book, or working on her photographs. And that solitary existence was wearing thin.

She poured herself another glass of vodka. When she had allowed fame to seduce her, she really had no idea the toll it would exact. *Before you knew it, you were living a life you didn't recognize.* One where every woman she met wanted something from her. Most didn't hesitate to reveal their motives, because they knew her reputation and didn't expect to have a second opportunity. A few, thinking themselves more clever, appealed to her for another fuck at another time, hoping to somehow grow closer to her and improve their odds of getting what they *really* wanted. *You've created a world for yourself where you can get laid any time, but forget being able to trust anyone. How is that world going to feel when you turn fifty?*

Taking this photo assignment was a mistake. She was going to have far too much time to *think* about things. And damn poor scheduling to happen so close to her birthday. Why hadn't she seen this coming? *Because you've been too successful at avoiding such introspection.*

Maybe you should hang out with Isabel and Gillian, at least some of the time. Do you good to be reminded about what the real world is like, outside of New York and Hollywood. What genuine people are all about. At least they would distract you. And any distraction right now was welcome. She could take some candid shots of Isabel and maybe a few photographs for herself. See if that artist inside of her was dead, or in hibernation.

❖

The first stop on Isabel's lengthy itinerary was the Louvre, only a fraction of which they'd be able to see in the three and a half hours she had devoted to it. But they still would manage to hit all the most important and well-known exhibits because she had mapped out a route for them on the floor plan in the guidebook.

"I thought you agreed to be more spontaneous," Gillian chided, when Isabel insisted they had lingered at the *Mona Lisa* long enough and it was time to move on to the Venus de Milo. As they trekked to the famed statue she put her arm around Isabel's waist. "Honey, you're starting to sound like a drill sergeant from hell, and we're only a couple of hours into the trip."

"There's a lot I want to see!" Isabel replied, nonplussed, without slowing her steps. "And you do realize that the sooner we get through my stops, the faster we can get to yours."

Gillian put her hand in front of her mouth. "Oops. My bad. Forget I said anything. Lead on, Sarge."

"By the way," Isabel said, "you're welcome to take off on your own tomorrow while I'm tied up doing these photo shoots, if there's stuff you want to see. Kash said it would take six hours—I have no idea how many stops that will involve, but you may be sitting around a lot."

"No prob, I'll hang with you guys. None of the clubs get going until late at night, and you'll be done long before then. And even if Kash is busy the whole time working, it should give me a chance to get to know her better," Gillian said. "She sure doesn't volunteer much, does she? Not really what I expected."

"Yeah, I've had that same thought." Isabel slowed to briefly admire a life-sized sculpture of three nude women. "I pictured her being more outgoing and gregarious. But I guess we *are* strangers, and this is only a job for her. Maybe she's more chatty with her friends."

"Probably right," Gillian agreed. "She sure seems to know *everybody.* She's on *Oprah*, and *Ellen*, and *Letterman* all the time. I'm probably dreaming to think she'd have any interest in me."

"Hey, don't sell yourself short," Isabel said. "You're hot. You're fun. And you have three weeks for her to get to know you." They arrived at the Venus de Milo and she took her time admiring the sculpture from all angles.

"Say, Izzy…" Gillian stood beside her and put an arm on her shoulder. "It's interesting that you want to spend all day admiring paintings and statues of women rather than the real thing. I mean, wouldn't you rather have the warm, breathing variety instead of cold, hard marble?"

"These are some of the world's greatest masterpieces, Gill," she said defensively. "Art enriches the soul and inspires the creative mind. These things fulfill me in the same way that music touches you."

"Okay, I'll buy that to a certain extent," Gillian replied. "But do you think that's really all there is to it?"

The question gave her pause. "Well, maybe you have a *small* point," she conceded. "I've had only disappointments with the real thing. And these always make me happy—guaranteed. They don't appear to be one thing one day and turn out to be something else entirely the next. What you see is what you get."

"That's true of some real women, too." Gillian squeezed her shoulder. "But you gotta give them a chance."

"I'll think about it. Now, Egypt exhibit next." Isabel put her arm through Gillian's and led her toward their final stop. "Then some lunch. And this afternoon…let's see. Notre Dame and a walk through the Latin Quarter…and I'd like to get in the Père-Lachaise Cemetery before dinner."

"We're going to a *cemetery*? You're kidding, right?"

"Oh, it'll be great, Gil—it's full of these unique old tombs and sculptures, and memorials to the victims of the concentration camps. And lots of famous people are buried there: Chopin, Jim Morrison, Oscar Wilde, Gertrude Stein."

"Izzy, you have *such* a weird idea of how to have fun in Paris," Gillian said, shaking her head.

Chapter Four

"Hi there! Gorgeous morning, isn't it? Mind if I join you?" The voice was gratingly chipper, much too loud, and entirely too close to her vodka-hammered skull. Kash struggled to crack open her eyes. *They need to make truly opaque sunglasses for mornings after.* She'd intended to have her coffee inside the hotel restaurant, in a quiet, dark corner. But the place had been packed and noisy, and she thought the fresh air might help her feel better, so she had carried her triple espresso to a quiet bench in the nearest park, at the Rue Balzac.

Isabel stared down at her with an amused expression, her face flushed from jogging. Her long blond hair was pulled back into a ponytail, and she wore navy blue running shorts, a baby blue T-shirt, and sneakers. "I was going to ask if you wanted to run a while with me, but I don't think an earthquake could shake you from this bench."

"Quite the comedy routine," Kash replied, shielding her eyes with her hand. "You should take it on the road, Pollyanna. And soon. *Very* soon."

Ignoring the suggestion, Isabel planted herself on the seat beside her. "Are you always this grumpy in the morning?"

Kash glowered at her. "Are you always this *perky*?"

The tone of her voice made the question sound undeniably like "go to hell and leave me alone," but Isabel decided to ignore it. *That's some hangover.* Under normal circumstances, she might be a bit more compassionate about someone in such a state. But it was a beautiful morning…she was in Paris…*Paris!*…and she was too damn happy to let Kash's sour mood bother her. "Yup, guess I am. Most days I virtually leap out of bed. For me, sleeping is a waste of time."

Kash sighed and shut her eyes. *I wonder if I can get the hotel to deliver coffee to me here?* "Do you mind if we put off the shoot until this afternoon? Say, two o'clock?"

"Whatever you like. I'm fine with skipping the pictures altogether."

Huh? Skip the pictures? Kash opened her eyes fractionally again, though the blinding glare stabbed at her hangover. She thought back to Isabel's wooden performance at their first shoot back in her studio. "If you're worried about how you'll come off on camera there's no need. I can make a star out of anyone." *That's what you all want, so that's what I do*, she added bitterly to herself.

"It's not that. I mean...no disrespect intended, to you *or* the magazine. Like I told you that first day, I think you take amazing photographs, and I'm really grateful for this trip and everything—"

"But?"

"But this makeover and being in the magazine is really my least favorite part of the contest." Isabel bent over and carefully retied her shoelaces as she talked.

It was one of the dozens of gambits that women had used with Kash to gauge her interest in them—find some way to expose a part of their body and see if she was paying attention. Some were more subtle than others. Kash likened it to the preening displays of exotic birds during mating season, and she reacted as she always did, more out of habit than anything else. She let her eyes linger on the smooth expanse of pale skin exposed on Isabel's lower back. *Nice ass.*

"I mean, you heard the story at the news conference. Gillian entered me in this—" Isabel stopped abruptly when she saw where Kash's eyes were. She jerked up and felt a rosy blush of embarrassment color her cheeks.

"I...uh..." Isabel was so surprised at the way Kash was openly leering at her, like she had in the limo, that she couldn't continue for a moment. She was shocked as well by her own reaction. She liked it, very much. Perhaps a little too much. "I..." *What was I saying? Oh, yeah.* "I...I never tried to get on any cover. I'd never even picked up *Sophisticated Women* until after I got the letter saying I'd won."

"Still, you *did* win." Kash frowned at her empty coffee cup, wishing it could refill itself and grudgingly admitting to herself that Isabel hadn't intended to flirt.

"I'd be deliriously happy to let someone else have my fifteen minutes of fame, thank you very much." Isabel plucked the cup out of her hand. "Stay put. I'll get you some more." She jumped up. "I saw a place down the block. Black?"

Kash squinted up at her. "Very considerate. A triple espresso, please."

"Coming right up," Isabel called back over her shoulder as she jogged away. *Now what was that all about?* She was glad to put a little distance between them while she regained her composure.

Kash slouched against the bench, head back, eyes closed. She was irked to think that anyone—let alone some naïve Middle America nobody—might decline the rare opportunity to be captured by her camera. *Ninety-nine out of every one hundred women would jump at the chance. More than that, probably. She can't be serious. This has to be some cockeyed, roundabout way to get my attention.*

She was still trying to figure out Isabel's story when the subject of her ruminations reappeared with her triple espresso and an orange juice for herself. "Thanks." Her head still throbbed. Caffeine alone would not be enough. "See any pharmacies nearby?"

Isabel grinned and set down her juice. "At your service. Within two blocks. Whatcha need? Aspirin?"

"And one of those instant cold packs." She reached for her wallet, but Isabel was already up and jogging away again.

"Got it," she hollered back over her shoulder.

What's your story, Isabel Sterling? Everyone had a motive. Everyone. And sooner or later, it always made itself known. All she had to do was wait.

It wasn't long before Isabel rematerialized with aspirin and a cold pack. "Shall I leave you alone now to battle your headache in peace?" she asked as she handed over her purchases and reached for her juice.

"Thanks, and no. Not necessary. Sit," Kash said as she popped three of the aspirin. "So why don't you want to be a cover girl?"

Isabel shrugged as she settled back on the bench. "It's not my thing."

"You don't strike me as the shy type." She activated the cold pack and held it against the back of her neck. It was hard to really relax and hold it there at the same time, but she knew it would help her hangover.

"Here, let me," Isabel offered.

Her hand rested on Kash's, and Kash slipped hers out and accepted the help. Elbows on her knees, she let the cold penetrate. "Oh, yeah. That's better."

Isabel had been keenly aware of the brief touch of their hands, and she was conscious now of the close proximity of their bodies. Kash had on black jeans and a snug black T-shirt that allowed a glimpse of the lean musculature of her back, shoulders, and upper arms. *God, Kash, you really have a nice body. No wonder all the women throw themselves at you.* "I hope you had enough fun getting this way that it was worth it." Isabel spoke with more humor than reproach.

"What does fun ever have to do with it? Don't change the subject," Kash said. "So if you're not shy, why don't you want to be in the magazine? Most women would consider it their big chance at fame."

"Well, I guess I'm not most women. Or perhaps just not like most of the women you know."

Kash had heard that line before. Women always wanted to be different. Special. They thought they could ask for anything then. Perhaps Isabel's approach wasn't that unique after all. *What do you really want?* "What is it about the attention that bothers you?" she pressed.

Isabel considered her answer for a while. "I simply have no desire to be recognized everywhere I go. I've never craved fame. It's even less appealing since the press conference. I can't imagine living the life you lead."

"It can get tedious with the paparazzi," Kash agreed, then paused. "That must sound odd coming from me."

"Oh, not at all. The only thing you have in common with them are the tools of your trade."

Coming from Isabel, the remark sounded sincere, and Kash mentally thanked her for it. Perhaps it had been true early on. But she thought again of what Dix had said and how far she had strayed from her once-noble career objectives. Perhaps she had more in common with the paparazzi than she was willing to admit.

"You shouldn't have such a bad time from here on." She sat up and took the ice bag from Isabel. "Thanks." Her head felt a lot better. "The press conference was worse than it should have been because I was there. The tabloid guys can get twenty grand or better if they catch me doing something really stupid, and it's rare for me to appear at a press conference where they can shout questions at me. Of course, they got real interested in you when you took a header."

Isabel grimaced.

"But as long as you don't do anything similar, you'll just have to endure a few months of being recognized, once the magazine comes out," Kash said. "And you'll probably get some interview offers afterward. So be careful of which ones you take. And remember, the more money they offer, the worse they'll make it for you—that's usually the case, anyway."

"Well, I don't intend to do anything I don't absolutely *have* to do to fulfill my obligations to the magazine," Isabel declared.

We'll see. Even those rare birds who claim not to want celebrity status succumb when it falls in their lap. "Fame does have its advantages at times," Kash said.

"I imagine it does. Like getting the Errol Flynn Suite whenever you visit Paris?"

Kash rubbed at her eyes. "Yes, there's that, among other things."

Isabel sat back against the bench and crossed her legs. "Why did you give us your suite? I'm curious."

"Eh, not a big deal." She waved off the gesture as insignificant. "I've seen that view and thought the two of you might appreciate the extra room." She hoped that a mention of the second bedroom might prompt a response from Isabel that would clarify her relationship with Gillian, but Isabel failed to take the bait.

"Well, it was incredibly sweet. Thanks."

Sweet? Now that's a new one. Kash chuckled. Not for a minute would she ever believe such a thing, and she knew it was probably only a line, but she had to admit that it felt nice to imagine someone might think that of her. "'Sweet' isn't a word that people often apply to me."

"No?"

"No."

"How do your friends describe you, then?" Isabel sipped her juice.

The question demanded more honest introspection than Kash was willing to offer someone she barely knew. Too often, when she had volunteered any kind of personal information to a woman, her words appeared verbatim later in some tabloid or blog, often out of context. "That would be for them to say."

She knew how Miranda would probably describe her, since she

wasn't shy about offering her blunt assessment of Kash whenever she needed a good smack to the side of the head. Guarded and controlling. She heard those two descriptives a lot, from her and others. And detached, because she didn't wear her emotions on her sleeve or volunteer a lot of what went on inside her.

Arrogant was another one that was becoming more popular, and she could see its validity. She hadn't always been so. But once she was able to have who and what she wanted with the snap of her fingers, she had never been reluctant to spell out her desires. Arrogance was the scar that frequent and easy acquiescence had left.

"If I'm being presumptuous, forgive me. I'll leave you to recover from your hangover in peace," Isabel said, getting to her feet. "I still have a lot of Paris to see. So I'll meet you at the hotel at two?"

"Yes, at two," Kash said. "And thanks."

"Don't mention it."

As she watched Isabel jog toward the hotel, Kash slightly regretted having been her usual abrupt self. Outwardly, Isabel had been nothing but friendly and thoughtful. And she seemed sincere and genuinely self-effacing. Could she be for real? Long ago, Kash had dared think that someone might be nice to her and show interest merely because they liked her. But it had been a long time since she'd allowed herself the luxury of that delusion.

❖

"So that outfit says *you*, huh?" Kash eyed Isabel's choice of attire for their first photo shoot. She might have expected the ensemble, which was well suited for Isabel's no-frills, natural look: low-waisted, faded blue jeans, sandals, and a loose-fitting pale yellow blouse. The blouse wasn't particularly stylish—in fact, it was a bit faded, which suggested it was a favorite garment at least a few years old. Still, it brought out the highlights of Isabel's long, honey blond hair, which shone like wheat in the summer sun.

"My lucky shirt," Isabel explained, following Kash's gaze. "And I'm in these jeans almost seven days a week. Is it okay?"

"It'll be fine," Kash said. "I'll shoot you in your own stuff before the makeover. Afterward we'll put you in your new wardrobe. I'll be doing mostly full-body shots, but some close-ups, too. Try to have fun. Move around, change your expressions, and don't be afraid to act silly."

"Isabel? Silly?" Gillian stifled a laugh. "She'd need at least a couple of drinks for that. Best you can hope for here is relaxed."

Isabel punched her in the arm. "Big help you are."

Since Miranda had challenged Kash to take more than the typical shots of the Eiffel Tower, she ignored the predictable snapshot that every tourist took—the one of a smiling vacationer standing on the terrace of the Palais de Chaillot with the tower as a dramatic backdrop.

Instead, she had Alain set up her equipment on the first stage of the tower, 189 feet in the air, and she photographed Isabel from angles that would utilize the brown girders of the superstructure and the scenery below to provide context.

There was one drawback to her plan. On this sunny July afternoon, a growing legion of tourists decided it was much more fun to watch them than to sightsee.

"Sorry, no autographs," she repeated ad nauseam as the gutsiest of the bunch thrust pens and assorted writing surfaces her way—Eiffel Tower programs, ticket stubs, Paris guidebooks, slips of paper. To the most persistent she added a slightly annoyed, "Hey, some respect, please. I'm trying to work here," which rarely made much of a difference. Gillian and Alain did their best to act as makeshift barricades, keeping an area clear around both her and her subject, but it was an impossible task.

Isabel watched a steady stream of people approach Kash, some shy and others incredibly forward, a few even positioning themselves in front of her camera so that she couldn't ignore them. She couldn't hear everything that was said, but Kash's body language and clipped tone plainly said she wanted to be left alone. *I would hate to have that kind of a life, not able to be out in public without people staring at me all the time and interrupting whatever I'm doing.*

"Okay, Isabel." Kash's exasperation became increasingly evident. "Let's try to wrap this up, can we please? I need you to give me something to work with here. *Move* a little. I have fifty frames with the exact same forced smile and rigid posture. Hell, I'd even settle for your perky morning self."

To Kash's surprise, Isabel grinned and responded with a whimsical series of poses and facial expressions that soon had most of the onlookers laughing and cheering. Not only did Kash get some good photos, but since the autograph hounds were diverted she was able to finish the job with a relative measure of peace.

"For someone who doesn't like attention and cameras, you sure got over it fast," Kash remarked once they were underway to their next stop. "That was like someone flipped a switch."

"Please don't use one that's going to make me seem goofy," Isabel pleaded. "I know I overdid it on some."

"Overdid it?" Gillian said. "I'd have thought you were *on* something if I didn't know you better. Gotta give you props, Izzy. Way to loosen up. What the hell happened?"

"Well…" Isabel ran her hand through her hair. She wasn't entirely sure what *had* come over her. "You're always telling me to go with the moment…" The first part was directed at Gillian, the next at Kash. "And I saw how the crowd was getting on your nerves, so I thought you might welcome a distraction." Also, the sillier she got, the bigger the grin on Kash's face had become. She liked that—a *lot*—but wasn't about to admit it.

For real? Kash's cynical nature was beginning to crack. More and more, she realized that Isabel was refreshingly genuine.

"Like I said, the more I see of fame, the less I want to be on that cover. You sure there's no way out?"

"Not a chance, I'm afraid. It's what we're all here for."

Isabel sighed and stared out of the window. "Ah, well. Can't blame a girl for trying."

Kash studied her face in profile for subtle signs of guile or pretense. There were none. *You're full of surprises, Isabel. Nice surprises.*

❖

They had three more setups that day for the magazine—at Notre Dame and the Louvre, then the Arc de Triomphe after nightfall.

While Alain and Kash unpacked and set up the equipment, Isabel and Gillian enjoyed the spectacular view from the top of the famous arch. They were seemingly at the center of a brilliant star, with twelve streaming avenues of white and red light radiating outward. They faced the brightest and most vibrant of the streams—the famed Champs Elysées, whose wide pedestrian walks were densely crowded on this warm summer night.

"I know we have all these other great places ahead of us, but it's going to be hard to leave Paris." Isabel folded her arms across her chest and hugged herself. "As often as I've dreamed about seeing all this, it's so much more beautiful than I imagined. No offense, Gill—but it's a shame I can't share the most romantic place on earth with that special someone, you know?"

"Maybe you can't spend it with that special someone," Gillian replied, "but tonight I will definitely increase your chances of finding some romance in Paris."

The day before, Isabel had kept them to a tight schedule, with a full day of sightseeing followed by dinner and shopping in the Marais district, then a boat ride on the Seine. Now it was Gillian's turn to pick how they spent their evening. "I don't know about finding romance," she said, "but I'm game for whatever you want to do."

"Cool," Gillian said. "Then prepare your tummy for Greek food. Alain told me about a great place near the club I want to try. Want to see if Kash wants to come along?"

"If you like. But I bet she'll say no. She's evidently got her own entertainment opportunities, from what I saw this morning."

"What happened?"

"While I was out for my run I stumbled upon her in a park near the hotel. She was slumped on a bench, and in the same kind of shape you were the morning after Connie and Shelley's engagement party. How long did it take you to recover from that all-night orgy of sex and alcohol?"

"Ouch." Gillian winced. "Hey! Maybe we should ask Kash where to go after we eat."

No, let's not, Isabel immediately concluded, but didn't say it aloud. It was pure gut reaction, and she knew it had to do with the way Kash had leered at her in the park. Certainly women had looked at her that way before—sexually appreciative and interested—but the attraction was rarely mutual.

This time it had definitely been mutual. Her shiver of excitement at Kash's overt ogling had surprised her, as did her wish that it would happen again. But it hadn't all afternoon, much to her disappointment.

A passing moment and nothing more, I guess. And it's not like it could lead to anything, anyway. She can have anyone she wants. Besides, Gillian's going after her. Best I stop thinking about her that way.

As much as she tried to talk herself out of her attraction, though, so far she was losing the battle. *Which is why I want to steer clear of Kash's favorite nightclubs,* she admitted to herself. Maybe it was silly, but she didn't want to go somewhere where she might see Kash with someone else. That didn't sound like much fun at all.

"They're about ready for me," she said, pushing off from the ledge to make her way to where Kash had set her camera. Isabel could see she intended to use the distant Eiffel Tower, now a mere string of lights against the darkness, as the backdrop.

How ironic. The photo shoots today hadn't been unpleasant, which she had expected after her experience in Kash's studio in Manhattan. Quite the contrary.

Since Kash had fueled her attraction this morning, she had been very much appreciating the opportunity to do nothing but watch her work, and she couldn't ask for a better front-row seat than being her model.

"Ready, Isabel?" Kash gestured toward the place she wanted her to stand.

"Yes, ready." She got into position.

"You've been doing great all afternoon," Kash said encouragingly as she raised her camera. "Keep it up and we'll be done in no time."

And then you can get back to wherever you were last night. For an instant, Isabel was tempted to be less than perfect with her poses in order to prolong the shoot. *Yeah, that's really mature. Get over it.*

Kash zoomed in on Isabel's face and brought the image into focus. In her years photographing people through the detached and extreme close-up view she achieved with her camera, she'd become adept at reading expressions. Now and then, she'd see something in someone's eyes or smile that intrigued her—some spark or hint of mischief she couldn't quite decipher. Usually she let it pass.

But today, she'd caught Isabel watching with a cryptic smile, like she had on right now, and she wondered what was behind it. *What is it you want? Who are you hiding that you think the camera might reveal?* And she was equally curious about the change that had come over Isabel. She'd been stiff and nervous during their first shoot back in Manhattan, but something had finally made her relax and even enjoy their sessions.

"Can I ask you a question without interrupting what you're

doing?" Gillian's voice was so near behind her Kash knew not to step back.

"Sure," she responded, as she continued to click.

Hell, Isabel thought. *Here it comes.*

"We're going to a Greek place in Pigalle for dinner," Gillian said. "And then out for a night on the town. I thought you might have some suggestions about where to go?"

"Depends on what you're in the mood for," Kash responded. *Click. Click.*

"Let's see…hot women, good music, dancing, drinks, and fun."

Kash paused long enough to acknowledge her.

"And you're welcome to come with us, *of course*," Gillian added with a seductive purr. "Maybe I can get a dance with you?"

Kash smiled. Spending time with Isabel and Gillian was a much more pleasant option than another night getting drunk on the balcony. She knew it was stupid to go out to a club. Someone would almost certainly recognize her and probably try to photograph her in some compromising position once she had a drink or two. Wind up on yet another tabloid cover.

But every time she warned herself to stay away from such places, her loneliness drove her back into temptation. *Screw Dix. I'm not going to let him or anyone else dictate where I go and what I do.*

CHAPTER FIVE

K ash! Welcome." The doorman of Vive la Vie recognized her at once. "How nice of you to honor us with a visit. See Vanessa, at the back bar. She'll make sure you're treated right." He stepped aside to admit the three of them, to a chorus of groans from the long line of women waiting in line outside.

It was midnight and the place was crowded, and the booming, driving beat of the music pulsed inside Isabel like a second heartbeat as Kash led them through the throng of bodies.

The club was immense, easily four or five times larger than any of the lesbian bars or clubs she'd visited back home. And scores of beautiful women, dressed to seduce and excite, preened in their perfect hair and makeup, and gyrated in amazingly explicit displays on the dance floor.

No, this was in no way like the bars back in Wisconsin.

Vive la Vie was a sleek, hip space, with modern décor. Square steel columns surrounding the central dance floor created dark and intimate seating areas behind them, with low square couches and matching hassock chairs. The lighting was dim throughout, except for the revolving spots of color on the dancers, so the pink-red neon balustrade around the long bar at the back stood out like a beacon. A matching neon strip on the rail led to an upper-level mezzanine, where more low couches gave their occupants a bird's-eye view of the dancers below.

Gillian, a veteran of the club scene, had begged a stop back at their hotel after the photo shoot so she could change into the low-cut clingy top and miniskirt she'd purchased at a boutique in the Marais. "How cool is *this*, Iz. My, my, *my*."

Kash also fit right in with the clientele. She was wearing low-cut black trousers with a wide-buckled belt, black leather boots, and a white shirt, impeccably tailored and crisply pressed.

Very hot, Isabel had thought when she'd spotted her getting off the elevator.

She herself hadn't changed and still wore her lucky shirt and jeans. She never felt out of place and was comfortable, which was usually enough. She didn't judge by appearances and hoped that others didn't either.

But as they navigated through the dancing women, she noticed the vast difference in the way the crowd responded to each of them. All eyes focused on Kash, in the lead, some in recognition, some not, but all with interest. Many of the women weren't at all shy either—licking their lips provocatively as they smiled or winked at her, or reaching out to lure her into a dance.

Since Kash was leading, she couldn't see her face or gauge her reaction to this attention. And that bothered Isabel more than a little.

Gillian, following Kash, got a lot of appreciative looks, too, and approving smiles at the miniskirt; and Isabel saw at least a couple of women touch her or give her an affirmative nod, like *see me later*.

When the women encountered her and noticed what she was wearing, their faces registered…something else, usually surprise. Some openly disapproved, their expressions virtually screaming *Who are you to be with Kash?* Or they saw her only in passing, barely registering before they moved on to someone more interesting. No one tried to entice her to dance.

The assessment was superficial, by women she didn't care one whit about, and so it shouldn't have bothered her. But she had to admit that it did, at least a little. *Shrug it off. I don't have to let them get to me.*

Meanwhile Kash claimed an empty space at the long bar, but before she could get the attention of the nearest bartender, an attractive brunette with short, spiky hair and Barbie-doll proportions tapped her shoulder.

"Welcome, Kash, we're so pleased you could visit us tonight," the woman said as she extended her hand. She spoke English like a Brit, with an underlying trace of a French accent. "I'm Vanessa, the manager." They shook hands. "May I offer you and your friends a place on the mezzanine with a bit more privacy?"

Kash turned to Gillian and Isabel. "Sound okay to you?"

"Sure!" Gillian answered before Isabel could open her mouth.

"That would be very nice, Vanessa," Kash said.

"What may I offer you to drink?" the manager asked as she waved over the nearest bartender.

"Vodka, on ice. Jewel of Russia, if you have it," Kash answered.

"Yes, we do." Vanessa smiled. "Ladies?"

"Screwdriver, please," Isabel said.

"Bourbon, rocks. Jim Beam?" Gillian asked.

"Of course," Vanessa said. "If you'll follow me?"

She led them to the most secluded small sitting area on the mezzanine, separated from the rest of the upstairs by a privacy screen and cordoned off with a velvet rope. Obviously the VIP area, it had three plush leather couches and the best view of the dance floor.

"Excellent." Kash turned to Vanessa as the bartender from downstairs arrived with their drinks. "Thank you, ladies. I'll remember the hospitality you've shown us this evening."

"Our pleasure. I'll have one of my girls check in on you from time to time, to make sure you have everything you need."

Vanessa had barely withdrawn when a statuesque woman with long blond hair and green eyes slipped past the privacy screen and headed straight toward Kash, intercepting her before she could sit.

Has to be a model, Isabel thought. She had much in common with the women who'd come to Kash's studio. The same height, thin build, beautiful face, and perfect execution of hair, makeup, and clothes that bespoke professional help. Her miniskirt and heels made her seem all long, lean legs. She was stunning.

The surprise on Kash's face as the blonde approached changed to vague recognition just before the woman planted a lingering kiss hello on Kash's mouth.

"Damn," Gillian whispered under her breath. She and Isabel had dropped onto one of the couches with their drinks and were watching the exchange with interest.

Yeah. Damn, Isabel concurred.

"What a surprise!" The stranger was bubbling over with excitement to see Kash. She had an accent, too, but Isabel wasn't sure what it was. German, maybe.

Isabel watched Kash's eyes narrow as though trying to place the woman.

It didn't take long—a slow, sexy smile spread across her face right before she offered up where they'd met. "Amsterdam."

"Yes." The woman smiled back at Kash with the same sultry expression. "Hilde."

"Hilde," Kash repeated, looking her up and down. "How are you?"

"Very well, thank you." She wore a low-cut blouse that showed considerable cleavage. "I have a featured role in a Tarantino film shooting here."

"Congratulations," Kash said.

"Thank you. What brings you to Paris? Business or pleasure?"

Kash glanced toward Isabel and Gillian, then back to the newcomer. "Business," she answered. "Hilde, may I introduce Isabel and Gillian. Ladies, Hilde is a Dutch actress I…became acquainted with last year."

"Nice to meet you," the woman said politely in response to their hellos, though she barely glanced at either of them before returning her full attention to Kash. "So, are you engaged in business tonight?"

"Nooo," Kash answered. A long, drawled response, as though she knew precisely what was coming.

"So you have the evening for pleasure?" the woman pressed, her smile growing.

Kash nodded.

"Have you already made plans?"

Kash shook her head, and the woman moistened her lips as she put her arm through Kash's. "Then let me steal you for a dance?"

"If you'll excuse me, ladies." Kash allowed herself to be led away.

"Well, that didn't take long," Gillian grumped as soon as they were out of earshot. She took a big sip of her bourbon and watched them as they descended the stairs and joined the crowd below.

No shit, Isabel concurred, downing nearly half her drink. She had to support Gillian and what she wanted, but she certainly wouldn't enjoy watching Kash live up to her sordid reputation. Not that she had much choice. From the VIP couches they could easily see all of the dancers below.

The two were dancing close, very close, and Isabel couldn't take her eyes off them. First they swayed face-to-face, their eyes pinned to each other. Hilde, a few inches taller, had her arms around Kash's neck, while Kash had draped her hands loosely on the woman's hips.

After a while, Kash spun Hilde around and hugged her from behind, and they gyrated hip to hip in a sensual bump and grind that was intoxicating to watch.

"Hey, so she ran into an old acquaintance." She tried to sound flippant but sounded unconvincing even to herself. *A drop-dead-gorgeous acquaintance. And I swear, they look like they're going to have sex right here in front of us.* "Maybe you'll get a dance later with her. Or another night, in another club."

"Yeah, you're right." Gillian brightened. "I've got lots of time."

They watched as the women dancing around Kash began to recognize her, many gravitating purposefully into her field of vision, trying to catch her eye. Now and then, one would dance close enough to rub a hip seductively against her or stroke her arm or back in passing.

"Boy, beautiful women sure throw themselves at her, don't they?" Gillian sighed and took another long sip of bourbon.

"Don't they, though," Isabel agreed with a frown. And Kash seemed to be right in her element, soaking up all the attention from the women buzzing around her. She winked at some or briefly released Hilde now and then for a bit of dancing with one of her admirers. All the while she smiled this oh-yeah-show-me-some-more-baby smile and leered appreciatively at the women around her, precisely the way she had at Isabel that morning.

Isabel was startled to realize how envious of them she was. "Come on, Gill, you keep telling me to stop sitting on the sidelines. Time to get in the game. Let's dance."

The surprise on Gillian's face quickly came and went. "All right, Izzy. That's my girl!"

They joined the throng as a well-known song came on, a remix of an old disco tune that played a lot in the club back home. They broke up laughing and immediately got into the groove, grateful for the sweet reminder of home in their otherwise foreign environment. Around them, the murmured comments and come-ons they could overhear were mostly in French, but the music lyrics were all about "Hot Stuff," which was a universal language.

Isabel was determined to try to forget about Kash and her growing harem and the fact that all the women in the place were acting as though she were invisible. *None of that matters. I'm damn lucky to be in Europe, and I'm going to enjoy every minute.*

And dancing with Gillian was always fun. They had a flirty ease with each other that was often mistaken for much more than the lighthearted frivolity between friends that it was. That was never truer than tonight, for the open sexuality in the air created an infectious spirit, and both caught the fever.

So Isabel put her hands around Gillian's neck, and Gillian put her hands on Isabel's hips, and pelvis to pelvis, they fell into a sensual dance every bit as hot and steamy-looking as the interactions all around them.

Their bodies were pressed so tightly together that Gillian had to lean in only a few inches to put her lips next to Isabel's ear. They were very near one of the speakers, so it was the only way to be heard above the music. "Have I told you how proud I am of how I hardly recognize you?"

Isabel threw her head back and laughed. She barely recognized herself, either. Something was happening to her on this trip. She wasn't sure what, or why it was happening now, but something was pushing her out of the controlled and structured rut her life had become. And though the change was a bit scary, it was incredibly liberating. She was almost literally waking up from a long sleep, to find a brighter and more vivid world.

When Kash happened to glimpse them through the crowd, Gillian had her thigh between Isabel's legs and her hands on Isabel's ass. Kash couldn't really tell what was going on, but their body language and the way they were dancing made it crystal clear that both were gay, *very* close, and also, she realized, not nearly as conservatively naïve as she'd presumed.

Gillian glanced her way and smiled provocatively. The tilt of her eyebrow seemed to say, *So, have you been thinking about my offer?*

And Isabel—well, Isabel sure knew how to move on the dance floor. *Nice ass.* No trace of any inhibitions. *Yes, indeed, maybe that threesome idea isn't dead after all.*

"Feels so good." Hilde's voice was husky, seductive, and very close to Kash's ear. They were dancing tight against each other, front to front again, and she massaged Hilde's ass as she watched Isabel shake hers. The combination of what she was doing and seeing thrilled her and began to arouse her, acutely. Then a buxom blonde, who actually resembled Isabel quite a bit, danced into Kash from behind, sandwiching her and thrusting her crotch into Kash's ass. *Fuck, yes.*

Hilde kissed her, and she responded hungrily, thrusting her tongue into her mouth. But she soon missed the view she'd had, so she broke free and returned her attention to Isabel and Gillian, only to find Isabel staring intently at her with an interested but unreadable expression.

Kash let her attraction and desire show, returning Isabel's heated stare with a seductive half-smile and faint nod.

Suddenly, Hilde put a hand firmly to her crotch and made her jump nearly out of her skin. Her trousers were paper thin and her clit so sensitive the touch jarred her.

Without breaking their dance, Kash removed the hand. That was not going to happen, no matter how turned on she was getting. She was too well known to be fucking in the middle of the dance floor. Not with all the cell-phone cameras in this room.

Isabel hadn't taken her eyes off her, all the while continuing her sexy gyrations with Gillian. Kash wished she could better read what the woman was thinking. *Damn, she can move.*

"Kash." Hilde pulled at her shirt.

When she turned her face to respond, Hilde kissed her possessively and put Kash's hand on her breast. Again, Kash knew better than to let that happen; several of the women around them had recognized her. But she had a real weakness for that particular body part, and she could feel Hilde's hard nipple through the sheer fabrics she wore, so she couldn't help but linger there a few seconds.

Kash hazily recognized a flash, but she had no clue where it came from. *You asked for that.* Much as she wanted to denounce those who took such pictures of her, she knew she really couldn't; to do so was hypocrisy. She was the ultimate voyeur herself and believed that anything viewed through her lens was fair game. *You hate not being the one in control, that's all. But you can't choose only the perks of celebrity and none of the downsides. Not if you insist on coming to clubs and groping women at every turn.*

She glanced around but didn't see anyone with a camera or phone. Her eyes met Isabel's, and Isabel pointed to a dark-haired woman barely out of her teens standing a few feet away. When Kash stared at her unflinchingly, the young fan averted her eyes, blushing, and tried to hide her cell phone behind her body.

Kash extracted some bills from her wallet. "I need that phone." She was friendly but firm as she held out five fifty-dollar bills, and after only a brief hesitation, the young woman sold her the phone.

"Sorry, I didn't mean anything."

Yeah, I've heard that before.

Vanessa suddenly appeared at Kash's elbow. "Is there a problem here, Kash? Is she bothering you?"

"No, we're good," Kash replied, and tucked the cell phone into her pocket. A hand seized her elbow.

"Let's go upstairs." Hilde tugged her resolutely toward the stairway.

Kash allowed herself to be led, glancing toward Isabel and Gillian as she and Hilde left the dance floor. Other couples now blocked her view, and though she couldn't thank Isabel as she'd intended, she figured she'd have ample time.

Once she reached the upper level, she spotted them again in the crowd below. To her surprise, a third woman had joined their sensual dance. An attractive, butchy brunette had sidled up to Gillian and was fondling her from behind, and the trio was previewing a delicious visual appetizer for the threesome she hoped for later.

"No cameras here," Hilde purred in her ear as she pulled Kash down on one of the couches.

The next thing she knew, Hilde was straddling her, pushing down against her, and of their own volition, her hips began to answer with slow, rhythmic thrusts. The short skirt that Hilde was wearing had hitched up, exposing the soft ivory skin of her endless thighs, and Kash traced lightly along the sensitive flesh in a teasing path intended to heighten Hilde's excitement. From the moans she was hearing she was having the desired effect.

"You're driving me crazy," Hilde panted breathily, rolling her hips to push against Kash's hands. "*Please.* Touch me like I need you to."

Kash was never one to deny such a request, so she slipped beneath the skirt and spread her hands over Hilde's ass, pleased to discover no barrier of undergarments.

Hilde groaned at the sensations and pushed forward, raising her body to allow Kash access to the growing wetness between her legs.

At the same moment, Kash felt a tug at her waist, and she looked down to discover that her belt was unfastened and her trousers open. It was a scenario that Kash had played out more times than she could remember, so she shouldn't have been surprised when Hilde chose then to reveal what she really wanted.

"I hope you'll give me your number this time," she said with playful reproach as she lifted her top above her head to reveal a lacy, crème-colored bra. "Let me get to know you better. Maybe see whether we can work together as well as we play together."

Usually this flagrant trading of sex for favors didn't bother her. It had become the de rigueur course of her life for the past several years. But maybe her approaching milestone birthday or Hilde's incredibly poor timing—making her *think* when she only wanted to *feel*—or maybe the fact that she had already been there and done that one time too many made her interest wane. She pushed Hilde off her and got to her feet. "I need another drink."

Isabel tried to keep her swirl of emotions in check as she watched Kash head upstairs with Hilde. Watching them dance together, seeing Kash kiss and touch the actress that way...*All the while staring at me like she wanted me instead. I didn't mistake that.* The desire in Kash's eyes had stirred something in her, made her deliciously and powerfully horny in a way that startled her in its intensity. But it had frustrated her, too.

What was she doing, anyway, to even think in those terms about some playgirl photographer at whom women constantly threw themselves? *So many, she apparently can't immediately recognize a beautiful actress she slept with a year ago.*

Besides, even if she is interested, and even if I did decide to do something totally against character for once, I still have to consider Gillian.

"Guess those tabloid stories about her are true," Gillian said, following Isabel's eyes up to the VIP area.

"Yup. I'd say so."

"Which is good, actually. I mean, I stand a better chance of getting a night with her, don't you think?"

Isabel kept dancing and tried to appear nonchalant. "You'd know better than I would. One-night stands aren't really my area of expertise."

"Don't knock it till you've tried it, Izzy. Speaking of which, if

Kash is otherwise occupied, it's time to start thinking about other opportunities for my evening's fun." She tilted her head toward the cute butchy brunette dancing near them. "That one's been winking at me. Time to start winking back." She maneuvered herself so she could flirt with the brunette while she kept dancing with Isabel. "Seen anybody here that does it for you?"

Kash does it for me, damn it. As for the rest…Isabel scanned the room, still amazed at how uniformly trendy and beautiful the clientele was. She also noted again that not a single woman was paying her any attention, though the club was full of nonstop flirting and touching. She glanced down at her clothes. *No wonder. This is the least sexy outfit in the place. Not wanting to judge by appearances is one thing, but I seem to go out of my way to avoid attracting any attention to myself. Why is that? Do I do it deliberately?*

"Don't worry about me," she whispered as the brunette Gillian was interested in joined them. "Appears you've got company. Be careful, huh?"

"No worries, Iz." Gillian slipped away from her embrace to welcome the cute stranger who was bumping against her from behind. The three of them danced together long enough for Isabel to catch the woman's name—Véronique—and for her to determine that three was definitely a crowd in this equation.

"I'll see you back at the hotel," Isabel told Gillian, kissing her lightly on the cheek. "Good luck, and have fun."

Threading her way through the dancers, she headed toward the back bar, not at all anxious to interrupt what she was fairly certain was going on upstairs. But the crowd was thick and the bartenders all occupied, so she detoured to the ladies' room. She spotted the small neon *Toilettes* over a doorway to the left and headed through it, only to find herself in a dark hallway populated by a dozen couples in clinches, their clothing in disarray. The heady scent of arousal hung in the air, and this far from the loudspeakers, as she walked by she could clearly hear the moans and guttural sounds of the women fucking.

Isabel had never been in a situation where women were publicly going at it like this, and the experience was more than a little exhilarating. There was certainly nothing like this back in Madison.

She was thinking what a shame it was to be all stirred up, with no suitable outlet for her sexual desires…when she ran headfirst into someone coming around the dark corner from the ladies' room.

And headfirst it was. When they crashed together, she started to lose her balance backward and reached out, flailing for something to grab. She found the front of the woman's crisp white shirt and ripped all the buttons off, then slid down her body until she reached the big buckle of her belt and it whipped out of her pants with a *swoosh*.

The stranger managed to cradle one hand behind Isabel's head, the other around her waist when they slammed into each other. Then, together, they hit the wall behind Isabel in a heavy thud of crashing bodies.

They remained frozen a long moment as Isabel realized this wasn't some stranger she had run into. *Kash*. Then she noticed how tightly they were pressed against each other, both breathing heavily. Meanwhile everywhere around them she heard, saw, and smelled women having sex.

She was hyperaware of Kash's lean and lithe body pressed up against the entire length of hers, her right thigh barely insinuating itself between her legs. She also became aware of the fact that she had Kash's belt in one hand and her other firmly planted on Kash's magnificent ass. *Oh, my. How did that happen*?

Kash's left arm was around her waist, possessively, while her right still gently cradled the back of her head. It hit her how close she had come to seriously injuring herself. She wanted to say thank you, but she wasn't sure she trusted her ability to speak. All she could think about was how damn hot Kash was at this distance, and how very much she wanted to be kissed. *God, she's got the most perfectly wonderful lips.*

Kash recognized that look in Isabel's eyes. Hunger. Desire. It was coursing through her own veins, too, in a way it hadn't with Hilde. She tightened her grip around Isabel, who gasped, and she liked that sound, very much. She slowly leaned in for a kiss, enjoying Isabel's expression.

Her lips were only a breath away when she became dimly aware of a flash, and Isabel must have as well, because she muttered "Damn," pushed Kash off her, and fled. Kash glanced about for the offender, but all the couples near them were still occupied. Then another flash brightened the hall, and she realized it had come from around the corner, in the direction of the restrooms. Three girls were playing around, photographing each other kissing and undressing.

Christ. She glanced down and saw her shirt open to the wind, exposing her sheer white bra. She couldn't help but smile. *Why doesn't this surprise me?* She tucked in her shirt, covering herself as best as she could and wishing she had buckled her belt after her aborted scene with Hilde, then elbowed her way out to the dance floor, surveying the crowd for Isabel. She spotted Gillian in one of the quiet alcoves, on the lap of the cute brunette she and Isabel had been dancing with. *Well, they certainly have an open relationship.* The two were going at it pretty heavy, Gillian apparently unconcerned whether anyone saw her without her shirt and bra. *Nice tits on that one.*

Isabel was nowhere on the lower floor, so Kash returned to the mezzanine.

Hilde pounced on her as soon as she spotted her. "Come on back to the couch and let's have some fun," she said, reaching for Kash's shirt and stopping when she saw it was unbuttoned. "Hey, what happened to you? Partying without me?" She fingered the clasp of Kash's trousers. "See you lost your belt, too. Aw. Couldn't you wait for me?"

Kash wondered whether Hilde had been quite so obvious and quite so irritatingly possessive the first go-round. She couldn't remember. "Party's over, Hilde. Thanks."

"Let me give you my number." Hilde went for her purse but Kash intercepted her.

"Don't trouble yourself. I'm sure I can find you if I want to get in touch."

Long after Hilde had gone she stood on the mezzanine watching the crowd below. For some reason, before she returned to the hotel she wanted to make sure Isabel really had left.

Then what? she asked herself. *You know what. You don't want a threesome at all, do you? You just want her.*

Chapter Six

When Isabel got back to the hotel, she ordered a cognac from room service and retired to the balcony with it to try to put the evening's surprising turn of events into some perspective. She felt restless, all jangled nerves and emotions, since her unexpected encounter with Kash in the hallway.

Closing her eyes, she let the memory of Kash's body pressed against hers flood her senses. *It's folly to be thinking about her like this. Where's it going to lead me?* Still, she couldn't help herself. Her body wanted what it wanted, and her mind refused to let go of the thrill that had ripped through her when she realized Kash was about to kiss her.

What the heck is happening to me? It was as though she had somehow switched bodies with someone, and the one she was now inhabiting had more ability to *feel* than the one she'd been living in all her life. She was so thoroughly and completely aroused that every part of her cried out for Kash's touch. *Why her? Why now? How can you go for thirty years thinking you have some idea of what it all means, how it all works, and suddenly find yourself realizing that so much more is possible?*

She'd never felt single-minded about sex. Sure, she'd been attracted to the women she'd been with and thought she'd known what it meant to *want* and *desire*. But nothing like this. This ache for Kash, this *craving*, was beginning to permeate her every thought, and her body refused to let go of this low-simmering buzz of arousal.

And now what? I took off out of there like a bat out of hell with no explanation. What a missed opportunity. She probably thinks I'm some kind of...who knows what she thinks?

Realizing that she might never get to kiss Kash disturbed her, but the prospect that she would bothered her even more. *And if she does want to kiss me? And more? What then?*

The cognac, the spectacular night view of Paris, the warm breeze on her skin, and the memory of Kash's musky perfume and strong arms around her eroded Isabel's tightly woven resistance to a one-night stand. *If she was here right now...Oh, if she was here right now.*

The cognac lulled her into a dreamscape of possibilities, and she let her imagination run wild. When she drifted off, she tasted Kash's mouth on hers, an escape so compelling she never heard the knocking at the door of her suite.

❖

Once more Kash rapped softly at the door of the Errol Flynn, but still no response. Either Isabel had not come back to the hotel, or she had gone directly to bed. *Damn.* No chance to finish what they had almost started.

She knew it would take only a few minutes back at the club to find someone to help her alleviate the knot of sexual urgency that had been twisting her insides since that clinch in the hallway with Isabel. But the alternatives lacked something.

She trudged to her suite, wishing she'd been able to confirm that Isabel had made it back all right. *Since when did you start caring about such things?*

Her body was tight as a drum, nowhere near ready for sleep, so she was pleased to see that Claude had replenished her supply of vodka.

❖

Late the next morning Gillian spotted Kash in the hotel restaurant. She was sitting alone, sipping coffee, an apparently untouched basket of fresh pastries on the table.

"Good morning," Gillian said. "Or am I interrupting?"

"No, of course not. Please sit." Kash removed her sunglasses and set them on the table. She had faint dark circles under her eyes and squinted.

"Hmm, apparently you had a late night, too?" Gillian inquired with a conspiratorial smile.

Kash sipped her coffee and shrugged noncommittally. "I saw you were enjoying yourself. Cute girl."

Gillian sighed. "Very cute. Say, by the time I got back to the room this morning, Izzy had already gone. You haven't seen her, have you?"

Kash sat up straighter. "No. I haven't."

"Well, she *is* an early riser." Gillian signaled their waiter and ordered coffee. "She left a note saying she was out seeing the town and would catch up with me at dinner, if I didn't have other plans."

"Don't you have a copy of that itinerary of hers?"

"No way. Are you kidding?" Gillian asked in mock horror. "She never lets it out of her sight. Besides, it changes every five minutes."

"Well, I was going up to Montmartre in a while to take some pictures. Great views of the city, if you want to tag along." Kash wasn't sure why she made the offer. It was a totally spontaneous gesture, made mostly because she didn't want to be alone. And she thought perhaps she might have an opportunity to get a better handle on what the deal was between Isabel and Gillian.

"Hey, that'd be great!" Gillian grinned.

❖

Isabel kept ahead of her itinerary all day, even without Alain as chauffeur. But she had gotten a much earlier start than she planned and had quickly mastered the Paris Métro system.

Her day began at four a.m. when she had awakened, stiff and sore, in the chaise on the balcony. Unable to go back to sleep, she had finished her run and shower and was off to find breakfast by six, so by four thirty p.m. she had run through her list with time left for a long pause for coffee and people watching, in a café on the Boulevard Saint-Germain.

It was the first real break she had allowed herself all day, so it was also her first chance to really think about the evening before. As soon as she settled and became quiet, she was transported back to the hallway and into Kash's arms.

Something warned her to prepare some reaction for the next time she saw Kash. Otherwise she would probably stutter and stammer or worse.

What she wondered the most was how Kash would react to *her* the next time they met. *If she makes no reference to almost kissing me, I'll have to take it that she wants to forget it ever happened. I mean, we do have to work together for another two and a half weeks.* The prospect of Kash acting as if nothing had happened thoroughly depressed her.

Of course, the other option is entirely possible. She hadn't mistaken the expression on Kash's face. *If it's still there when I see her again, I'll just melt and give in, and damn the consequences. I know I will. God, I'm almost ready to beg for it, where she's concerned. Why the hell doesn't it seem to matter how many women she's had, or whether being with her will make me only one of the masses she won't recognize a year from now? Why?*

"Live like there's no tomorrow," Gillian kept telling her. "Let the moment take you where it will for a change. Sometimes those chance, fleeting experiences make lasting memories." It sounded like as good a plan as any.

Maybe she should tell Gillian she was going to have some friendly competition for Kash's attention. *Why not? She won't care. I know she won't. She'll understand completely. Maybe she can even explain to me what's going on—how you can be so damn attracted to someone that you can't think of anything else but how much you want to be naked with them.*

Even as she thought it, though, she suspected there was a big difference in the way she and Gillian wanted Kash. Gillian would be happy with an evening, but she knew she wanted more. Much, much more. One night with Kash would never be enough. She glanced at her watch. *Time to face the music.* Excitement ran through her. *Please let Kash look at me like that again.*

The nearest metro station was only down the block, so she was on a train headed for the hotel within five minutes. She made it only halfway there, however, before a power outage shut down one-third of the massive subway system, including the line she was on.

Three hours later she finally arrived at the hotel—grumpy, sweaty, and starving. Gillian had left a note in their suite, which read:

> *Where are you?*
> *Having such a great day you lost track of the time, I hope. We waited forty minutes, then decided to head to dinner because we'd made reservations.*

We? she wondered. *We who?*

> *If you find this before eight, dress up and come find us at…*

The note gave the name and address of a restaurant in Pigalle, but Isabel quickly skimmed that part since it was already eight fifteen.

> *If you get back after that, we'll be at Vive la Vie. Kash will tell the doorman to expect you.*

Well, that explained the *we*. Her heart sank. So Kash and Gillian had dinner together. Gillian was getting her one-on-one chance to see if Kash was interested in something more.

She *had* to go to the club. Gillian would probably worry if she didn't hear from her soon. But she wasn't excited about seeing the two of them together. *I want her for myself, Gill. So much so that any notion I had about helping you get her has evaporated. I sure hope you understand. After all, I'm only doing what you advised. I'm letting my body take me where it wants to. And it sure as heck is making it all too clear it wants her.*

After a shower and plate of Boeuf Bourguignon from room service, she got ready to return to the club. *I walked through half of Paris today. Why didn't I come back with something to wear?* The clothes she'd brought with her were nothing like what she'd seen women wearing at Vive la Vie. She'd packed only a few comfortable things because she'd been told she'd get her new wardrobe the first week of her trip.

Gillian was always offering to loan her things to wear, and they swapped clothes so routinely that she didn't hesitate to go through Gillian's closet when her own failed to produce a suitable garment. She selected a short skirt that under normal circumstances might have made her a bit self-conscious.

But she was in the mood not to be invisible tonight.

In the end, she wore her own blouse, a plain white cotton number, but tied in front to show off a bit of stomach. Added a pair of heels—also Gillian's and a tad large—and a bit of makeup.

Her hair took another twenty minutes of fussing over to get it the way she thought would fit in with what she'd seen.

The person who stared back at her in the mirror was almost unrecognizable. She was sexy and mischievous and ready for fun. And totally in keeping with this new hypersensitized body she was inhabiting. *Tonight I won't be Izzy at all. Tonight I'm Isa. And Isa is a wild child, it appears. Think I've got it in me?*

❖

By the time she sat down to dinner with Gillian, Kash knew quite a lot about both her and Isabel. As they had explored the streets of Montmartre, she had got Gillian talking. Likes and dislikes, schools attended, jobs, and interests. And along the way, Gillian volunteered a lot of information about Isabel. In fact, she talked about nearly everything except the true nature of their relationship.

Kash brought up the subject over dessert in an effort to get more detail. "So you two have known each other a long time." She said it casually, repeating information Gillian had already shared.

"We met in college," Gillian confirmed. "She taught me to swim, actually."

"Did she?" This was new.

"I'd always been afraid of water," Gillian began. "I never had a chance to learn to swim growing up because there were no lakes or pools near us. Anyway, I went to the college natatorium because I heard they taught beginner classes. To make a long story short, I slipped and fell into the pool the first day, and she jumped in to get me."

Kash was impressed.

"Isabel is a very caring person, though she tends to be rather routine-driven."

"I would never have guessed that by that itinerary she's drafted," Kash observed wryly.

Gillian cracked up. "Oh, that's nothing."

"No? What do you mean?"

"Well, let's see. She's up at six. Swim or run until seven. Breakfast—usually granola or fruit or something healthy. Then off to decorate cakes. She's very good, by the way. Her cakes are edible works of art. Anyway, after work she either teaches swimming or sits home and reads. In bed by eleven. Weekends she bikes instead of runs. She plans every detail of her vacations months in advance and remembers every friend and coworker's birthday."

"I'm getting the picture," Kash said. "Creature of habit personified."

"Yup. Kind of a throwback, too. A real die-hard romantic. Not many of them left." Gillian finished off her crème brûlée and groaned with satisfaction.

"What does that mean, exactly?"

"Oh, the kind you find in fairy tales," Gillian said. "The fate-will-bring-me-my-soul-mate kind of girl. Lightning will strike or something when she meets 'the one.' They'll get married and live happily ever after. The end."

Kash couldn't help laughing. "I'm sorry, I don't mean to make fun…" She didn't want Gillian to think she was ridiculing Isabel. "I got the image of a lightning bolt, and Isabel, and it somehow seemed so appropriate, somehow—"

Gillian laughed, too. "In her defense, she's really not a clumsy person, Kash, or normally this accident prone. I suspect it's because she's been pulled out of her rigid routine so much lately that she's distracted."

"So…the two of you…aren't…" She left the question hanging.

"Oh, we're only friends! *Great* friends," Gillian said. "Sisters, really. And neighbors."

"From the way you two were dancing last night, I thought—"

"Oh. Well, having fun, that's all. Trying to loosen her up a little, when I can," Gillian explained. "She's not into going to clubs, unless I drag her out."

Couldn't have guessed that from the way she was dancing last night, Kash thought. "So she wasn't there to hook up?"

Gillian laughed. "Let's just say it would shock me if she ever did that. Izzy *dates* women—sometimes for weeks—before she sleeps with them."

Aware of her company, Kash didn't frown, though the information was a most unpleasant development. The idea of spending an evening with Isabel had been very attractive. Worth a nice night in the hotel, she'd decided, and not a mere quickie on some couch. But it didn't appear as though that was going to happen. *Yup. Like I thought. The type with way too many strings attached. Pity. But…other fish in the sea, as they say.* "So, you ready to head to the club?"

"Sure am." Gillian had a glint in her eye and a coy smile.

"What?"

"Oh, I'm trying to think up a way to get a dance with you once we get there."

Gillian had been good company, engaging but not pushy, and Kash was happy to agree. "Sure. You got it." *Any more than that happening? Well, she would determine that later.*

The doorman at the club didn't immediately recognize Isabel, but when she mentioned Kash's name he let her through. Inside, the crowd was as dense as it had been the evening before. As she waded through the sea of women, she felt a small glimmer of satisfaction when she realized she was drawing a few of the same kind of interested looks that Gillian had the night before.

Isa, not Izzy, she reminded herself. *Party girl. Don't think about tomorrow. Be open to seeing where the evening leads.* She wasn't sure what she was trying to prove. The opinion of these women really didn't matter to her. Her ego had been bruised a little the night before, she had to admit. *But mostly I want Kash to notice me. That's why it took me an hour to dress, when it usually takes ten minutes.*

First she glanced up at the mezzanine, but she couldn't see the VIP area from where she was. Next she surveyed the ground floor as she danced her way through en route to the bar. Every now and then, a woman would break off from her partner to engage her for a step or two as she passed, and she was enjoying the flirtations.

She was at the far edge of the dance floor, directly under a pulsing red light, when she saw them. Kash and Gillian, six or eight feet away in the shadows. Kash had apparently learned her lesson from the phone-cam incident the night before.

Isabel had anticipated this possibility, but the vivid reality still rattled her. Kash and Gillian were pressed together in a provocative hip-grinding sway, and Kash's hands were all over Gillian's ass. Kash was facing Isabel, but her eyes were closed and Gillian was turned away, so Isabel stood where she was, watching them, oblivious to those around her.

Her heart sank. *I'm too late.* The urge to party evaporated as quickly as it had flared, but before she could take a step toward the exit, Kash opened her eyes and looked right at her. Time froze for several heartbeats before she turned to flee.

The first three hurried steps in Gillian's borrowed high-heeled pumps were so unsteady that Isabel paused to pull them off. Only the horrific possibility of falling again could make her hesitate, for her insides were so twisted up she felt a little sick to her stomach.

Could I possibly make a bigger fool of myself? She was ashamed at how much she had allowed her hormones to rule her as far as Kash was concerned. *So obsessed by the idea of having sex with her that I've lost my common sense. Primping to get her attention. Ready to throw myself at her, even for only one night. And now, seeing her dance with Gillian, I'm acting like some jealous teenager. Get a grip. And for what? Whatever made me think she'd take any interest in me?*

❖

It took Kash a few seconds to wrap her mind around the transformation and really accept that the hot blond sex pistol standing before her was Isabel.

It took her a few more to realize that the expression on Isabel's face before she turned to leave was one of surprise and... *disappointment*?

Suddenly, it all made sense. Isabel *was* interested, and though she'd given off hard-to-get, strings-attached vibes initially, she'd changed during their time in Paris. The city was a wonderful aphrodisiac, it had loosened her up a lot, and Kash planned to take advantage of that edge.

Kash had already decided there would be nothing more between her and Gillian. It had only been a dance. She didn't want any complications. She wanted Isabel, not her friend.

It was time to let Gillian know that. *Then she'll tell Isabel.*

"Hey, Gillian." Kash loosened their embrace. "Isabel's here."

Gillian glanced around. "She made it? Great! Where is she?"

"She was headed toward the front." Kash let go and stepped back. "Thanks for the dance."

Gillian caught the tone and message and took it in good humor. "No chance of another dance or something later?"

Kash put a hand to Gillian's cheek. "You're a very nice woman. Beautiful. Sexy. And fun to be with. Maybe we can do some more sightseeing together on this trip. I'd like that. But that's all."

"Yeah, no problem. I understand. I enjoyed the dance."

"My pleasure."

"Well, guess I'll go find Izzy."

Kash watched Gillian disappear into the crowd, then sauntered to the bar for another vodka.

She stayed for a third and consented to a couple of dances, but none of the women at the club interested her for either conversation or other pursuits. Her mind kept returning to Isabel, long after it was obvious that she had gone and wasn't coming back. Though Kash rarely wasted a brain cell worrying about someone else, it had bothered her—that surprised and unhappy expression on Isabel's face. But she'd make it go away and replace it with a very satisfied smile.

Kash had never apologized for how she was with women, and she wouldn't now. She always made her intentions very clear. The women she fucked all knew not to have any future expectations, and none of them were unhappy when they left her. It appeared as though Isabel might be receptive to her lifestyle now.

On her way out, she spotted Gillian with a tall, lanky blonde in leather. Ordinarily, she'd have waited until Gillian was less occupied, but the kiss had gone on for a few minutes already, and it was only getting hotter.

So she grasped Gillian's shoulder and waited to be acknowledged. This would only take a second. Isabel had seemed the most upset by the fact that she thought she and Gillian were getting it on. *I'll sleep better knowing Gillian set her straight about that.*

"Oh, hey, Kash." Gillian was breathing hard, and her face was flushed. They both had to speak up to be heard over the music.

"Sorry to interrupt. I'm going back to the hotel. Did you find Isabel?"

"No. I guess she left." Gillian didn't seem at all concerned. "Like I said, she's not really into clubbing. She was out all day, so I bet she was tired and went back to the hotel."

"Want to make sure she got back all right?" Kash pulled out her cell phone, dialed the number, and handed the phone to Gillian.

After a long delay, Gillian spoke. "Hey, Izzy, it's Gill. Everything cool with you?"

Kash wished like hell she could hear what Isabel was saying.

"Yeah. That's what I thought." Gillian smiled, then laughed. "Well, I'm doing my best." A pause as she listened. Then she glanced at Kash. "She's right here." A long pause. "No, darn it."

Kash relaxed a little. *At least she knows we're not together.*

"Well, you're on your own there. I'm going to sleep in," Gillian said next, then listened some more. "Sounds like a plan. Sleep well." She closed the phone and handed it back to Kash. "Like I figured. She'd been out running around like crazy and it all caught up with her, so she went back to the room. Said not to worry about her. Oh—and she said since our flight isn't until noon, she's packing tonight so she can go out sightseeing again very early in the morning. I told her she's on her own."

"Well, guess I'll head back, too," Kash said. "Have fun."

"Boy, you two are such party poopers."

❖

Isabel was usually not one to drink to excess, but once back in the suite she ordered a bottle of wine and had downed a good bit of it by the time Gillian telephoned. She had anticipated the call so had prepared her answers in advance and tried to deliver them with the same casual, cheery tone she always used, though she felt anything but cheery.

"Hello?"

"Hey, Izzy, it's Gill. Everything cool with you?"

"Hi, Gill. Yeah, I'm fine. Exhausted, though. I've been on the run since this morning and suddenly it all caught up with me."

"Yeah. That's what I thought."

"I'd have stopped and talked to you, but you were dancing with Kash and seemed way too content to interrupt. So, are you having lots of fun?" She heard Gillian laugh.

"Well, I'm doing my best."

Isabel pictured the two of them wrapped up together on one of the VIP couches. Knowing Gillian, she wouldn't be surprised if her friend was missing a few garments by now. "So, is Kash somewhere within earshot?"

"She's right here."

"Well, there's no reason for either of you to waste any time worrying about me. So I'll let you go." Isabel wondered whether the two of them would end up back here or in Kash's suite. *Kash's, certainly.* Wouldn't they? *What if they don't?* She didn't relish facing the two of them, fresh out of bed, over her morning coffee. "Hey, by the way, have you figured out yet where you're sleeping tonight?"

"No, darn it."

"Well, I was thinking, since we don't fly out of here until after noon, I'm going to pack tonight and get up early to hit a few more places."

"Well, you're on your own there. I'm going to sleep in."

"I figured you would. If I'm not back by the time you're ready to leave for the airport, bring my suitcase with you, will you, and I'll meet you there?"

"Sounds like a plan. Sleep well."

"Thanks, Gill. Have fun. See you when I see you." She hung up the phone, wishing she could get the image of the two of them dancing together out of her mind. *Please don't come back here tonight.*

CHAPTER SEVEN

Isabel ventured out of her bedroom at five thirty the next morning as quietly as possible, weary from lack of sleep and with a Richter scale headache. Though she hadn't heard anyone come into the suite, she had managed to doze briefly so it was possible Gillian and Kash had slipped into the other room.

That door was ajar, as she had left it after rummaging through Gillian's closet the night before. She held her breath and glanced through the opening. Once she confirmed the bed had not been slept in, she exhaled shakily.

She was both relieved and disappointed. *Ah, well. At least I don't have to deal with them all over each other. Perhaps with Kash wearing a lot less than usual.* She recalled the softly sculpted perfection of Kash's upper body that she'd glimpsed when she'd changed her shirt during their first meeting. *I don't think I could stand it—seeing her parading around in next to nothing, smelling of sex, let alone consider the possibility she might like to walk around in the nude—and not be able to have something myself with her. That would be pure and absolute torture.*

Isabel didn't think it likely that Gillian would return this early, but she still hurried to leave the suite, anxious for some fresh air and black coffee, and reluctant to consider how she could possibly act normal and unaffected when she saw them together at the airport. That was as long as she could delay the inevitable. But at least seeing them together there would be easier than seeing them in the afterglow of sex.

And if Kash truly deserved the worst of her reputation, Isabel considered, then perhaps by the time she next saw them, their affair might already be over.

On paper, absolutely not the woman for me. She flirts with anyone and everyone and apparently drops her pants at the slightest provocation. Who knows how many women she's had? She doesn't, I'd wager. No, I couldn't possibly pick anyone more unsuitable. At least not for the kind of life I've always claimed to want, not for the person I've always claimed to be. So why, then, am I so drawn to her that I can't put her out of my mind? Does Isa have no common sense at all?

❖

Kash was sitting in precisely the same seat and even had her sunglasses on again, though the day was so overcast it was much darker inside the hotel restaurant that morning than it had been the day before.

The coffee and basket of pastries were the same, too, the pastries still obviously untouched, and Gillian finally realized they were an offering to Kash's celebrity.

"You look like I feel," Gillian said in a low, raspy voice. She was smiling in a way that said the evening had sure been worth it, though it was taking its toll now.

"Sit," Kash said. She signaled the waiter and ordered a pot of coffee. "The blonde in the leather?"

Gillian grinned and nodded very slowly several times. "Françoise. One delicious long drink of Perrier, let me tell you."

Kash laughed. "Aren't women the most wonderful creatures?"

"Indeed they are." Gillian let out a long, contented sigh. "I'll certainly miss Paris."

"Wait until we hit Rome," Kash said. "Mediterranean women are a rare breed. Fiery, passionate."

"Know any good clubs there?"

"I know clubs everywhere, Gillian. Public and private. I get invited to their openings, anniversaries, special events."

Gillian slapped herself in the forehead, the universal symbol for *duh,* and smiled. "Oh. Of course you do."

"So anytime you want to go out at night, say the word." Kash put her hand on Gillian's. "I'm glad you understand about…well, that we can't be more than friends. I'm very tempted, and I wanted you to know that."

❖

Isabel had intended to avoid returning to the hotel. But though the sky had been clear blue when she set out that morning, a storm blew in unexpectedly while she was strolling through the Tuileries Gardens. Before she could find shelter she was soaked, so she had hurried back to the Napoleon, praying she wouldn't walk in on something she didn't want to see.

She let herself into the suite as quietly as possible and paused for a few moments, listening. Relieved to hear nothing but silence, she headed toward her bedroom to change, pausing briefly at Gillian's open door to glance inside. Gillian's clothes from last night were strewn across the bed. *So she's been here. And then what? Back to Kash's suite?*

All she knew was that she was going to take advantage of the break she'd been given. She changed in record time and headed back out, grateful for the brief respite.

She crossed the lobby, hyperalert to her surroundings, half expecting to see either Kash or Gillian or both at any time. Under most circumstances, she'd have missed them—she got only a glimpse as she passed the door of the restaurant. But she stopped abruptly.

They were sitting opposite each other at a table, engrossed in conversation. As she watched, Kash took Gillian's hand.

Why am I putting myself through this? Isabel pushed herself forward, out of the hotel, vowing not to let what she had seen bother her or ruin her last morning in Paris. But she was in no mood for art, or architecture, or anything else the city had to offer. She wandered the streets without purpose until, finally, she recognized what was eating her up inside.

The revelation made her sit down hard on the nearest bench, stunned beyond belief. *I'm jealous*, she realized. *Jealous. Me! And not only a little bit, either. I'm insanely and unbelievably jealous.* She didn't think herself capable. The emotion was entirely new, and though she didn't like it at *all*, it was powerful, and driving, and made her feel incredibly alive. *Why now? Why not with Sylvia? What exactly does that mean?*

In her previous relationships, she'd never experienced the slightest bit of jealousy, though she'd had ample opportunities to. Not when the woman she was with flirted with a waitress, or ogled a passing stranger, or even shared a dance with someone a bit too provocative to be entirely innocent. When it happened, she merely recognized that her girlfriend was losing interest and that the end was near.

She'd never even been jealous with Sylvia, her most recent relationship and the one that appeared to have the most long-term potential. When Sylvia had bluntly told her, after two years together, that she'd fallen in love with someone she'd been secretly seeing from work, Isabel had been only hurt and disappointed. Felt rejected, yes. But not jealous.

Isabel certainly was jealous now, however. *In spades, as they say.* And the reason wasn't so hard to figure out. *I've never wanted anyone this much,* she realized. *Not nearly. I've been settling, all this time. Settling for what and who was offered. Even when it didn't fulfill me or stir me the way I knew it should. The way Kash stirs me, merely by being close to her.*

Why is that? she asked herself again. *Why does Kash make me feel as though I'll do anything—even make a fool of myself—just to have a chance with her?* She couldn't answer that question. She could only move in a new direction.

I won't interfere if it's Gillian she wants, Isabel vowed. *I'll grin and bear it, and be the supportive friend that Gillian has always been to me. But if I get any sign at all that it's over between them, and it's me that Kash wants…well, then, Isa will get another chance to come out and play.*

❖

"I can't believe Izzy's not here yet." Gillian scanned the crowd congregating near the departure gate. Their flight to Rome was scheduled to start boarding in the next few minutes. "She's, like, the most punctual person I know. Always early, never late."

Kash was also watching for Isabel, but less obviously. She was unable to forget Isabel's obvious disappointment. She didn't like to hurt women unnecessarily, and she hoped Gillian let Isabel know soon that they hadn't slept together. *She* certainly couldn't tell her.

"Here she comes." Gillian waved to get Isabel's attention, and she headed over to join them.

Something's wrong. Isabel appeared too serious and preoccupied, lacking the trademark ebullience that usually radiated from her. Her shoulders were slumped and her steps leaden.

And Kash noticed that Isabel barely glanced in her direction. *I was right. She's got it bad for me. The only question now is where and when.* "Hello, Isabel."

"Greetings, ladies." Isabel dropped into an empty seat next to Gillian, trying hard to act nonchalant around Kash. *What the hell is the matter with me? I've known her only a few days, but after running into her in that hallway I get three feet from her and my body has this insane visceral reaction.* Her heart was drumming and her skin was hot. *God! I want her hands on me so bad I can't think straight.*

"How you doing?" Gillian asked. "Get a chance to see everything you wanted?"

And a few things I didn't want to see. "Guess so. Ready for Rome. Oh—thanks for bringing my bag." Isabel massaged her temples. "I'm fine except for a headache that won't quit."

"Join the club." Gillian chuckled. "Kash and I were comparing hangovers earlier. But I'm not complaining, mind you. A little discomfort after a great night in Paris certainly isn't a bad price to pay."

Great, huh? Yeah, rub it in. "If you say so." Not that Isabel begrudged Gillian her night with Kash. She just wanted one of her own.

As Kash observed Isabel, she was a bit let down. As annoying as the unrelenting optimism she had come to expect from Isabel could sometimes be, she missed it. It was as though a spark had gone out of her. *Talk about mixed signals. Make up your mind, Isabel.* Maybe it was better to pass on her, after all. *Too much baggage there if she's acting all bent out of shape from seeing us dancing together.*

Their flight began to board, which ended conversation for the time being. The senior flight attendant, recognizing Kash, offered to seat her in the spacious first row of the Airbus, several feet away from Isabel and Gillian.

She accepted. The fun had gone out of being around these two. Gillian could obviously take care of herself, and Isabel...well, Isabel needed to grow up. They could have a little fun if she'd let herself go, but Kash didn't have the time or inclination to play nursemaid.

Perhaps it would be better to let them go their own way, except as necessary for the photo shoots. And of course, she would live up to her promise to show Gillian some clubs, if that came up. But it would be more for Gillian's amusement than her own. The club scene, and her transient approach to sex and relationships, was less satisfying by the day. *It's the age thing again, that's all. Stop thinking about it. Your birthday will get here soon enough.*

❖

A handsome Italian lad named Massimo met them at Fiumicino Airport with a sign that had all three of their names on it, but it was clear he didn't need it. He called out, "Kash! Kash!" and waved as soon as he recognized her.

He was the Roman equal to Alain in every way, with the same fawning admiration for Kash's talent and boundless zeal to serve her every whim.

His enthusiastic greeting ensured that everyone around them immediately realized that a celebrity was in their midst, and in no time Kash was surrounded by autograph seekers and flashes from cameras and cell phones, increasing exponentially as they walked toward the exit.

By the time they reached the car, the crowd was getting worrisome. People were pushing to get close to her and raising their voices to get her attention, so Isabel and the others were happy to get underway.

"That was almost scary," Gillian said, shaking her head. "What a mob."

"For some reason, I'm particularly big in Italy," Kash said drolly.

Gillian chuckled, but Isabel didn't find the reference humorous. It was merely another reason not to be so damn attracted to Kash.

She had set off an international scandal a year earlier, when she had been photographed at an after-the-Oscars party, kissing the young Italian beauty who had collected the Academy Award for best supporting actress. It would have been less newsworthy, perhaps, if Kash hadn't also had her hand on the woman's breast. And if the actress hadn't just been televised kissing her producer husband with considerably less enthusiasm when her name was announced.

They rode through scarily congested traffic, with Massimo occasionally pointing out a building or site of interest. Isabel asked a few questions about some of the major landmarks, but was nowhere near the chatterbox she had been with Alain during their first hours in Paris.

The sights and sounds of the Eternal City captivated Isabel as much as Paris had. Rome, on this warm fourth day of July, was bustling and noisy, the sun-baked streets of the city alive with people and cars. The blend of ancient and modern mesmerized her.

But Isabel's delicious proximity to Kash also distracted her. They sat nearly shoulder to shoulder in the back of the tiny Fiat, so she could smell Kash's earthy perfume and surreptitiously watch the gentle rise and fall of her chest.

Kash spent the trip to the hotel staring out the window, humming something under her breath. Isabel had noticed her doing that now and then, usually so low it was barely audible.

This time the tune was one she'd heard before. Isabel tried to place it. An old Beach Boys number. "I Get Around." It was so pathetically appropriate she almost wanted to laugh. But Kash didn't intend it to be humorous—that was clear from her distant, distracted expression. *I don't think she's even aware she's doing it.*

Their accommodations were every bit as opulent as their suites in Paris had been. The prestigious Aldrovandi Palace Hotel was an oasis in the heart of Rome, adjacent to the lush and tranquil Villa Borghese Gardens and very near the Via Veneto and Spanish Steps. The posh interior of the hotel was perfectly in keeping with the elegance of its nineteenth-century exterior. Rich fabrics graced the upholstered antique furniture and elaborate window dressings, the finest linens adorned the beds, and the artwork on the walls celebrated the Italian masters.

"The magazine sure is doing all right picking where we stay." Gillian stood at the window, admiring the view of the gardens, while Isabel unpacked.

"It's great," Isabel replied automatically. Just then, she came across Kash's belt, which she had neatly rolled and stashed in her luggage, awaiting its return. The memory of when she had gotten it flashed into her mind: Kash in the dim light of the club hallway, shirt open, her body pinning her against the wall. She had fled the scene so fast she had been halfway back to the hotel before she realized she still held the belt.

"Okay, that does it." Gillian abandoned the view and stretched out on the king-sized bed, giving Isabel her full attention. "Out with it. What's bothering you? Where is that eternal optimist I know and love?"

"Nothing's bothering me." Isabel tried to put some conviction behind the statement, but she was a terrible liar, and Gillian could spot any attempt at evasiveness.

"Izzy, come on. You'll tell me eventually. You always do. So let's get it out of the way right now, huh? Maybe I can help."

"Sometimes I wish you couldn't read me quite so well." Isabel kicked off her shoes and climbed onto the bed next to Gillian, with her back against the ornate carved headrest and legs stretched out in front of her. "Let me ask you something first," she began, chewing nervously on her lip. "Is this thing between you and Kash…is it going anywhere, do you think?"

Gillian glanced up at Isabel. "Huh? Thing between me and Kash… what are you talking about?"

"You know…are you going to sleep with her again, I mean?"

Gillian's forehead creased in confusion. "Again? I haven't slept with her once, Izzy. Not that I wouldn't like to. But she declined. What makes you think we did?"

"You didn't? Really?" She couldn't keep the glee out of her voice.

"No, I spent last night with a wonderful blonde in leather named Françoise." Gillian yawned. "Who, by the way, was one of the most insatiable women I've ever had the delight to spend time with." The grin on her face told Isabel that Gillian wasn't at all unhappy with the way her evening had turned out, Kash or no Kash.

"Well, I saw you dancing together last night," Isabel said, "then in the restaurant together this morning…so I thought—"

"We had one dance. She left—after asking about you, by the way—and then I ran into her today when I went to get coffee. That was all." Gillian studied her face. "Hey. You're really happy about the fact we didn't…aren't you?"

Isabel nodded, once. Slowly. Deliberately.

"What a *moron* I am!" Gillian smacked herself playfully in the forehead. "You? And Kash?"

Isabel nodded again, and her smile got bigger.

"Does she know?" Gillian asked. "Have you said anything to her?"

Isabel shrugged. "Hell if I can tell. I've caught her watching me like she's interested. But no, I haven't said anything."

"You know what they say." Gillian got up abruptly and pushed Isabel off the bed. "No time like the present. Strike while the iron is hot. Get your groove on. Okay, I'm all out of clichés, and I need a nap. Now go!"

Isabel knew if she stopped to think about it too long, she'd never do it. She grabbed Kash's belt and caught the elevator to the penthouse level, but began having second thoughts as soon as the car began to rise. *What the heck am I doing?*

Kash had been upgraded to the Royal Suite, which had a view of both the gardens and the hotel's private park and swimming pool. She was staring down at the pool, considering a dip, when she heard the rapping at her door.

"Hi."

She couldn't have been more surprised to see Isabel standing there, smiling uncertainly, a faint flush to her cheeks as though she had run all the way.

"Hello."

"I hope I'm not disturbing you." Isabel held up Kash's belt. "I wanted to return this. And…and offer to buy you a new shirt." *Don't stare, idiot. Don't stare.* But it was hard not to. In the heat of the late-afternoon Mediterranean sun, Kash had removed her shirt and wore only a very tight tank top. Black. *God, she's got great breasts.*

Kash couldn't help but smile, remembering when her buttons went flying and they had ended up all wrapped around each other. "Hey, it was an accident. Don't give it a thought. I have plenty of shirts."

"Okay. Good." Isabel shifted her weight from one foot to the other, as though trying to find a reason not to leave. "Oh, I also wanted to say…thank you. For…catching me."

Kash was struck by the look in Isabel's eyes. It was hard to describe. *Hungry* came close. *Passionate.* The kind usually reserved for those times when a woman is well worked up and needs it badly.

Her reference to when their bodies had been pressed together, hearts beating out of control, surrounded by writhing bodies, breathy moans, and the heady smell of sex, sent Kash's libido into sudden overdrive. She took in Isabel with a slow and lingering leer of appreciation, head to feet and back again, lingering on her breasts, hips, legs. Whetting her appetite, acknowledging the invitation.

"I have very fond…if unfinished…memories of that experience." She held out her hand for the belt, and when Isabel extended it, she took Isabel by the wrist and pulled her into the suite.

"Should we? Do you…" Isabel was breathing hard, pupils dark with excitement.

"Do you want to analyze this, or do you want to fuck?" Kash spoke even as she shut the door and turned Isabel to face it, planting Isabel's hands on the door at about shoulder height to brace herself. It was a purely rhetorical question, but the next one was not.

She pressed their bodies together, her crotch against Isabel's ass, her hands around Isabel's waist, and put her mouth close to Isabel's ear. "Tell me that you want this."

"So much, Kash. So much." Isabel's voice was breathy and low, and as she spoke her desire, a shudder ran through her body that Kash felt as a ripple against her chest and groin.

She skimmed her hands over Isabel's breasts, making the nipples rigidly erect by the third pass, and as Kash put one thigh between Isabel's legs to urge them farther apart, she heard her first murmured moan of pleasure.

More sounds followed as she let her hand stray from breasts to stomach to hips, stroking in ever more firm and purposeful passes under Isabel's tight cotton T-shirt and dipping low into the waistband of her khaki shorts. In no time, Isabel's ass began to move against her crotch.

She slipped Isabel's shirt over her head, unfastened her bra and removed it as well, and smiled inwardly when Isabel dutifully returned her hands to the door. Now she found only naked flesh, and the passes over Isabel's breasts and stomach produced more breathy sighs and moans, louder now.

It didn't take long. She knew it wouldn't. But she waited until she heard the plea to proceed.

"Please. Oh, please, Kash!" Urgent. Insistent. Exactly the way she liked it.

Then she unfastened the clasp of Isabel's shorts and slipped them and the sheer white panties beneath down and off.

Isabel tried to turn around, but Kash reacted instantly, pressing her hands firmly back against the door. "No." Only the one word, but the message was clear. *Move again, and I'll stop.*

There was a faint nod of acquiescence, and Kash rewarded it by pushing her crotch back roughly against Isabel's ass as she reached around and slipped her fingers into the silky wet folds between her legs.

"Oh!"

Isabel's gasp of pleasure shot through Kash and settled low in her belly. She could feel her own arousal rising rapidly as their bodies swayed against each other, and she fought to keep from touching herself. But Isabel excited her, more than any woman had in a long while, and she barely stayed focused on what she was doing as she stroked Isabel higher, playing lightly over her clit, taking it slow.

Then, easily and naturally, she withdrew from Isabel and quickly shed her tank top, so that when she resumed, her naked chest pressed against Isabel's back, warm flesh to warm flesh.

The brush of her nipples against Isabel's back sent a jolt of pleasure straight to her groin, and she bit back a groan before reaching down, one hand in front of Isabel and one behind, to resume her intimate caresses.

She took her time, getting Isabel deliciously wet and open before she pushed into her. Then she let Isabel set the pace for her thrusts by the rocking of her hips, a driving tempo that quickly sent her over the edge.

Isabel cried out when she came and slumped back against Kash, panting heavily, eyes closed. Her hands slipped off the door finally, and to her sides, and Kash embraced her, supporting her weight, as Isabel regained her breath.

After a very long moment, Isabel put her head back on Kash's shoulder, and Kash caught the floral fragrance of her hair. It roused her from her haze as though someone had shaken her.

She slowly pulled back a step and retrieved her top, slipped it over her head, and allowed a final lingering study of Isabel's perfect nudity before she spoke. "Probably time you dressed and got started ticking off stops on that itinerary of yours," she said gently. "I have some things to do to prepare for our shoot here."

Isabel looked at her with heavy-lidded eyes, so lost in the aftermath of her orgasm it clearly took her a few seconds to realize what Kash had said. Then her face registered confusion and a hint of disappointment.

"Oh. Sure. Of course." She reached for her clothes, quickly dressed, and waited by the door for several beats as though hoping

Kash would embrace her, kiss her, or in some way acknowledge what had just happened.

When Kash stood her ground, unflinching, Isabel gave her a half smile and put her hand on the doorknob. "I'll...I guess I'll see you tomorrow, then."

Soon, only her lingering fragrance remained, and Kash was surprisingly unsatisfied and empty.

CHAPTER EIGHT

Stop! I demand a break for espresso or something," Gillian groused. "My feet are killing me, I have to pee, and my stomach has been growling for the last hour, at least."

"Okay, already." Isabel glanced down at the map in her hands to orient herself. She had kept them to a strict schedule all day, first to the Spanish Steps, then the Roman Forum and the Pantheon. She still couldn't quite believe what had happened the day before with Kash, so she kept them constantly on the move, too preoccupied to spend much time trying to make sense of it. Her sexual encounter with Kash had left her breathless, but also in a semistate of shock. It hadn't gone at all as she imagined.

The way that Kash had *taken* her, for that was what it felt like—without any discussion or foreplay, without the kind of gentle interaction she was accustomed to—and without the reciprocity that usually marked her sexual encounters—all of it had surprised her, especially her own reaction.

Do you want to analyze this, or do you want to fuck?

The entire experience had been so unbelievably exciting that merely remembering it sent her into a mild state of arousal. Kash stirred her up and made her feel *more* in those few minutes than any woman she could remember. Including women she'd known well, women she thought she might be in love with. But even as the experience had thrilled her, it had left her wanting, as though they had unfinished business.

But she apparently doesn't share that thought. Her dismissal of me couldn't have been clearer.

"Izzy? Earth to Izzy! You going to stare at that map all day or make a decision?" Gillian's words shook her out of her reverie. "Is everything okay with you? You've been awfully quiet. Ever since you went to talk to Kash, as a matter of fact. Did something happen?"

Is that ever an understatement. "Everything's fine, Gill. No worries." It was rare for her not to confide in Gillian. Normally neither of them hesitated to discuss other women they were interested in. But she wanted to keep what had happened with Kash to herself. At least for now. Until she could put it in perspective somehow. Right now it was too fresh, too raw. "Should be a toilet somewhere. We'll stop at the first place that seems promising."

"*Buon pomeriggio, signori.* May I help take you somewhere?" The offer, in heavily accented English, came from one of two young Italian men who seemed to materialize out of nowhere.

All day, whenever they stopped to study a map or appeared uncertain about their surroundings, some handsome, swarthy stud or two would appear, charming and gracious, and offer assistance and sometimes more—dinner, drinks, a guide for the afternoon. Gillian's miniskirt got a lot of attention, as did Isabel's long blond hair and fair complexion.

They learned fairly quickly to firmly decline the offers if they expected to keep to Isabel's schedule, for many of their would-be good Samaritans were more than a little persistent.

"Thank you, no," Isabel responded politely.

"We're fine. But thanks," Gillian chimed in.

"*Prego. Come desideri.*" One of the men sighed dramatically before they took the hint and departed.

"Damn shame that Italian women aren't as anxious to introduce themselves as the men are," Gillian said wistfully. "I've seen some absolutely breathtaking women."

"This is true," Isabel agreed. *But still nothing to compare to the one we came with.*

They came upon a pleasant café where they could sit outdoors and people watch. Over espresso and biscotti, Isabel studied her list. "I wish I didn't have to do this makeover thing. It sure eats up a lot of hours that we could use seeing the city."

"Did she tell you? Kash is going to do shoots at the Colosseum and Trevi Fountain," Gillian informed her. "I tried to grill her about what's ahead when we were out to dinner."

"No, we didn't talk about that." *We hardly talked at all.* Isabel ordered a couple of bottled waters they could take with them. Once they sat down, she realized how hard she had driven them. Her legs and back ached their appreciation. *All to keep from thinking too hard about Kash. Not that she's very far from my thoughts no matter what I do.* "Did she tell you anything else about what's coming up?"

"Nope. I did good to get that out of her. She's pretty tight-lipped."

Don't talk about Kash's lips, Isabel wanted to say. *I don't need any encouragement to start obsessing over them.* She'd wanted so much for Kash to kiss her, the way they had almost kissed in the hallway—she *still* wanted her to—and wondered why it hadn't happened. *She kissed that actress. But with me…*She'd never known that sex could feel so intimate and impersonal at the same time. It was a confusing mix.

"The women here sure know how to dress. Have you noticed?" Gillian asked. "Even more so than in Paris. I mean, like her—the babe in the red skirt? Very hot—that look is only now hitting the States." Picking another chic native out of the crowd with a tip of her head, she continued, "And that one, the whole package—the jewelry, the shoes. And there—the redhead." The latest reference was to a buxom beauty meticulously put together, from makeup and hair to the three-inch designer heels she wore with practiced ease. "Very stylish."

"You're a far better judge than I am," Isabel said. "Beautiful, I can absolutely agree with. But you know I have no clue what's new in fashion."

"I wonder what kind of clothes they'll give you for your makeover wardrobe. Since you're getting it here, I bet it'll be Versace, or Dolce and Gabbana. Maybe a Fendi purse and some Ferragamo or Sergio Rossi shoes. Oh! Maybe Armani. Wouldn't *that* be the bomb?"

"Yes, Gill." Isabel patted Gillian's shoulder reassuringly. "You can borrow whatever and whomever, whenever you like."

Gillian laughed. "I'm kind of glad you're not into clothes the way I am. Leaves more for me to choose from."

"Okay, enough of a break. Still got a lot to see." Isabel glanced down at her itinerary as she got to her feet.

Gillian reluctantly followed suit. "Yes, Drill Sergeant Sterling," she said, saluting. "Don't suppose we can fit in a club tonight?"

Isabel considered her answer. She knew Gillian would be happiest spending another night out drinking and dancing, but that prospect held little appeal. Her mind kept returning to Kash, despite her best efforts to distract it elsewhere. *You're obsessing over her.* If given the choices among an evening with Gill, seeing the sights of Rome alone, or more time with Kash? It wasn't hard to decide. Maybe Kash would reject her, maybe not. But Isa the wild child wanted to return to her suite and see if she and Kash could finish what they had started, and she would apparently not be denied.

"I know you want to go out tonight," she said. "But I'm not really in the mood. Why don't we hit another stop or two and then head back to the hotel. You can change, and I'll see if maybe Kash is up for showing me a bit of Rome at night."

Gillian nodded with a sly smile on her face. "Sounds like a great idea. For both of us. I approve of this new being-more-spontaneous Isabel, by the way, hon. You wear it well."

Isabel punched her lightly on the shoulder. "Well, I have to admit, you've opened my eyes to some new possibilities."

❖

Kash spent much of the day scouting locations with Massimo. He was the perfect assistant, even if his driving kept her heart in her throat as they wove in and out of traffic—he, cursing loudly in Italian and missing every obstacle or impediment by centimeters. They checked out several possible locations and finalized arrangements for her photo shoot.

She was recognized nearly everywhere, and Massimo did an admirable job keeping people from getting too close. But one of his best qualities was his sensitivity to her mood. He obviously realized as soon as he picked her up that she was preoccupied, so he avoided idle chatter, leaving her alone with her thoughts.

And those thoughts were almost exclusively about Isabel.

She knew that her celebrity status had spoiled her. She could usually have whatever she wanted immediately, be it a new Jaguar or a pretty face and sexy body.

And rationally, she knew how easy it was to develop an obsession for what she could only want, but never have. The tantalizing allure of forbidden fruit. Some of the e-mail she had received from fans and admirers was testament to that kind of fixation.

She'd thought for a time that this dynamic was responsible for Isabel's allure. That she'd developed this desire for her because Isabel didn't, at first, appear to be available.

But if that had been the case, she should now be over that fascination. She'd had her. And in the past, fucking a woman had always been the way to exorcise her from her thoughts. Not this time.

Screwing Isabel had only made her more desirable. Now she absolutely couldn't get her out of her mind. She was surprised as well by how quickly and easily she had discarded what had become for her a well-established boundary in regard to sex. She had shed her shirt and embraced Isabel, allowing and relishing the contact of their naked bodies.

Most distressing of all, she had been wondering all day about what Isabel had thought of their encounter. *You shouldn't have dismissed her like that. Not her.* Her preoccupation—*No, not preoccupation. It's worry, for Christ's sake. I'm worried about whether she's okay with what happened. What have you done to me? This isn't like me at all.*

She felt so off-center that she decided to opt for a quiet evening back in her suite, with a room-service meal and a book to distract her. But the concierge presented her with another option as she strolled through the lobby en route to the elevators.

The message he handed her was from Isabel. It was simple and to the point.

> *I'd like to see you tonight. I'm in my suite if you're interested.*
>
> *Isabel*

She slipped the note into her pocket as she continued toward the elevators, considering whether to accept the invitation. A part of her wanted to run in the opposite direction. But she suppressed the urge with little effort. She needed to figure out why this woman was different, more compelling than most, and also perhaps remedy how coldly abrupt she'd been. After all, they were going to be spending another couple of weeks together—so she headed to Isabel's room.

CHAPTER NINE

When Kash knocked, Isabel's perfectly imperfect smile greeted her, and she felt uncharacteristically awkward. No, not exactly awkward—*shy? me?*—about the way Isabel was undressing her with that piercing gaze.

"Hi, Kash. Come on in. I was hoping you'd take me up on my invitation." Isabel stepped aside to let her pass, but kept staring at her with that same hungry expectancy that had started things up between them the previous afternoon.

It made her feel off balance. Too much so. Like they were on Isabel's turf now, and she was setting the agenda. The loss of control bothered her. *Maybe this wasn't such a good idea.* She stepped over the threshold but stopped once inside. "I wanted to see if you were okay," she lied. "I have other plans. I can't stay long."

"Oh. I see." Isabel frowned, and that spark of eager anticipation in her eyes vanished.

Kash felt like a heel, but refrained from soothing the damage.

"Yes, Kash. I'm fine. I have to admit, I was kind of hoping we might…well, I guess…pick up where we left off yesterday."

Usually when women wanted more from her, more than she could give them, she simply said no. She never explained or justified her actions. But for some reason, she wanted Isabel to understand. "Isabel, we didn't 'leave off.' You got what you wanted. And so did I. And that's *all* I wanted."

Isabel studied her with an unreadable expression for a very long while before she replied. "Okay, I think I get it. You don't like to be touched, correct?"

"No. Not there."

Isabel cocked her head, seeming surprised. "Ever?"

"No."

Another long silence between them. "Do you ever touch the same woman more than once?" Isabel asked.

Kash never answered such personal questions because whatever she said inevitably ended up in print somewhere. But she took a leap of faith with Isabel. "Yes. Sometimes. If it's fun and uncomplicated."

"So…what?"

Isabel had been clearly irritated with Kash only moments before. But now she seemed mostly curious.

"Touching me wasn't…fun? Or uncomplicated? Which?"

Kash flashed back to how it had felt to make Isabel come. "Fun" wasn't the word for it. "Amazing" might do, but she could never admit that to Isabel. "The latter. Listen, you wanted it, and you got it. It was fun. End of story. Why keep pushing? Is one more evening that important to you?"

Isabel's eyes grew moist as she considered her answer. "Yes," she said softly. "I guess it is."

Most women readily accepted what Kash said when she told them it was a one-time thing. If they asked for more, usually they hadn't yet gotten what they really wanted from her. But she didn't feel that was the case this time.

She wasn't certain which she feared most: that Isabel would turn out to be like the others after all, or that she would be the rare woman who might be interested in *her*…with no ulterior motive. The *real* her, too, the messed-up one, not the celebrity one. The one who felt ill equipped for any kind of authentic relationship. "What's this really about? What do you want from me?"

"Only what you're willing to give, Kash," Isabel said. "If you have boundaries, I'll respect them. I want more time with you, that's all. Is that so unexpected?"

"*Why*, Isabel?" Kash repeated.

Isabel went to sit on the couch a few feet away, and in a while she said simply, "I'm drawn to you. I want to be around you while I can be, because when I am…I'm totally and completely *happy*. You know? Savoring the here and now, not existing for that somewhere-down-the-road time that I usually spend all my energy fretting about and planning for."

Kash had heard nearly every conceivable story, flirtation, and phony come-on line possible. She could smell one coming long before it actually materialized. This time in her gut she felt certain that these were the words of a sensitive, caring woman.

"I know your affairs are fleeting," Isabel continued. "I'm not asking for more than is possible. I simply enjoy your company and want to know you better, Kash. I want more time with you, as much as you will give me, because I want to remember you long after we go our separate ways."

"Isabel, I have lots of...issues. Personal issues. I do sex, not getting-to-know-you, like you do. I'm not that type of woman." *God, it's getting hot in here.*

"Can I ask why?"

Again, she sensed only naïve curiosity from Isabel, not the probing query of a woman who might be seeking information to sell.

It was so hard for her to trust anyone. Miranda had earned a good measure during her steadfast friendship of many years—for putting up with her moods and occasional bursts of thoughtless or inappropriate behavior.

After knowing Isabel only a few days, Kash wanted to trust her. Some instinct told her that she could.

"No easy answer to that." Kash slumped back against the door, her legs suddenly rubbery. She had long managed to avoid too much self-examination, but lately she had been more introspective than usual.

"I'm not close to many people." *Talk about understatement.* "Because people usually try to get to know me because they want something from me."

"I can imagine how celebrity would make for a rather cautious individual," Isabel observed. "Especially if personal things you've shared with someone end up in a magazine article."

"Yeah," Kash replied wryly. "That's happened a time or two."

"I realize you haven't known me very long, Kash," Isabel said. "But I wish you could believe I would never reveal anything private you might share with me."

Kash regarded her thoughtfully. "I don't think you would, Isabel." *Why do I want to tell you things? Confide in you in a way that is so completely foreign to me I'm not sure how to start?*

She stuck her hands in her pockets because they were starting to shake.

"I'm a bit of a control freak," she began. *A bit? Miranda would say I'm an Olympic gold medalist in that regard.* "I need that sense of control when I'm with someone sexually."

Isabel regarded her with an unflinching expression. "That wouldn't be an issue with me, Kash. Like I said, I have no problem respecting any boundaries you might have. Or with letting you…call the shots."

Isabel's consent to whatever Kash might desire made it even more difficult for her not to summarily discard any further contact between them. *She wants this, even though she knows what it means. Or what she thinks it means, anyway. But she doesn't know the whole story.*

"There've been a couple of women who have…well, who've meant something to me. Who got close to me." She was astounded to realize she had known Christine Shaw more than half her life ago. "The first was my college roommate, freshman year. Chris was beautiful, and fearless, and impossibly easy to tell all my secrets to. She was the first girl I ever felt attracted to, and I finally told her, right before spring break, even though I knew she was straight."

Kash closed her eyes and suddenly felt all of nineteen again. "It's not like I expected her to suddenly become gay or anything. But I guess I wanted her to know because I was tired of hiding my attraction." She sighed, remembering the shocked expression on Chris's face.

"She'd always been one of the most open-minded people I'd ever known, and we were close, so I thought she'd take it fine. But she freaked and completely closed me out. Moved out of the dorm and in with a guy she barely knew, and stopped returning my calls. To this day I don't know whether she really was rabidly homophobic or…Well, later I wondered whether she didn't perhaps feel something for me, too, but couldn't deal with it when I brought the issue front and center. Anyway, that ended the only real, significant friendship I'd ever had. I'd always been pretty…solitary, and she was the first person I really deeply trusted."

"I can't imagine how difficult that was for you."

"It was hard to trust again, after that," Kash confirmed. "Until I met Lainie, about four years later. After Christine, I kept all my relationships with women casual and brief. No strings."

"No expectations meant no disappointments," Isabel said.

"Yes." Remembering Lainie was much more difficult, for no amount of time could make that wound feel any less painfully fresh. *Why, when I remember her, don't I ever see her during one of her cruel moments, there at the end? Why do I insist on picturing her as she was the day I met her?*

"I was blown away the minute I saw her, which was during one of my first jobs out of college. Lainie was breaking into modeling, and she came to the studio in New York where I was working to get shots for a portfolio." Kash could still recall the patchouli undertones of her perfume as she swept by, all confidence. "I was only an assistant then, right in off the street, and she barely noticed me."

Her voice had dropped to a lower register than normal. She wished she had some water; her throat felt constricted. "Our paths crossed a couple more times after that, at one shoot or another, but I still never registered with her. Not until *People* magazine did a story on me. The next time she saw me, backstage at some awards show, she introduced herself as though we'd never met. But I didn't care, because suddenly she couldn't wait to spend time with me."

"You were in heaven," Isabel said.

"Yes." It was easy to talk to Isabel, perhaps a little too easy, but she couldn't stop now. "I hadn't been famous long enough yet to know about women who will throw themselves at you for the right phone number, invitation, or introduction. She made me believe she loved me, that we had a future together, for six months. Until she had gotten everything she wanted from me and had snared someone who could give her more. Oh, and as a parting gift, she sold everything I had ever told her in confidence—most of it in bed—to the tabloids, a chapter at a time."

"Oh, Kash." Isabel's voice was so soft Kash barely heard it.

"It was a long time ago." But it had changed her, hardened her, badly. She had never been the same, and she knew it. "After that, I rarely let a woman get close. The few who did? Well, they always wanted something from me, too. So I started making everything clear and obvious, right up front. A fuck for a favor. No illusions about what was involved."

"*Always*?" Isabel asked. "Surely some women have been genuinely interested in you?"

"No," Kash insisted. "Never."

"No disrespect intended, Kash, but maybe you hang out in the wrong circles. And when was the last time you really gave someone a chance?" There was no challenge or malice in Isabel's tone, only gentle inquiry. "Or honestly opened yourself up to the possibility? You didn't with Gillian, who had no interest in asking for any favors or anything else from you. And you're pushing me away—and I want nothing from you except your company, as long as I can have it. I don't want the photos, the cover, the magazine…all of that stuff. I really don't. I'm doing these shoots only because I'm obligated to, and because they're a way to be near you."

"Gillian's your friend and a lovely woman, and I don't mean to criticize her unfairly. But I would bet she wouldn't have come on to me if it wasn't for who I am."

Isabel didn't refute the assertion, because she wasn't sure she could. "Well, your celebrity isn't a selling point as far as I'm concerned, Kash. I respect your talent, of course, but I'm not interested in you because of what you can do for me." She settled back against the couch. "I know probably nothing I can say will convince you of that. But it's the truth."

"Isabel, if I didn't believe you, I wouldn't have told you all I did." Kash took a couple of steps closer. "I do think you're one of those rare women who say what they mean and mean what they say, and don't have some hidden agenda. It's a refreshing change, and I won't deny that I'm powerfully attracted to you. That's pretty obvious. But I guess it's precisely because you *are* different from the type of woman I'm usually with that my usual…well, let's say that the way I usually *am* with women…doesn't feel right with you. I'm not sure I can explain it better than that."

"I wish you could, Kash. I want to understand, because I don't see anything standing between us."

Kash ran a hand through her hair. *Jesus, I'm terrible at this.* "Isabel, ever since Lainie, I can't *be* with a woman unless I can absolutely control *everything* that happens. I don't know any other way to be."

"Okay, I think I understand that."

"I'm not sure you do," she said, exasperated. "To put it bluntly… what I mean is…I can't get off unless I completely dominate whoever I'm fucking. They become an object to me, in a sense."

Isabel studied Kash's face intently but didn't interrupt.

"I don't want to think about what *they* might want. It's about what *I* want. It's part of the deal. If I screw them, then I don't mind so much when they screw me." *God, I wish I had a drink.* "Oh, I make sure they leave happy. I know if I don't, that will end up in the tabloids, too." She couldn't keep the bitterness out of her voice. "But none of them will get the satisfaction of making me come. Most of the time, they're not even around. I wait until I'm alone."

The next admissions were the hardest. "I can be very…demanding and aggressive sexually, Isabel. And rough, particularly if the woman I'm with is blatantly trying to deceive me that she doesn't really want something *else* from me. It's always consensual, but…" She paused. "Sex has become, for me, a way of doing business." She knew that sometimes women probably agreed to do things with her they might not ordinarily, only because they wanted a favor badly enough.

"Don't you see?" Kash was suddenly tired of trying to explain and understand. "Do you get it now? I can't *be* that way with you. It doesn't feel right, somehow. You're too different for me." *I think about what you want too much. And I don't feel the same need to dominate you, but if not that…then what?*

"Is there anything I can say…or do…to make it possible for you?" Isabel asked. "To change your mind?"

"No. Nothing. I can't. We're from different worlds."

The irony wasn't lost on Kash. *Brief affairs are totally against her nature, but she'll make an exception for me. Of course she would be the rare woman I can't just fuck and forget.* "I'm sorry, Isabel. From now on, we should keep things between us strictly business. It's better that way."

She turned to go, trying to erase the image frozen in her mind of the disappointment on Isabel's face.

❖

When Isabel and Gillian left the hotel the next morning for Isabel's makeover, Kash was already waiting in the car with Massimo. Isabel, in the lead, slipped into the front seat next to him, leaving Gillian to get in the back with Kash.

She and Kash exchanged few words beyond perfunctory good mornings, and they avoided eye contact. Isabel was a little afraid that Kash might somehow be able to sense how her day had started out, and she guessed that Kash was trying to keep her distance.

Isabel had awakened that morning in the middle of a very hot dream, in which Kash was fucking her while "I Get Around" played in the background. It was far more realistic than most of her dreams. In fact, she was still trying to convince her stirred-up hormones that it had all been imaginary and that she wasn't going to be getting any more real opportunities to experience Kash's touch. *Doesn't seem to matter that she wants nothing further with me.* And her self-confessed "issues" weren't a deterrent either. In fact, Kash's sexual-control proclivities—much to her surprise—were extremely enticing.

Morning rush hour was a nightmare, with Massimo demonstrating amazing kamikaze driving skills and his command of every conceivable Italian curse. But they arrived at the salon with all body parts intact and only a few minutes late for Isabel's appointment.

Clifton Mengam had gained the same kind of acclaim for doing hair that Kash had achieved for taking pictures, so he had long since dropped his last name from his business cards. He had established a chain of salons in Rome, Milan, New York, and Los Angeles and often created the cutting-edge and always highly flattering coiffures of actresses attending red-carpet events.

One of his assistants settled Isabel comfortably into a chair, under an aubergine cape with the large swirled *C* that was Clifton's trademark. Her cappuccino arrived in the hands of the man himself.

The famed stylist was a handsome black man with a broad, welcoming smile, whose soft-spoken demeanor contrasted to his imposing six-foot, three-inch height. He seemed casually dressed in faded jeans and a white linen shirt, but she could tell the shirt was finely tailored and his shoes looked expensive. In his early thirties, he wore his hair cut very short, with neatly trimmed edges.

"*Buon giorno*, ladies," he warmly greeted them all, then presented Isabel with her cup and saucer, also adorned with his trademark *C*. "Miss Sterling, *benvenuta*. Welcome. May I call you Isabel?" Both his English and his Italian carried a faint accent, a suggestion of his Surinamese heritage.

"Of course."

"*Grazie*, Isabel. I am most pleased to be the one chosen for your makeover."

"Very nice to meet you."

"Kash!" Clifton smiled broadly at the photographer, who was setting up her equipment. "Wonderful to see you again. *Come va?*"

"*Non c'è male*, Clifton," Kash replied. "How is it you seem never to grow a day older?"

They hugged and exchanged the customary duet of cheek kisses, and Clifton introduced himself to Gillian before he returned to stand behind Isabel.

He ran his hands through her hair, taking measure of the texture and weight, as he studied her face in the mirror for a full minute or two. "Beautiful hair," he said at last. He spread the long blond locks over her shoulders. "You have not cut it for many years."

"Hmm. Twelve or fourteen, or so," Isabel said. She was impressed by his gentle touch and unhurried assessment.

"So are you excited about this change, or a little nervous?" Clifton had a twinkle in his eyes, like he could see through her veneer of polite enthusiasm.

Isabel couldn't contain a smile. "I know I'm very lucky to be the beneficiary of your talents, and believe me, I'm appreciative. I admit, however—hoping you won't take offense, please don't—that I'm happy with the way I am. I didn't enter myself in the contest that won me this makeover, you see." She pointed to Gillian. "My friend there did. So although I'm sure I'll be happy with the result, because I know you're a whiz at this…it's not like I'm seeking a change."

Clifton nodded knowingly. "It is wonderful to be content with how you are, as you should be—you're a beautiful woman. Very beautiful." He continued to run his hands through her hair, considering the possibilities. "But I am willing to bet that if you trust me completely, you will leave here not merely happy with the result, but really thrilled."

"Thrilled, huh?" *Unlikely. I'll be happy if I don't leave here with a blue Mohawk. It can always grow out.*

"Thrilled and amazed," Clifton promised with a smile and a wink.

"This I gotta see." Isabel sighed resignedly.

Clifton rattled off instructions in Italian to one of his assistants, who busily began to mix two colors of hair dye.

"First, I will add highlights and lowlights to your hair," he told Isabel. "They will add a lot of shine and depth to your beautiful natural color. Then I will cut it, to a couple of inches below your shoulder." He indicated the length with his hand. "And give you some soft bangs, long. Here…" Sweeping over her forehead with his fingers, he indicated the path his razor would take. "They will better frame your face, show off those high cheekbones. And your eyes. You'll see."

As Clifton worked with his colors, Kash started clicking away, circling them. She was happy for the chance to study Isabel's face in her viewfinder while Isabel was distracted and unguarded. *He's right. She's lovely just as she is.*

When she got into photography, her camera was her artist's easel, her method of connecting with the world. But her long zoom lenses had also made her the ultimate voyeur, bringing faces and bodies intimately close for study and appreciation while allowing her to maintain her distance and veil of disinterest.

Her eyes really are the most interesting shade of blue. Deep and endless, the sky on a perfect cloudless day. Calming. She felt buoyant whenever Clifton said something to make Isabel laugh or smile that marvelously imperfect smile.

He was a master at it, too. Kash had seen him in action often, behind the scenes at some awards show or runway event, taking care of the hottest of the hot. Like bartenders and psychiatrists and priests, stylists heard all types of stories and confessions. While maintaining total discretion, he still managed to tell marvelously entertaining stories about his clientele. And between what he learned on the job and picked up as the voracious reader he was, he could talk to absolutely anyone about anything.

Kash was enjoying both the view through her lens and the bits and pieces of new information she was learning about Isabel through the warmly gregarious Clifton.

"Cakes! How wonderful. My medium is hair, yours is fondant. They are actually not so different." Clifton motioned his assistant for another cappuccino for Isabel. "It is all about making the vision a reality and that delight on the client's face when they see it for the first time."

"Exactly," Isabel said.

"So tell me," Clifton said, "your most challenging task, most rewarding, something along those lines. The memorable ones."

"Hmm." Isabel pursed her lips.

Kash zoomed in and focused. *Click. Click.* Zoomed in some more. *Such nice, full lips. And soft. Christ. So soft. Why the hell didn't I kiss her when I had the chance?*

"Well, I'm kind of known for my kids' cakes. You know, for birthdays, mostly. Whatever the child likes, I try to do something appropriate. Making a football cake—now that was a challenge. A three-dimensional one, mind you, to scale. With frosting the right color and texture. The stitching. Only with the kid's name instead of *Rawlings*."

"Sounds marvelous." Clifton finished administering the color to her hair, and while they waited for it to set, he sipped espresso with her.

"I was the most proud of a cake I made of the Disney castle—you know the one I mean? It's patterned after one in Germany."

"Neuschwanstein," Clifton supplied. "King Ludwig the Second."

"Hey. I'm impressed. Exactly right."

"Izzy, they've got a computer here," Gillian chimed in. "You should call up your Web site and show him pictures."

"You have a Web site?" Clifton set down his coffee and went to retrieve his laptop, which was currently displaying his day's schedule of appointments.

"Yes. Izzycakes dot com," she answered. "I do freelance work, mostly for bakeries."

"They're so amazing that people are always saying they can't bring themselves to cut into them," Gillian enthused.

Clifton typed in the address, then grinned. "Brava! Incredible work, Isabel. I had no idea you could do something like this with flour and sugar. The castle must have taken a very long time. It is so wonderfully detailed it could almost be a photograph."

The comment drew Kash's attention to the screen.

Clifton wasn't exaggerating. Isabel's cakes were stunning in their complexity and meticulous attention to detail. The windows in the castle were thin sheets of colored sugar as translucent as stained glass. And the roses and leaves on her wedding cakes were so realistic Kash could swear they had been plucked from a garden that morning.

"All of this is handmade?" she asked. "That's all really edible?"

"Every bit," Isabel said. "Hate to have a client bite into something that's going to choke them. Wouldn't be very good for business, now would it?" Her teasing tone helped to defuse the tension between them.

Kash met her eyes. "I really have to apologize, Isabel. When Miranda told me you decorated cakes, I sort of made fun of what you do. I was picturing those big sheet cakes with *Happy Birthday, Junior* written on them and little plastic football players stuck into the icing. But this is truly impressive. You're much more artist than baker."

"You're forgiven."

Kash wondered how else she had underestimated Isabel. There was certainly more to her than was readily apparent.

"Your cakes for children are quite something, indeed. I can see how you are known for them," Clifton said. "So…you like kids, obviously. Do you have any of your own?"

"No," Isabel said. "Not yet. Maybe some day, though."

"And no wedding ring," Clifton observed. "Such a beautiful woman like you is not married? How is this possible?"

Kash thought the faint blush of color that appeared on Isabel's cheek more appealing than any painted by mere cosmetics.

"Not happened upon Ms. Right yet." Isabel grinned shyly. "But it'll happen."

"Of course it will. You are a lovely girl. So full of life." Clifton checked her hair, then put his hands on her shoulders and smiled at their reflection. "You must go out tonight and let the world see how beautiful you are. Romance is everywhere in Roma." He lowered the chair she was perched in. "If you'll follow me?"

After a rinse and an absolutely divine scalp massage that almost put her to sleep, Isabel was back in Clifton's chair, but this time she faced away from the mirror.

"Will you indulge my wish that you not get a glimpse until I'm done?" Clifton gave her puppy-dog eyes, well practiced.

Isabel laughed. "Sure. Why not?"

"So I understand you will be on *Sophisticated Women*." Clifton selected his razor and glanced at Kash, who was changing lenses. "When will you be taking the cover photographs?"

"I've got some space in a studio here to take some later today," Kash said. "And I can take additional shots back in New York if I need to."

"Oh, you won't need to. You'll adore what you'll get today." He started to cut, using his razor with delicate precision, like a sculpting tool, taking only small bits at a time. "Isabel, you are in excellent hands with Kash."

Isabel and Kash looked at each other. Isabel smiled first, but Kash wasn't far behind. What most surprised Clifton, who missed nothing, was that his comment made both of them blush profusely.

"Kash will capture you in a way that will make everyone who sees that cover want to know more about you," Clifton continued, but he knew at once he'd said something wrong. Most women adored attention, but Isabel cringed at his words. And Kash? Kash couldn't take her eyes off Isabel. *I don't think she has even realized she has stopped taking pictures and is staring at her.* "Have I said something wrong?"

Isabel shook her head. "No, not at all. It's only that—that's so not me. No offense to Kash. She takes amazing photographs."

"But it will be splendid!" Clifton paused to study what he had cut so far. "A cover is a taste of appreciation, that's all. A little stroking is good for the soul."

"Hear, hear!" Gillian said. "It's nice when good things happen to worthy people, Izzy. No one is more deserving of winning that contest and being pampered than you."

"Hardly," Isabel protested.

"Well, maybe the *no one* is a slight exaggeration," Gillian said, "but you deserve it more than anyone I know. All those weeks you were down in Louisiana, helping out after Katrina. And that work you do every year with the AIDS/HIV awareness group."

"Hush, Gillian," Isabel said.

"And the senior swim classes," Gillian continued. "And how many times have you cooked a meal for someone who—"

"Enough!" Isabel's tone was firm.

Kash had captured the entire sequence of Isabel getting redder and redder from embarrassment. *She really doesn't want this cover. And she's humble about her altruism as well.* She had so rarely come across a truly selfless individual that the experience was wonderfully refreshing. *There's some substance to this one.*

"You must have faith in Kash's ability to represent you well, *bella*," Clifton told Isabel. "She captures the essence of someone, so that you feel you understand them, somehow—what they are thinking and feeling, or what kind of people they are at their core."

"I'm not paying you nearly enough, Clifton," Kash deadpanned.

"So have you had some fun photo sessions together so far?" he asked.

Kash feigned horror and stepped between her tripod and Isabel protectively, which made Gillian snort with laughter.

"Comedians," Isabel complained good-naturedly.

Clifton chuckled, too. "So you are the type with two left feet?"

"Not on the dance floor," Kash supplied.

Isabel's cheeks warmed as she glanced at Kash. *Click.* The

photographer circled her, snapping several shots in quick succession. *I wish she'd put that camera down more often so I could see her face, tell what she's thinking.*

Kash was absolutely mesmerized by how much a simple haircut could change Isabel's appearance. *Click.* Clifton was a perfectionist, so he was still taking tiny bits here and there, studying her hair from all angles. Roughing it up to make it playful and sexy. *Click.* It was truly a masterpiece; the added shades of caramel and blond added a wonderful depth and shine to Isabel's hair and complemented her complexion perfectly. The cut was modern and chic but suited her personality well and made her deep blue eyes really stand out. She was more woman than girl now. *Click.*

Kash zoomed in on Isabel's face. *You've got that expression in your eyes again. Hungry. Like you're imagining me with my clothes off.* It made her feel both exhilarated and somehow also kind of...*nervous? Women never make me nervous.*

"Kash? Everything all right?" Clifton's amused tone snapped her out of her thoughts. His simple question contained undertones of *Oh yes, you're not fooling me. You really like this one, don't you?*

She realized she hadn't snapped a picture in quite a long while. "Yes, fine," she said, depressing the shutter only so she could hide behind the camera. *Click.* It wasn't easy for her to regain her equilibrium with Isabel staring at her like that. *Damn. How can I go another two weeks with her?*

Gillian had been so busy watching Isabel's transformation that she didn't immediately see the sparks flying between her friend and Kash. But Clifton's tone alerted her, and then she felt like slapping herself. *Something has certainly happened between these two. Something great, it would appear, from the way they can't keep their eyes off each other. But there's a problem, too. And that's why Izzy has been acting so weird. Perhaps these two need a little help to get past whatever is keeping them apart.*

"My part is done and I will now turn you over to Cosma." Clifton put his hands on Isabel's shoulders. "But you are not to see yourself... and neither are they...until she finishes your brows and makeup. I have also arranged to have one of your new outfits delivered here. We'll have a big unveiling."

"Is this really necessary?" Kash complained.

"Yeah," Gillian said. "It's fun watching the whole transformation."

"Call it my flair for the dramatic. Come on, ladies. Indulge my one request." Clifton wouldn't budge.

"You're going to flip, Izzy." Gillian shook her head in wonder. "It's incredible. Amazing. Don't you agree, Kash?"

"Clifton, as usual…you're the man."

Gillian noticed that Kash seemed to have missed the nuance that suggested she was clued in to the attraction between her and Isabel.

"Now you're really making me want to see it," Isabel griped as Clifton lowered her salon chair. "Come on. Let me peek?"

"Patience. I promised you would be thrilled, and thrilled you will be. Trust me."

CHAPTER TEN

Isabel knew from the looks on their faces that she was going to see a dramatic difference. Clifton was supremely self-satisfied. Gillian let out a low whistle of approval, and Kash was...well, Kash was staring at her in a way that made her pulse race.

"I don't know that I would have recognized you, Izzy," Gillian said finally. "It's awesome. You *rock*."

Kash still hadn't said anything. But Isabel was quite enjoying the smoldering expression on her face. *I'd say it definitely meets with her approval. Perhaps there's a chance for more between us, after all. She's got that same intensity about her she had right before she pulled me into her suite, only more so. Oh yes. I think a door has definitely opened.*

"Ready?" Clifton asked.

"As I'll ever be." Isabel faced the mirror, her heart fluttering with anticipation. She knew the clothes themselves would make a big difference. She had arrived in sneakers, jeans, and a polo shirt, but now wore black heels and a simple black dress, cut to mid-thigh, with a plunging back and a front that exposed the valley between her breasts. It was far more provocative than anything she had ever put on before, so she imagined it was more the dress than anything else that had put that glassy-eyed expression on Kash's face.

But when she faced the mirror, she gaped at the image that stared back at her. *Jesus. I'm not sure I would have recognized myself, either.* The overall effect was astonishing. Her makeup was understated and elegant, perfect for her coloring, the smoky tones befitting an evening out on the town. Her lips shone with a bronzed lip gloss, and her eyebrows had been shaped and dyed to match the new dark honey hues in her hair. The haircut itself was stylish and modern, and greatly contributed to an overall effect of sexy sophistication.

"Thrilled, eh?" Clifton asked with a complacent nonchalance.

"Way beyond thrilled," Isabel managed. "It's truly mind-boggling."

Kash tried to will herself to stop staring and say something. She knew she was gawking like a pubescent boy with his first copy of *Playboy,* but damned if she could do anything but drink in the decidedly sexy splendor that was the new Isabel. *Christ, she was driving me crazy before. But now…*

Her eyes met Isabel's, and Isabel winked at her. *Oh, great. She can see exactly what she's doing to me.* Arousal twisted in her groin.

Isabel embraced Clifton. "'Thank you' comes nowhere near being enough. It's totally unbelievable. What a difference!" *Not to mention the fact that it appears to be exactly what I needed to get Kash's undivided attention again.*

"I only enhanced what is already there," Clifton responded warmly, hugging her back. "As I said earlier, you are a very beautiful woman, Isabel. We have merely showcased you in a new way." He spoke to Kash. "You see why I know you will take some wonderful photographs today."

"No doubt," Kash managed. *If I can keep my hands from shaking long enough to shoot them. Christ, Isabel. How will I ever keep my promise to myself not to touch you again?*

While Isabel excused herself to retrieve the clothes she had come in with and Gillian went out to find their driver, Kash packed up her cameras and equipment under Clifton's watchful eye.

"Kash, I have seen you in the company of models, actresses, many of the world's most beautiful women," Clifton commented. "But I don't think I have ever seen you quite so taken with someone as you obviously are with this one."

Kash straightened and glared at him. "What? What are you talking about? That's nonsense."

"It could not be more obvious, my friend. That surrender in your eyes when you saw her? Priceless. Don't tell me someone has finally captured the heart of the world's most confirmed playgirl?"

"Captured my heart?" Kash snorted dismissively. "You sound like some drippy romance novel, Clifton. Okay, I admit Isabel is positively stunning in that dress, and I certainly can appreciate a sexy, beautiful woman. That's all."

"Whatever you say, Kash. Whatever you say."

❖

Massimo had been idly chatting with Gillian when Isabel and Kash emerged from the salon and slid into the backseat of the Fiat. When he spotted Isabel, he stopped in mid-sentence and muttered something that sounded like a prayer under his breath.

"*Sembrate incredibili*," he concluded, staring at her in the rearview mirror. "You are very, very beautiful, Isabel."

"Thank you, Massimo." Though Isabel had based her whole life on the concept of not judging people by appearances, the reaction to her new look excited her nearly as much as the makeover itself. Especially Kash's. Kash kept glancing surreptitiously in her direction, most frequently at her breasts or her legs. Their thighs were almost touching. *I can tell she likes what she sees, but she hasn't said one word to me directly. I wonder why? Still determined to resist this attraction between us?*

Gillian swiveled around in the front passenger seat. "I have to say I feel woefully underdressed now, next to you two. Why don't you drop me at the hotel so I can change, and pick me up when you're done with your shoot? Then we can all go out to dinner and find a place to show you off."

"Sure, fine with me," Isabel answered. She didn't think it really necessary. Gillian was always more than presentable, and her beige linen pants and matching shell were every bit as dressy as the classic black trousers and black silk shirt that Kash wore. But she was beginning to understand that the right outfit could make all the difference.

After the detour to drop Gillian, they continued to the photo studio where Kash had rented space for the day. Somewhat to Isabel's surprise, once they arrived, Kash dismissed Massimo and told him to pick them up for dinner in ninety minutes.

There had been the occasional bit of small talk in the car, but Kash still had avoided commenting directly about her transformation, which was making Isabel nuts. *Why the heck isn't she saying anything?*

Kash couldn't comment on Isabel's transformation because

everything she thought to say sounded far too obsequious. She had used or heard every line imaginable, and now that she had met a woman truly worthy of a few superlatives, they all sounded hollow and overused. *And what good would it do anyway? She can tell what she's doing to you. To compliment her will only make her think there can be more between you, and you can't let that happen. Not only because you have to work with her for the next couple of weeks, but also because she'll make everything much too complicated. She's not like you are. You have to remember that.*

But Kash certainly couldn't ignore the incredibly sexy allure of the new Isabel in that little black dress. It was a damn good thing she could take photographs in her sleep, because she was too distracted for anything too demanding. *That dress should come with one of those warning labels. Do not operate heavy machinery when Isabel is barely wearing this.*

"Why don't you relax while I set up," she told Isabel in a more businesslike tone than she'd intended, gesturing toward a couple of couches in one corner. She was grateful for the familiarity of the studio routine, because Isabel was making her feel entirely too self-conscious. Every time she met Isabel's eyes, the fire of arousal flared hot, low in her belly, and she had to glance away. If she didn't, she might have to acknowledge and answer the yearning she saw in Isabel's eyes.

"You've been awfully quiet," Isabel said as she settled onto one of the couches and crossed her legs. "Everything all right, Kash?"

Oh, I don't like that tone at all. Not at all. She's trying to push my buttons, and she's succeeding all too well. "Fine," she answered, trying to calm the drumming of her heart with deep, even breathing. Her strategy wasn't working very well, and her hands were trembling as she set up her tripod and lights. *Come on, what gives? Women simply don't have this effect on me.*

"You sure?" Isabel pressed, amusement in her voice. She got up and ambled slowly toward Kash. "You seem kind of…distracted."

Yup. She knows exactly what she's doing. Kash fought to keep her mind on her work, but it was increasingly difficult. She could feel Isabel behind her. Unnerved, she fumbled for one of the light stands but missed, and the stand toppled over with a crash.

"Watch out!" Kash instinctively reached out to block Isabel from the spray of glass. When the noise subsided, she looked over, chagrined, to confirm what she already knew. Yes, she had indeed just placed her hand rather perfectly on Isabel's left breast.

She snatched it back as though burned, but not before memorizing the sensation of the soft swell beneath her fingers. "S...sorry."

Isabel laughed. "For which? Being clumsy? Or feeling me up?"

"Uh...for..." Kash felt completely flustered and she didn't like it one bit. "Hey, let's get to work, huh? Want to take a seat, please?" She tilted her head toward a stool she'd placed against a plain background, as she got her camera ready.

"Sure, sure," Isabel said smugly. She perched on the stool, then shifted forward, and Kash could see maximum cleavage. "I'll sit, I'll stand. Whatever you want. Do with me what you will."

Oh, Christ. The invitation and her provocative pose conjured up the vivid memory of Isabel's satin skin, and how she sounded when she came. *I know what I'd like to do with you in that dress. And out of that dress.* She raised the camera, grateful to escape behind her viewfinder for a while. *Click. Click.*

One thing she knew for damn sure. *Click. Click.* One of these photos was going to burn up the cover of *Sophisticated Women*. Isabel would get her fifteen minutes of fame, and then some. Whether she wanted it or not.

"Can you give me three-quarters, please," she asked in her most professional manner, but not to give her a perfect perspective for pictures. She had to force Isabel to stop teasing her with her cleavage, because that's all she could focus on. *Click.*

"Sure thing." Isabel crossed her legs, hiking her skirt up to an almost obscene height.

That's not helping. Kash kept snapping away, humming absentmindedly. Her body sang with desire. *If she dances in that dress tonight like she did the other night...shaking her ass that way. Man, oh, man.*

Isabel had been relatively certain of the effect she was having on Kash, and when she started humming, her suspicions were verified. Kash's behavior and body language suggested that she was entirely unaware that she was humming and that her tune of choice might reveal what was going on behind her neutral façade.

Isabel tingled with excitement when she recognized Kash's current selection: "I've Got You under My Skin."

When Clifton had introduced her to that stranger in the mirror earlier that day, all of the changes that had been taking place in her on this trip had blossomed fully. The wild child Isa, fully realized. Sexier, more impulsive, and far hornier than the Isabel of old ever remembered being. An intensely sexual part of her had evidently been patiently dormant all these years, but now that Kash had awakened it, it was screaming to be heard.

"How about…" Climbing off the stool, she stood in front of it, her back to Kash. *Let's see what this pose does.* She braced her elbows on the stool, which gave Kash the best possible view of her ass, then peered back over her shoulder at her. "This? What does this do for you?"

Kash froze. *Oh, fuck, yes.* Her mind flashed back to their sexual encounter in her suite. "Spread your legs."

She wasn't aware she had spoken the words aloud. She hadn't meant to, but she knew she had when Isabel complied, smiling that perfectly imperfect come-on smile at her all the while. *Oh, fuck. What the hell are you doing? You can't let this happen again.* And they certainly wouldn't use a pose like this in the magazine. Well, not in *Sophisticated Women.* One of the men's magazines would certainly snap it up, not that she would ever consider offering it to one. *But you can take a few shots for yourself. No harm there. Click. Click. Click.*

Isabel's heart was racing. *I can't believe I'm doing this.* Her body was on fire. She could feel Kash's eyes on her, and that husky undertone in her voice when she had told her to spread her legs had been like a verbal caress, urging her acquiescence. She was getting wet. *I wish you'd put that camera down and come over here and touch me again. I can tell you want to.*

For a minute or two, the only sounds in the room were the steady clicks of Kash's camera and Isabel's rather loud breathing.

With each trigger of her shutter, Kash stepped closer. She couldn't help it. Isabel's breathing did it. Each ragged inhalation and exhalation tugged at her, drawing her nearer. Before long Kash was too close for the lens she was using, and she finally lowered her camera and met Isabel's eyes. They were only a few feet apart.

Isabel said nothing, but the plea in those deep blue eyes couldn't have been clearer. *Fuck me. Take me. Want me.* And Kash did. She couldn't remember when she'd been this excited.

That nagging inner voice that had been telling her this wasn't a good idea faded under the roaring of blood to her brain, and her mind went hazy. She wasn't used to denying herself what she wanted, and she certainly didn't want to start now. Possible consequences and complications ceased to matter. All she knew was what her body demanded—to touch Isabel.

Kash closed the distance between them. She swore she could see Isabel's pupils dilate in anticipation.

She skimmed her hand over the soft skin of Isabel's back as she nestled her pelvis against Isabel's ass.

At the exquisite moment of contact, Isabel moaned, closed her eyes, and pushed back against her.

"Isabel..." Kash spoke gently, but her body reacted instantly to Isabel's encouragement. She drove her groin into Isabel's ass and instantly got hard. Her left hand hung loosely at her side, the camera she held all but forgotten, while she wrapped her right hand around Isabel's waist, ready to pull them tight together. Heart pounding, she started to move against Isabel, and Isabel's body responded, matching her rhythm thrust for thrust.

"God, Kash." Isabel braced herself against the stool. "*So* good."

The muscles of Isabel's taut stomach tensed beneath Kash's fingertips, the material of the dress so sheer it was virtually nonexistent. Her hand was inches from Isabel's breasts, and she knew without being able to see them that the nipples were erect. But before she could confirm her suspicion, which was all she could think about, someone rapped at the studio door.

"Kash?" It was Massimo. A little early, but not much.

"Damn," Kash rasped under her breath as she released Isabel and stepped away. Then, louder, "We'll be out in a minute!"

Isabel straightened and faced her, one hand on the stool for support. Her eyes were penetrating, her lower lip swollen and pink where she'd bitten down on it. "Jesus, Kash. How you make me feel—"

"Isabel..." Kash fought to control the incredible torrent of arousal that made her want to lock the door and throw Isabel down on the couch.

You can't do this. You can't. Pull your shit together and stop letting your clit rule your life. The conscience she rarely heard spoke up and insisted that she couldn't do this without complications. Serious complications. She didn't want to examine why it mattered, why she didn't want to hurt Isabel, because she probably would if they succumbed again to the heat between them.

Something else in her subconscious tried to tell her that maybe she was trying to protect herself from hurt, too, because Isabel was beginning to make her *feel*, and she never, ever *felt*. But she managed to push all of those inner voices aside as she regained her normal breathing. Her hard-on would persist, unfortunately, as long as Isabel kept looking at her that way.

"This shouldn't have happened." Her voice shook and she turned away, grateful for the distraction of having to pack her equipment. "I… I should apologize." She wasn't sorry at all.

"No," Isabel cut in. Her voice was breathy—she was obviously still on fire. "I wanted you to. I *want* you to. *Please*, Kash. Let it happen. Don't hold back."

Kash stood and faced Isabel, but kept her distance. "I won't pretend I don't want it, too, Isabel. That dress…the way you're posing…the way your body feels…I'm so turned on I want to…want to…" *I want to kiss you until I can't breathe. I want to spend the night with you. Do everything with you. Not just fuck you like some anonymous stranger and then leave. But the most I could offer still isn't nearly enough for a woman like you.*

"But it's a bad idea." She took a deep breath. Her clit was still throbbing, and it was hard to maintain eye contact with Isabel and still get through what she had to say. "I mean, we have to work together for the next couple of weeks. I don't want things to be any more awkward and complicated than they already are."

"They won't be," Isabel reassured her. "Kash, I know this is only some fun. I don't expect anything else, if that's what you're worried about."

"Isabel, I appreciate that." Kash resumed packing her gear. "But you're not a casual-sex kind of woman. So it's better this way. It shouldn't have happened the first time."

"What do you mean, I'm not a casual-sex kind of woman?"

"Well, Gillian told me that you…that you…" Kash ran her hands nervously through her hair. "That you date women before you sleep with them. That you weren't at the club to hook up. I know what happened between us wasn't something you ordinarily do."

"Maybe this isn't my normal routine, to go for a…quickie, or one-night stand, or whatever. That's true." She put one leg up on the rung of the stool. "But you do something to me, Kash. I want whatever I can have with you. One more night. One more hour."

Kash's sex twitched. She knew she could make good use of one night with Isabel. *You make it hard to refuse. But I have to, or somebody's going to get hurt. I'm not sure why I know this, but I do.* She shook her head. "I'm sorry, Isabel." *You have no idea how sorry.* "It's better we don't have a repeat of the other day. I think we both know that was a mistake."

Isabel frowned, making no effort to hide her disappointment. *Maybe for you it was a mistake. But you'll never convince me of that, Kash. I'm very glad it happened.*

Gillian knew immediately that her plan to leave Kash and Isabel alone together hadn't produced the desired results. Sparks were flying, that was for sure. The sexual tension was so thick it was like an extra person in the room. But they were both being awfully quiet, and neither was happy. By the time they had finished their appetizers, Gillian had decided they needed a bigger push in the right direction. *Some sexy music, a dance floor, and a couple of drinks to loosen them up would be a good start.*

"So, Kash," she said, "know a good club where we can go show off Isabel's amazing new look?"

Kash pursed her lips. The prospect of going out with the two of them, of watching Isabel on the dance floor in that dress, both thrilled and frustrated her. She couldn't refuse—she'd promised Gillian, after all. And even if it was frustrating, it still sounded better than drinking alone. "Yeah, I have a place in mind."

Chapter Eleven

K ash knew of three lesbian clubs in Rome: two large establishments that weren't much different than the one they'd visited in Paris, and a smaller, more intimate joint where entry was restricted to the chosen few.

Gillian wanted to try one of the bigger places first, but Kash was mobbed almost immediately, so they opted instead for SoHo, a private club whose interior was fashioned in the style of the hip, trendy lofts that its namesake Manhattan neighborhood was known for. Posters of Broadway shows adorned the brick walls, and other New York touches made them all feel as if they had been transported back to the States.

Kash was just as quickly recognized, but celebrity and money were routine here, and so the clientele, for the most part, was more respectful and women kept their distance. As in Paris, the manager of SoHo was quick to offer Kash and her party VIP accommodations—a partially curtained-off sitting area in the back, with an L-shaped couch and minimal lighting.

As the manager led them through the crowd of dancing women, Gillian noticed that Isabel was definitely a hit—women were flirting with her as they passed by almost as much as they were with Kash. And she also noticed that Kash seemed to be much more preoccupied with Isabel than with any of the Italian sirens who were trying to catch her eye. *Oh, yes. This is good. This is very good.*

Gillian waited only until they had placed their drink orders before she grabbed Isabel's hand and pulled her back toward the crowd. "Come on. Time to show off this new you." She made sure to choose a spot on the dance floor where Kash would have an unobstructed view of Isabel's backside.

"You really look phenomenal, Izzy," she said, initiating the same sexy routine with her friend that they had danced in Paris. She barely got the words out of her mouth before two women joined them. The taller of the dark Mediterranean beauties came at them from the side, putting one arm around Isabel's shoulder and the other around Gillian's. The other wrapped her arms around Isabel's waist and pressed against her from behind.

The music had a driving beat, erotic and provocative, and all four women surrendered to it, brushing bodies and letting hands wander over thighs and waists, shoulders and arms. Gillian was thoroughly enjoying the experience but kept one eye also on Kash, who watched from the sidelines, her face hidden in shadow. *Come on, Kash. You know you want her. Don't tell me you're going to sit there and let someone else take her home.*

Kash sipped her vodka and brooded, wishing she had chosen a different pair of trousers that morning. The ones she had on were too tight in the seam when she was this aroused, and too thin as well—she could feel how wet she was every time she moved. The experience wasn't altogether unpleasant, but it disconcerted her because she couldn't satisfy her need for release in the way she most wanted to.

She knew she could likely have any woman here. But it was Isabel she craved, and only Isabel would do.

Watching her dance was torture. Every time Isabel's hips rocked against Gillian's, Kash's own pelvis rose. And when the two locals joined in and started running their hands over all the smooth skin revealed by that little black dress, she could barely control herself. She was not used to having to watch others claim what she wanted.

Isabel had been simmering in a state of semiarousal ever since the photo shoot, and she'd had a couple of glasses of wine with dinner, so her body welcomed the strangers' attentions—the heated, teasing caresses and the press of insistent hips. When Gillian paired off with one of the women, she slipped easily into the arms of the other. But she closed her eyes and imagined Kash's hands were fondling her ass, and Kash's thigh was insinuating itself between her legs.

Warm breath glanced over her cheek, then moist lips pressed against the delicate skin of her jaw, traveling downward. She gave in to the soft moans she imagined came from Kash and threw her head back, allowing her companion access to the exposed flesh of her neck and chest.

The wet kisses increased in intensity as they descended slowly toward her cleavage, and the hands on Isabel's ass roughly pulled her closer. The thigh between her legs rocked relentlessly against her sex, and the friction sent a shudder of excitement through her.

She might have come like that, her mind half convinced that Kash was delivering her from her fevered state, except that the music changed and her dance partner spoke, a whispered plea in Italian that, by the tone of it, begged something entirely sexual.

The spell was broken. She stiffened as she opened her eyes and pulled back from the dark-haired stranger, shocked to find she had come so close to surrendering to someone whose name she didn't even know.

"I'm sorry," she sputtered, embarrassed. She glanced about for Gillian and spotted her near the bar, kissing the other Italian beauty who'd broken up their dance. Then she scouted around for Kash, but the VIP area was empty. *She couldn't have left already. Could she?* "Excuse me," she told the woman, who caught her arm as she began to leave.

"*Non andare. Balliamo un po' di più.*" At Isabel's confused expression, she smiled and added in heavily accented English, "Stay. Dance."

"No, I'm sorry. I can't." *It's Kash I want. Only Kash.*

It took her only a few minutes to determine that Kash wasn't there. And her absence was all it took to throw a cold shower on Isabel's heated hormones.

Gillian had moved to the VIP area with her Italian squeeze by the time Isabel located her.

When she spotted Isabel approaching, she extricated herself from the woman's lap.

"You're going already? Where's Kash?"

"I think she left," Isabel said. "You didn't see her go?"

"No. Sorry." Although Gillian had set out to play matchmaker that evening, she had lost track of what was happening between Isabel and Kash as soon as her fiery-hot dancing companion, Ambra, began describing in delicious detail what she wanted to do to her later.

"I wonder if she went back to the hotel," Isabel said. *Hardly seems she was here long enough to pick up anyone, but I guess it doesn't take much if you do this all the time. An invitation. An acceptance. And if you're Kash, you'd want to do it away from here, after all the near misses with cameras in clubs lately.*

The thought that Kash might be screwing someone else right now depressed the hell out of her. "Well, anyway, I'm going back to the room," she told Gillian. "It's been a long day. Have fun, and if I don't see you in the morning before we go, I'll leave a copy of Kash's shooting itinerary. We're starting at the Roman Forum."

"Okay, Izzy. Sleep well."

Fat chance of that, since I'm apparently doomed to remain preoccupied with a certain sexy and very frustrating photographer.

❖

As Isabel taxied back to the hotel, the romance of Rome on a warm summer evening, with its bridges and monuments lit with an orange glow, infused her with a renewed determination to follow her instincts.

Right now, her gut was telling her to go to Kash, even though at the very least she expected Kash to push her away again.

Quite possibly, Kash might have brought someone from the club back to her suite, and interrupting them didn't appeal to her. But she knew she wouldn't be able to sleep tonight until she tried once more. She detoured by her room only long enough to check her hair and makeup. The reflection that stared back at her was still that of a virtual stranger, though a pleasant shock.

It took her two minutes outside Kash's door to gather the nerve to knock.

It took even longer for Kash to answer. When she did, she held a large glass in her hand, half full of vodka. Still dressed in the clothes she'd left the club in, she seemed surprised to find Isabel before her. "What are you doing here?" The *what are you* came out in a drawled slur, *whutter-yu,* and Kash was so wobbly on her feet she steadied herself against the door frame with her free hand.

"Kash? Are you drunk?"

Kash stared forlornly at her glass. She had had one drink after another, trying to erase the feel of Isabel's body against hers, trying to forget the sight of Isabel in someone else's arms, trying to deny how much she wanted this woman. All unsuccessfully. There wasn't enough vodka in the world for that. "Maybe."

"Are you alone?" Isabel held her breath, waiting for the answer.

Kash met her eyes and nodded. "Are you?"

Isabel stepped forward, took the glass out of her hand, and draped Kash's arm over her shoulder. "Come on, let's get you to bed." She closed the door and set down the vodka so she could put her arm around Kash's waist. It was clear that getting her to the bedroom might be a challenge.

As soon as she hugged Kash close, supporting her weight, Kash sighed and slumped against her. "Izzzabel," she slurred. "I want to kiss you so damn bad."

Isabel started them off toward the bedroom. "Me, too, Kash. Hold that thought until you're sober, and I'll definitely take you up on it."

"Now," Kash protested, then stuck out her lip in an inviting pout.

"Nope. I want you to remember it."

"Aw, c'mon. I will," Kash insisted as Isabel deposited her on the bed. But she was fading fast. Her limbs were limp, and she shut her eyes as soon as her back hit the mattress.

Isabel managed to get her shoes and belt off and covered her with a blanket. As she reached to click off the light beside the bed, Kash stirred and looked up at her with heavy-lidded eyes.

"I wanna dance wit' you next time," she mumbled, then fell asleep.

Isabel kissed her lightly on the lips, the briefest of touches. "I surely hope you do, Kash," she whispered. "With all my heart."

Chapter Twelve

Kash dreamed of Isabel and awakened early, in somewhat the same state as when she went to sleep—with a hard-on that wouldn't quit and a brain fuzzy from vodka. She had a remedy for both. Two aspirin, a long, hot shower, and a pot of coffee would help her head. To work off her sexual frustration, she needed the hotel's exercise room. A call to the concierge ensured the necessary equipment would be there for her.

Punching a heavy bag had been a regular part of her routine for more than a dozen years, a perfect way to remain toned and strong, and also often successful in dispelling anger, frustration, or other negative emotions. She was pleased to find the room unoccupied and a new pair of gloves in her size waiting for her.

The effort to reconstruct what had happened the night before was driving her crazy. Oh, she remembered the club. Every detail of that part of the evening was ingrained in her memory. Isabel dancing in that amazingly revealing black dress, making her remember what it had felt like to touch her. Thinking about that too long, too much, had forced her here. *Wham.* She leveled a series of blows to the bag, exhaling with a grunt with each one.

However, she only vaguely recollected what had happened later, in her suite, and wasn't even entirely certain Isabel had been there. Her hazy memory of Isabel leaning over her as she lay in bed differed little from the dream that had roused her, in which their positions had been reversed and she had been on top of Isabel, fucking her, about to come.

Since she'd awakened with her clothes on, she thought it fairly safe to assume the fucking part was pure fantasy. But in her wasted state she couldn't have placed her shoes so neatly by the bed, so she suspected Isabel had come by sometime during the night. *Wham.* She damn sure wished she could recall anything whatsoever about that part. *Wham.*

"You're the last person I expected to see here this morning."

Isabel's voice startled Kash so much she lost concentration as she was unleashing an uppercut, and the hesitation in her follow-through pulled her off balance. She grabbed for the bag and barely managed to keep from falling.

Behind her, Isabel snickered.

Scrambling to regain her cool, she straightened and turned to respond. But her words caught in her throat. *Oh. Oh, my.* Isabel wore brief jogging shorts and a matching cropped running top, which showed off her toned swimmer's body and emphasized her breasts to perfection. And Isabel's mischievous smile made Kash wish all the more she could remember what had transpired in her suite.

"I shouldn't give you a hard time." Isabel was clearly fighting the urge to laugh, not very successfully. "You're probably feeling poorly this morning. But after all, you did it to yourself."

Kash was breathing heavily from her exertions. *So you were there.* "I guess I should thank you that I woke up in a bed this morning and not on the balcony or floor."

"You're welcome." Isabel got on a treadmill and started it, setting off at a fast walk to warm up. She was ten feet or so from Kash, with a great view of her as she worked the bag. *I could stay on this thing all day with you to look at.*

Kash wore a tight black tank top, gray shorts, and a half-lidded, brooding expression, and the raw power in her stance was incredibly sexy. The muscles in her arms, shoulders, and taut thighs glistened with sweat, and the rapid rise and fall of her chest as she regained her breath made her appear highly aroused.

Isabel was captivated. "I'm glad to see you doing something positive to take care of yourself. I was beginning to think all you did was drink a lot and stay out late."

"Tone down the perky, huh?" Kash grumped good-naturedly. Although she resumed her work on the bag, she had lost the fervor she'd exhibited when she thought she was alone.

"Spoilsport. You're no fun." Isabel increased her pace to an easy jog and fought to keep from staring at Kash. It wasn't easy, because watching the muscles of her shoulders and arms flex and bunch as she hit the bag exhilarated her. Kash met her eyes frequently, but almost always immediately looked away.

Do you still want to kiss me, Kash? And dance with me? And more? Did you leave the club because I was dancing with someone else, like I had to when I saw you with Gillian? Kash's drunken confession and the way she had pressed their bodies together during the shoot after her makeover encouraged her. Oh, yes. Something was definitely simmering between them, and they still had almost two weeks left. Anything could happen.

The roar of a sudden downpour drew their eyes to the large windows that faced the private garden.

Kash paused in her workout and went to study the sky. She'd been trying to come up with a way to put some distance between her and Isabel so she could get her overheated libido under control, and nature had provided her an answer. "Guess we'll have to postpone our shoot until tomorrow. It probably won't let up anytime soon, and every setup I want to do here is outdoors."

Isabel frowned. "That's all right. I can do Vatican City. Most of that is indoors."

"Good." Kash peeled off her gloves. Her heart was still thundering, but it was her proximity to a scantily clad Isabel rather than her work with the bag that caused it. "Guess I'll see you tomorrow morning, then." As she wiped at her face and neck with a towel and prepared to leave, she glanced over at Isabel.

The look of disappointment on Isabel's face was unmistakable, though she did try to mask it with a faint smile.

Guilt made Kash's chest ache. *It's for the best. Just get out of here, and get your mind off her any way you can.*

"Okay, see you then." Isabel slowed from a jog to a walk. "Have a pleasant day, Kash."

"You, too." All the way back to her suite, Kash tried to tell herself she'd forget about Isabel as soon as the trip was over. But her arguments didn't ring true.

Kash worried that nothing could dull this desire for Isabel, because it only seemed to get stronger. With Isabel, she wanted to memorize every detail of every encounter. Somewhere along the line, her voice had become music and her smile a tonic. And the memory of their brief encounter haunted her. Now, when they were in the same room together, she couldn't focus on anything else.

A couple more weeks, that's all. You'll get through it, you'll say good-bye, and things will be normal again. She'll go back to her life and you'll return to yours, none the worse for wear.

Even as she said these clichés to herself, she could sense the lie. Oh, they might never see each other again, but it would be a very long time before her mind let go of Isabel Sterling. And when she got back home she'd have to reevaluate whatever had been "normal" for her before this trip. Her carefree, no-strings lifestyle wasn't cutting it anymore.

Not that it had ever really made her truly happy, but at least for a time it had become a usually pleasant routine, and she'd had no motivation to wish for anything else. Now it was increasingly unsatisfying, and Isabel only added to her discontent with the status quo. She longed for something more; she just didn't know what.

❖

By the time Isabel showered and changed, Gillian still hadn't returned to their suite, so she left her a lengthy note with her plans for the day and set off for the Holy See.

She had long dreamed of seeing the Sistine Chapel, Saint Peter's, and the treasures and art in the massive Vatican Museum complex. But all she could do was think about Kash and regret they weren't spending the day together. *Jesus, I am totally taken with her. How did I let this happen?*

Kash obviously didn't feel the same about her, despite how she'd acted right before she'd passed out. She had quickly accepted the opportunity to postpone their shoot to do her own thing. *I wonder what she's up to today? Catching up with friends? She knows everyone who's anyone. Probably has all sorts of company to choose from, much more exciting than mine.*

One thing was pretty clear. Gillian had spent the night elsewhere. Isabel had hoped to hook up with her for dinner, but a note was waiting for her instead:

Hey, Izzy!

Hope you're having fun! I'm still with Ambra, that incredibly hot woman who interrupted our dance last night. Details when I see you, which may not be until our flight out. Have a great shoot!

So Isabel ate alone at a quaint café around the corner from their hotel. The waiter gave her the best table by the window and flirted with her incessantly, but it was not his company she craved. *Such a damn shame to be in these amazingly romantic places all by myself. How wonderful it would be to spend this trip with someone I'm falling in love with.*

She imagined Kash there, holding her hand across this candlelit table. But that was foolishness talking. *She doesn't do getting-to-know-you, and she's not one for relationships. She told me that in no uncertain terms.* But unrealistic or not, she wanted much more than another sexual encounter with Kash. It might have started as an incredible physical attraction, but she was developing real feelings for her. *Better to at least keep my fantasies within the realm of possibility, Isa. The most I can hope for with her is sex, and even that's certainly not a given.*

She returned to her suite and went to bed early. *Amazing how I hated the thought of these photo shoots when we started out, and now I can't wait for them because it's my chance to spend some time with her.*

❖

Massimo had two strangers with him when Isabel found them waiting in front of the hotel the next morning. And instead of the little Fiat, he drove a small van, the back loaded with large black cases of lighting and photography equipment. Massimo introduced the behemoth of a man sitting next to him as Ecco, a fellow photography student, and the glamorous twentysomething woman in the back as Francesca, Isabel's hair and makeup stylist.

Well, there's definitely going to be more than the two of us today. Pity. They would be outdoors and not alone in a studio again, but Isabel had hoped she'd get the chance to talk to Kash without a lot of other people listening.

Kash joined them a few minutes later, slipping into the seat beside her without meeting her eyes. "Good morning, everyone."

"Hi, Kash." Isabel's spirits lifted from merely being next to her, but Kash remained coolly professional, avoiding sustained eye contact as she explained the plan for the day.

"We're going to stop at a couple of the design salons to pick out a few things from your new wardrobe. The rest of the clothes will be sent to your suite. As you've probably already gathered, today's shoots will be more elaborate than what we've done so far. The 'before-makeover' photos will get used as inserts with the article on you. The shots from here on will be the featured stuff—at least a couple of them will probably go full page. So we'll use different makeup and clothes for each location."

For the first shoot, at the Roman Forum, Kash put her in a sheer, gauzy white dress and sandals, an outfit as timeless as the backdrop. Her pale makeup and structured hairstyle helped her resemble a Michelangelo sculpture.

"So you can see the premise," Kash explained as she positioned Isabel in front of an ancient column. "Statue in the garden. I'd like something evocative of that image. Think serene. Tranquil."

Since Isabel had recently studied statues at the Louvre and in the Vatican, she had a variety of material to draw upon, and she did her best to please Kash, recreating every pose she could recall. And she must have been doing all right, because Kash was taking lots of pictures without giving her much additional direction.

Most of all, she was hoping to break through that businesslike attitude and get a smile or a laugh. Something, *anything*, to acknowledge what they had shared, that Kash was also finding it impossible not to think about their bodies rocking together.

But nothing seemed to crack Kash's polite aloofness. Isabel was frustrated. *It must have been the alcohol talking when she said she wanted to kiss me.*

After the Forum, they moved to Trevi Fountain. Massimo and Ecco set up the equipment while the women adjourned to the ladies' lounge of a nearby café so Isabel could change. From the large garment bag of clothes, Kash selected a chic blue silk suit and a blouse with a scoop neckline.

"We're going for sophisticated urban professional in this one." Kash handed the suit and matching shoes to Isabel. To Francesca, she said, "Daytime makeup, nothing too edgy."

"*Sì*. I understand."

"I'll try to be quick," Isabel said as she removed the clothes from their hangers.

"See you out there, then, whenever you're ready." Kash left without waiting for anything further from Isabel. Having to stare at her all day was torture enough. But being this near her, smelling her perfume and, God forbid, watching her change clothes…the thought was intolerable.

Kash had spent the entire previous day trying to take her mind off Isabel. She wandered the streets of Rome, dressed in jeans and a T-shirt, sunglasses, and a ball cap, to minimize being recognized. She carried a small gear bag and her camera, and for the first time in a long while, she took pictures only for herself.

For the most part, they were pictures of people, captured in their environment in a way that told the story of who they were, often in black and white. The baker taking fresh loaves of filoncino from the oven, the doe-eyed girl on the balcony with her cat, the wizened old man entertaining tourists with an accordion as ancient as he was. The day was relaxing and one of her better ones creatively in weeks. But nothing could push Isabel far from her thoughts.

It was damn disturbing, how she had memorized so much about Isabel—from which moods raised that dimple in her cheek, to the way she could appear shy and provocative at the same time, to the nice definition of musculature in her calves when she danced.

She already noticed too much detail about Isabel, far too much. And today, protected by her camera, she couldn't escape the opportunity—no, the *responsibility*—to capture the essence of Isabel's beauty, admiring her with her lens, showing off her sweet side, her sexy side, her sparkly, effervescent side.

Being close to Isabel this way was killing her. In a good way, but it *was* killing her. And not showing it was the *worst*. Her words rang in her head. *I want whatever I can have with you. One more night. One more hour.*

The possibilities played through her imagination like a slide show of nude photographs. The two of them, doing all sorts of things to each other. *One hour wouldn't be nearly enough. I'm not at all sure one night would be, either, to get you out of my system.*

The object of her musings reappeared wearing the new blue suit, which gave her a more powerful and confident air than anything Kash had seen her in before, while she maintained an aura of sensuality. The color emphasized her eyes, and Kash was drawn there, endless depths to drown in.

Oh, fuck. Get a grip. You have a job to do. She steeled herself and tried to act entirely professional. "Perfect. Hold out your hand."

Isabel's face registered pleased curiosity as she complied.

Kash gave her a few coins. "Of course we have to do the traditional throwing a coin in the fountain. Probably a few times to get a good shot. Then we'll do some other poses." She started to turn away, toward her tripod. Nothing said she had to go into the whole tradition thing, make any explanations. It wasn't necessary and would eat up valuable time. But she did it anyway, because Isabel was the type of woman to like such sentimental things. "Do you know the tradition?"

"Hmm. Well, I know you're supposed to get something great, but exactly what, I'm not sure," Isabel said cheerily. "Good luck? Oh no, wait—I know. A wish granted, I hope?"

Kash knew from Isabel's smoldering expression that any wishes being made here today would involve the two of them getting naked together. *Get your mind back on the job at hand. Do* not *let her see how she is affecting you.* "Not exactly. You get a guaranteed return to Rome." Kash forced herself to respond casually, then walked back to her tripod and lined up her first shot. "You have to stand with your back to the fountain and toss the coin over your shoulder."

"Oh, right," Isabel said. "I did read that in the guidebook. Shame you can't get your wishes granted around here." *Kash is ignoring every single flirtation and innuendo. She's not the least bit interested in more with me. But still I keep trying.*

Logically, she shouldn't let herself get so worked up over Kash, read so much into one quick sexual encounter and a few drunken sentences. *The way I was posing, I was throwing myself at her, for God's sake. But apparently she's not going to bend from her vow not to let anything further happen between us.*

She couldn't help herself. No matter how silly it seemed, she was hurt that Kash wasn't acknowledging the chemistry between them, or what had happened in Kash's suite. *Not only that, but she's actually being kind of...cold. And there's no need for that.* She smiled ruefully. *Cold, hard Kash. I wonder how many women you've heard that from?*

None of Kash's actions deterred her fascination, however. *Why do I still want you like crazy, even though you're beginning to frustrate and irritate the hell out of me?*

"Can we *please* pay attention, Isabel, and *move*? You're not giving me anything to work with here."

Case in point, Isabel thought. *You could be a little nicer.* Okay, so her mind had wandered a bit, but only for a moment. She didn't deserve *that. Is Kash hungover again from another night out?* She didn't seem to be, but something was definitely going on. Her body language was stiff and guarded, and her demeanor icily remote.

"Sorry. Perhaps if you were more precise in telling me what you'd like me to do?" Isabel had tried to be cheerful and cooperative, but there were limits even to her good nature, so she let her answering tone convey her annoyance. "I'm not some urban businesswoman, you know, so I have no idea what you want."

Kash stepped out from behind the camera and frowned. She had immediately regretted her reprimand, even more so when she saw that it had spoiled Isabel's up-to-now buoyant mood. *Brilliant. Can't you deal with not screwing her again without becoming a total asshole?*

But any spoken regret died on her lips as she stepped over to position Isabel. She wasn't one to apologize, anyway, and the only way she knew to be right now was remote. Otherwise, she couldn't endure being this close to Isabel and having to touch her, but not as she most wanted to.

Willing herself to appear more calm and cavalier than she felt, Kash put one hand on Isabel's shoulder, the other on her back, and gently positioned her. "Let's do a few from this angle," she said. "Hands on your hips. Good. You're a self-made woman, with a Fortune 500 company. Think power. Confidence." She briefly touched Isabel's chin, to tilt it up defiantly.

Damn, her skin is so soft. She couldn't resist a quick glance to Isabel's lips, currently adorned with a cinnamon lipstick that complemented the earthy tones in her eye shadow and blusher. *I want to kiss her so damn bad.* So bad she wanted to blurt it out. And for a split second, she almost felt as though she had.

She had this almost weird sense of déjà vu about kissing Isabel, like it had actually happened. Only she had been drinking…

It was so hard to recall exactly what had happened. She barely recalled Isabel walking her to the bedroom. *Did I? Did I blurt out something about wanting to kiss her?*

Her breath caught in her throat. *Or did I actually kiss her? Could I have and completely not remember it?* She didn't think it possible, but she had a big blank space in her memory about that night. A lot of hours unaccounted for. *Oh Christ, if I've already kissed her and totally blotted it out…talk about the ultimate injustice.*

After the Trevi Fountain shoot, they broke for a bite to eat at Taverna del Lupo, a quiet restaurant specializing in Sicilian fish and pasta dishes. The food was fabulous, and Kash was frankly relieved when Massimo and Ecco peppered her with photography questions because she could concentrate on something other than how much Isabel was getting to her. She didn't want to think about all the days they still had to spend together, and how she was going to get through them. But even more, she didn't want to think about saying good-bye to Isabel and resuming her mostly solitary life.

"We have two more locations, yes?" Francesca asked as Kash summoned the waiter for their bill.

"Yes," she confirmed. "We'll do a casual ensemble and makeup for the setup at the Spanish Steps. That's next." Glancing at her watch, she did some rough calculations. "I want to finish that by six thirty or seven at the latest, so we have plenty of time for the final shots at the Colosseum. Sunset is a little before ten."

There she would face the toughest challenge of keeping her mind on the task at hand, because of the dress she had selected for Isabel to wear.

CHAPTER THIRTEEN

Y ou're kidding, right?"
Isabel held up the dress and tried to picture how much of her body it would cover. *Not nearly enough.* It was fire engine red, and floor length, the kind of dress you'd see on a Paris runway or a red carpet in Hollywood. But the wearer would have to take precautions to avoid any embarrassing wardrobe malfunctions.

The low-cut back, she figured, would come to just above her ass. The incredibly high slit up the side would reveal not only her legs, but much more if she wasn't careful. And the front—well, the front was going to be obscene any way you looked at it.

"And these." Kash ignored her protest and handed her a pair of matching stiletto pumps that she knew she would have trouble walking in.

They were high up in the Colosseum and thankfully were being completely ignored by the myriad of tourists who were exploring the lower portions of the giant amphitheatre.

"And where do you expect me to change into this scanty excuse of a dress?" Isabel asked. "I'm not walking all the way back up here in these heels. That's begging for a broken leg."

"Not necessary." Kash checked on Massimo and Ecco, who had arrived with their second load of gear from the van. "I packed a portable screen in one of those cases. The guys will set it up while Francesca does your makeup."

"So I've gone from garden statue, to businesswoman, to well-heeled tourist, to…what? This seems like something a high-priced call girl might wear."

Kash couldn't suppress a smile. "I want you to think *diva*, Isabel. Classy and sophisticated. Confident in your sex appeal and allure. You're on your way to a gala event somewhere, and everyone will be watching you, as they should be."

"Oh, yes. That is *so* me." Isabel wasn't at all keen on how well she could pull off what Kash was asking.

"Trust me, Isabel. We'll make it work. Now we need to get you ready…the light is almost perfect for what I have in mind."

The sky above them was brilliant blue, but to the west, a smattering of high thin clouds was already taking on subtle hints of pink and purple from the lowering sun. A light breeze cooled them, and their protected location high above the city muted the usual blare of traffic.

Francesca gave Isabel dramatic evening makeup, with smoky eyes and deep red lips to match her dress. Her hair's elegant but casual style included a few loose tendrils that gave it a playful appeal.

The dressing screen consisted of a panel covered in thin muslin fabric, barely large enough to conceal her, but Isabel still viewed it as a much better option than hiking all the way down to the floor of the arena to find a better place to change.

Kash finished her camera preparations as Isabel stepped behind the panel and started to undress. Only then did she realize that the men had set up the screen so that the setting sun would be behind it, illuminating Isabel's silhouette on the fabric with vivid clarity. *Oh, my.* She'd been in hundreds of dressing rooms while models undressed, and this should have been tame by comparison.

But it wasn't. When Isabel started to strip, top first, then bra, Kash's heart started to race. She swore she could see the bump of her nipples on the fabric. *Fuck.*

"*Mama mia, che* sexy. *Mi raccomando una notte,*" Ecco said to Massimo from somewhere behind her. While she couldn't translate exactly, his tone and the words she could understand—*sexy* and *one night*—made it entirely too clear what he had said.

"*Neanche per sogno,*" Massimo replied with a chuckle.

That does it.

Kash never felt or exhibited any kind of protective attitude toward someone she was working with. Nudity in the fashion industry was so commonplace it didn't rate a raised eyebrow. But Isabel was no jaded model, and Kash became increasingly angry that the two men had deliberately placed the screen so they could ogle her. She wheeled around and glared at Ecco and Massimo. Her voice was ice. "I won't need you for at least an hour. Make yourselves scarce."

Disappointment registered on both men's faces, and Massimo, at least, also seemed remorseful. "*Mi dispiace*," he muttered, hanging his head before tugging at Ecco to leave.

As they departed, Isabel poked her head out from behind the screen. Undoubtedly, from her silhouette, she was now entirely nude. "Is there a problem?"

"No. No problem," Kash said, her voice betraying only a hint of her discomfort. "Hurry, please. We're losing the light." *And you're making me so fucking horny with your striptease I'm about to start touching myself.*

"Sure, okay." Isabel resumed what she was doing, and Kash, despite herself, enjoyed every bit of the show.

The sky behind the dressing panel was growing more beautiful by the moment as the sun sank lower on the horizon, but once Isabel stepped out from behind the screen, she was all that Kash could see.

The little black dress had been eye-catching, no doubt about that. But seeing Isabel in the sexy red number took Kash's breath away. Dumbstruck, unmoving, she could do nothing but immerse herself fully in the vision before her.

The dress conformed to every curve and swell of Isabel's body as though it had been cut and sewn for her alone. She spun around in a slow pirouette, giving Kash the full effect. The scoop back allowed an unimpeded view of the ivory skin of her back, flawless in its beauty. The long slit up the right side displayed the length of her leg to her upper thigh, the tall stiletto heels accentuating the firm musculature built by swimming.

But the full frontal view left Kash unsteady on her feet and made her heart flutter.

It wasn't merely revealing. This dress would have live TV censors sweating, their hands twitching on the time-delay switch.

The V cut into the front of the dress extended nearly to Isabel's navel and was open enough at her cleavage to expose a good portion of her breasts. Her nipples were barely covered and seemed ready to appear with the slightest provocation. Her hair and makeup added to the overall effect of sexy allure personified.

Lord have mercy. Kash knew she shouldn't be staring like she was, but she was completely captivated and also marginally aware that as she gawked unabashedly at Isabel, time was passing, and with it, the perfect light she had been waiting all day for.

She might have stood there gaping until dark had not Francesca brought her back to reality with a tentative hand on her shoulder.

"Kash? Is everything all right? This is not what you wanted?"

"Uh…no! I mean…yes. Yes, it's good. Fine." *Perfect. Too damn perfect. How is a girl supposed to get any work done with that kind of distraction?* Only then did she completely realize how quickly the light was fading.

"Where do you want me?" Isabel asked, the smile on her face clear evidence that she knew precisely how Kash would like to answer that question.

Under me. That's where I want you. I want to be on top of you so bad it's taking every ounce of my willpower to keep from touching you right now. But if I do, I won't be able to stop. All the air seemed to have been squeezed from her lungs, and she feared her legs would give way. But she reached automatically for her tripod, determined to see this shoot through. Then she could push Isabel from her mind, go back to the hotel, and do something about the hard-on that was about to drive her mad.

"Over here is good." She gestured, keeping her distance. To be anywhere near Isabel in that dress was inviting disaster. "So…like I said…I want you to think *diva.*" She cleared her throat, wondering why her voice sounded like she'd just rolled out of bed. "Confidence. Mystery. Sex appeal." *Though you certainly don't need any help with that last one. Any more sex appeal and I might need oxygen.* She escaped then behind her viewfinder, grateful for a brief respite from her responsibility to maintain a cool exterior. *Click.*

Isabel had been so self-conscious getting into the dress, she wasn't sure she could bear to be photographed in it for all the world to see. Its cut and clingy fabric dictated that she couldn't wear anything underneath, so she felt constantly at risk of exposing herself. But as soon as she stepped out from behind the screen and saw Kash's reaction, her misgivings evaporated.

That carefully controlled exterior, that damned frustrating air of aloofness that she had been trying to break through all day, shattered right in front of her. She watched Kash's eyes widen and faintly heard her sudden intake of breath as her gaze trailed up and down the length of her body, lingering on her half-naked breasts. For a couple of minutes, Kash's expression was unguarded and her desire evident.

Kash's appreciative attention swept over Isabel like a warm caress, and her bruised ego and sagging spirits lifted. *There's no mistaking that look. Now I just have to find a way to break through whatever the hell is keeping her from letting something more happen between us. And perhaps this dress is exactly the ammunition I need.*

She hadn't felt particularly sexy or confident, not until she saw Kash's reaction. That gave her the courage to pull off the diva attitude. Mindful not to reveal too much, she emulated some of the sassier, sexier poses the models had used during her first visit to Kash's Manhattan studio.

Kash kept quiet, except for the occasional minor directive, like, "Tilt your chin down," or "Turn a bit more toward me." She was taking pictures nearly nonstop, so Isabel figured she was doing all right. But that frustrating veneer of reserve was quickly and firmly back in place again, and apparently unshakable, regardless of how seductive her poses might be. *I saw it in your eyes. What do I have to do to get you to admit you want me as much as I want you?*

Right before the sun hit the horizon, Massimo and Ecco rejoined them. Kash paused to glare at them with reproach, but no words were exchanged, and Isabel wondered what had precipitated the chilly atmosphere.

"That's all we can do, the light is gone." Kash stretched, suddenly feeling the tension that had been simmering all day right between her shoulder blades. "I suggest you change into something casual," she told Isabel. "You shouldn't be walking down in those heels, anyway, and I'd save that designer number for a special occasion." The advice was really for her own benefit. She couldn't fathom sitting next to Isabel in that dress all the way back to the hotel.

"Well, I *am* a little worried I'm about to expose myself," Isabel said. As darkness began to descend in earnest she went to find her casual clothes. The spotlights that illuminated the Colosseum came on and allowed them light enough to see, but shadows were growing all around them.

"You can start carrying the equipment down," Kash told Massimo and Ecco. "And Francesca, if you would, go with them on this first trip and wait with the van while they come back for the rest."

The men packed the gear for the first load in only a couple of minutes. While they worked, Kash walked a short distance away and sat by herself on a low wall. Her body was strung so tight she was shaking and needed time to gather herself. *What the hell is happening to me?*

Isabel's sexy poses had short-circuited her brain and electrified her body. *Why should I refuse more of what we both want?* She rarely allowed herself to care about ethics or the repercussions of her actions on someone else's feelings. And she didn't want to speculate on why it seemed to matter now, with Isabel. She only wanted to talk herself out of her reservations. *She's an adult. She can make her own decisions, and she was clearly all right with what happened before. I shouldn't worry about whether she'll regret this later or whether this might hurt her.*

Kash wanted desperately to convince herself to give in to Isabel's seductions, because she was beginning to believe she might not be able to get her out of her mind and body any other way than to have her again.

All the while she had been taking pictures, she had been getting more and more aroused, imagining her mouth on those breasts…her hand, slipping into that slit in the skirt to find Isabel's sex, swollen and wet and ready.

Her own clit had been worked up but good by those fantasies and was coiled tight. She knew it would take very little, once she got back to the hotel, to get herself off. But the wait to get there was excruciating.

Kash heard a sound behind her and swiveled around to find Isabel, still in that damned dress. Her chest felt suddenly as if it was being squeezed; she could barely breathe. *Dear God, you're lovely.* The men had just left, and it was a good hike to the van and back. They'd be alone for several more minutes.

As Isabel slowly walked over and faced Kash, she smiled that damned irresistible smile, ripe with that same hungry yearning that had obliterated her resistance back in her suite. She feared she could be no better now at refusing that plea. But she had to try. She got to her feet.

"Isabel…" Her voice was shaking as badly as her hands. This close—only an arm's distance away—her need to touch Isabel again flared fiery hot inside of her, a blinding heat that threatened to consume her. Every nerve ending in her body sang out. "I don't think this is a good—"

Isabel took her hand and pulled it to her lips, kissing Kash sweetly on her palm, then placed it in the valley of cleavage between her breasts and held it there. "Can you feel how my heart is pounding, Kash? How much I want you? So much it *hurts*."

Her words, the dress, those lips, and the sensation under her palm—for she could indeed feel the rapid hammering of Isabel's heart—crumbled her final resolve. She couldn't live with the regret of never having tasted Isabel's lips.

Kash wrapped her free hand around Isabel's waist as she closed the distance to kiss her. The thundering in her ears matched the rapid pulse beneath her palm, and when their bodies came together both she and Isabel let out a breathy gasp.

Time slowed as she found Isabel's mouth with her own. That first brush of lips was so light it was barely discernable, but a flash of heat from the contact shot through her, heightening her senses. Isabel's musky perfume was intoxicating. The soft skin of her back begged to be touched. Isabel's rapid breathing mirrored her own.

On the next light brush of their lips, Isabel moaned and tried to extend the contact, but Kash pulled back just out of reach. To answer Isabel's sigh of disappointment, on the next pass she licked Isabel's lips with the tip of her tongue, a teasing, light caress.

"God, Kash. You make me feel so *much*." Isabel's voice shook.

Kash responded with deeper, more prolonged contact, using more of her tongue to wetly explore Isabel's soft and yielding lips. Isabel's arms snaked around her neck, then her fingertips glanced along the back of her head, raking lightly along her scalp.

When Isabel moaned again, a deep sustained sound, and parted her lips, Kash pushed her tongue past them and found Isabel's eager, answering tongue. The kiss deepened, and her heart began to beat so hard and fast in her chest she felt light-headed. Her knees began to buckle again and she pulled Isabel even closer to steady herself.

The sounds of their rapid breathing and Isabel's moans filled her ears, and she trailed her fingertips down Isabel's spine and slowly past the loose barrier of her dress to roughly massage her ass.

When she did, Isabel sucked hard on her tongue, and she felt the pressure as an urgent pulse of sensation between her legs. An unbearably exciting mix of pleasure and pain.

Her right thigh rocked lightly against Isabel's center as she scraped her nails more firmly over Isabel's ass. Their kiss abruptly ended when

Isabel claimed the sensitive skin of Kash's neck with wet strokes and soft bites.

The throbbing in her clit intensified, and she threw back her head and closed her eyes, losing herself in the feel of Isabel's mouth on her. *Fuck, yes. Right there.*

Her thigh suddenly slipped between Isabel's legs, and Kash looked hazily down to discover that Isabel had hiked up her dress. That long slit in the skirt proved invaluable, providing her thigh the opportunity for direct contact with Isabel's sex.

She pressed harder, firmer, into the warmth between Isabel's legs, and felt the wetness of her arousal through the thin material of her trousers. She rocked her hips forward, slowly, purposefully, and glancing down, glimpsed the faint triangle of hair beneath the dress.

The hitch in Isabel's breathing hinted that in another minute or two, she would surely come.

Kash was so far gone, so lost in Isabel, that she failed to hear the men approach until they were almost on top of them. "Isabel...I..." Straightening, she reluctantly released her hold on Isabel's ass.

Isabel barely heard Massimo and Ecco's approach. The only sensation that mattered was the building pressure, an urgent, insatiable need for release greater than any she had known and more powerful by far than she had expected. She wanted Kash with a ferocity that scared her, made her feel wonderfully but dangerously out of control.

When Kash pulled away from her, all she felt was the stab of loss, the ache of separation. She had been swept away completely in Kash's arms, and the sudden return to reality made her reel. Not at all certain she could walk, she steadied herself against the low wall Kash had been sitting on.

"Isabel, we need to go." Kash forced herself to put a few feet of distance between them. This was not the time or place. Her clit was calling the shots, which was never a good idea, and they had company. She'd learned to somewhat accept having her own misdeeds splashed across the tabloids, but she would forever regret it if a picture of a compromised Isabel got into one of the rags because she couldn't control herself.

Massimo and Ecco started packing the rest of the gear without overtly paying them any attention. The two women were in the shadow of the wall, but Kash knew the men could see them clearly because of the ambient light from the Colosseum lights and the full moon. "Do you want to change?" Kash asked. She tried not to stare at Isabel's cleavage, or lips, or into her eyes. If she did, she would surely take her right here and now, consequences be damned. Her body was on fire from their kisses and stroking, and she could still feel Isabel's wetness on her thigh.

"You know what I want," Isabel answered in a breathy whisper the men couldn't overhear.

"We can't." Kash tried to still the beating of her heart. "Do you want to change or not?"

Isabel sighed, accepting that Kash would not relent. At least for now. "Probably would be much easier walking out of here in the clothes I came in with." She started unsteadily toward the dressing screen, but paused long enough to grip Kash's shoulder as she passed. "You'd better finish what you started."

Imagining the possibilities, Kash felt another sharp stab of arousal.

Chapter Fourteen

A battle raged inside Kash as they returned to the van, though she gave no outward sign of it. The strongest voice commanded she treat Isabel the way she treated most women in her life. *Fuck her good, get her out of your system once and for all, and move on.* The caged frustration of their interrupted encounter, the memory of their previous coupling, and a growing need to resume her predictable way of life fueled that voice.

Then Isabel's words rang in her ears. *I want whatever I can have with you.*

But Isabel was so sweet and real and honest that she deserved better.

So maybe give her more than the usual twenty minutes or half hour. A nice dinner out first, and a full evening back at the suite. Some candles, champagne to fulfill any responsibility you may think you have. Then you can have what you want and not guilt yourself out about it anymore, and finally get her out of your mind.

There was scant conversation in the van as they rode up the Via del Corso toward the hotel. Isabel sat next to her, and Kash could feel her staring, but she avoided prolonged eye contact by looking out the window. She was still like a lit fuse, and she knew if she allowed herself to focus on the desire and arousal in Isabel's eyes, she wouldn't be able to stop from taking her at the first opportunity.

After they stopped to let Francesca off, Isabel and Kash were alone in the back. Isabel stroked Kash's arm gently.

Her sense of touch always became acutely heightened when she was aroused, and she couldn't remember it being more so. The sensation along her arm reverberated throughout her body and jerked her right back to the edge of dangerously losing control.

"Drop us here," she said abruptly to Massimo, and he braked near the massive Piazza del Popolo, a short walk from their hotel. The square was busy with people: locals enjoying the warm summer evening and tourists admiring the Egyptian obelisk of Rameses II, the fountains at the center, and the historic churches at its edge.

After the men had departed, Kash faced Isabel, whose expression was expectant. *Oh, Isabel. You reach right inside of me and stir up something.* "Let's get some dinner, all right?" She was surprised at how normal she sounded. "I know a quiet place near here."

"Sure," Isabel replied with delight, taking Kash's arm. "I'm all yours. Lead on."

The completely alien and disturbingly delightful feel of Isabel's hand gently resting in the crook of her elbow startled Kash. The gesture was far too intimate for her to initiate or even tolerate under normal circumstances, and she stiffened, but Isabel failed to notice.

"Gosh, it's such a beautiful night. The full moon, the warm Mediterranean breeze," Isabel said as they strolled along. "Really couldn't ask for anything more perfect."

Kash said nothing, let none of the continuing turmoil inside of her show. *Perfect for you, maybe. But me? This isn't me. I don't do romantic. At least I haven't before. Why do you make me want to* do *things,* feel *things,* be *things that are so contrary to all that is recognizable?* Isabel caressed her arm again, and Kash wondered how such a small and simple gesture could feel so wonderful and terrifying at the same time. Although her every instinct told her to pull away, she decided to let it be, at least for now.

"It's still early, and it's so nice to walk with you like this," Isabel said. "I'm not really that hungry yet. Maybe we can soak in some of the sights before we stop?"

"If you like." Kash made it sound as though it mattered not in the least, like she did this all the time. In reality, though, every day she spent with Isabel made her feel more unsettled. This caring, sensitive woman was weaving a spell over her, and the incredible allure of Rome at night was playing right along. She was powerless to resist such a powerful combination.

"I've dreamed so long about seeing Rome and Paris," Isabel was saying, but it was difficult to concentrate on the words because, in addition to the hand on her arm, a warm body pressed up against her side as they ambled along. "It's much better to share some of this with you than be alone."

Well, this was obviously an incredibly stupid idea. This diversion to dinner was supposed to make Isabel stop thinking there's anything more to this attraction than a quick fuck. Now she's getting all mushy and romantic. What was I thinking? I can't deal with this.

She was angry at herself for her error in judgment, for letting Isabel cloud her reliable ease of detachment. *I can't even bring myself to take my arm away, for Christ's sake.*

But she had to do something. She didn't want to hurt Isabel, but Isabel was reading far too much into this little walk. And her own enjoyment of this silly sentimentalism was entirely too disconcerting.

They were walking along the Tiber River, when Kash halted abruptly beside a bench and pushed Isabel down onto it. She had to free herself from Isabel's wretchedly magnificent embrace so she could think. Isabel seemed briefly surprised at the unexpected interruption of their moonlit walk, but apparently content to let Kash set the course for their evening.

"Listen, Isabel," Kash began, as she started to pace in front of the bench, with Isabel her rapt audience. "This sharing Rome thing…I told you, I don't do sharing. I don't do romance, or dates, or whatever you're turning this into in your mind. I thought I made that clear, but apparently you haven't gotten the message." She knew she sounded a little angry, and she was, but only at herself and her inability to cope with the chaos of emotions Isabel had churned up.

"I…I didn't mean to…I wasn't…" Isabel's face darkened in confusion.

That reaction only compounded Kash's determination to return to her comfortable routine, to push Isabel into the safe category of screw-them-then-forget-them that she had managed to put almost every other woman in her life into. It was already far too late for that, but she was desperate to find a way to get Isabel out of her system.

"Whatever you thought, or meant, or wanted," Kash continued, still pacing, "for me, it's all about sex, always, and *only* about sex, or it's about nothing at all. I want to make that clear. The choice is yours, but you can have no expectations beyond that, Isabel."

There was a lengthy silence before Isabel responded.

"I'm sorry if I did or said something to make you think I have any notion about anything beyond this evening." Isabel's voice was soft, apologetic, but Kash couldn't mistake the tone of hurt. "I enjoy spending time with you, and I let myself get a little carried away. I did mean what I said earlier, Kash. I won't ask for more than you're willing to give. I guess I thought that because you invited me to dinner, we were going to kind of make a date of it."

"Well, you were wrong. That's not me."

"So now I know. It's crystal clear. It was *you* who suggested dinner, Kash, not me, so I don't know why you're getting all bent out of shape." Isabel glared at her. "All I want is sex. Is that what you need to hear? Are those the magic words for you?" she said with an almost childish petulance.

"I don't screw someone merely because they want to. If I did, I'd never get any work done. Or sleep, for that matter." Kash knew she sounded arrogant, but she was angry, and frustrated, and damn it if Isabel wasn't completely irresistible when she was petulant in the moonlight.

"I didn't imply that you did," Isabel shot back. "If you'd slept with all the women who were throwing themselves at you in Paris, you'd still be there."

"Jealous?" Kash asked testily. *Why am I asking her that? Since when did I care if she's jealous or not?*

"Get over yourself," Isabel replied, equally exasperated. *How did this wonderful evening spin so out of control?* She jumped to her feet. "Yes, you're a beautiful woman, Kash, and you obviously know it. But you can also be a real pain in the ass. I said all I wanted was sex, but I'm not going to beg for it." She stormed away.

Isabel's abrupt departure deflated Kash's anger, but did nothing to stem the current of arousal that had been simmering since their heated kisses in the Colosseum. *Well, that certainly went well, idiot.* She sat on the bench for a full thirty seconds, watching Isabel's rapidly retreating figure and debating with herself about whether to follow. *Leave it. Let her go. It's better this way,* said the voice that always counseled distance and self-preservation. These methods had always helped her escape any situation that threatened loss of control.

But that voice couldn't compete against her body's desire and that persistent, although extremely annoying, sudden conscience she had grown that hated to see Isabel hurt.

She caught up to Isabel as she was threading her way through a throng of people on the nearest bridge, the Ponte Cavour, a picturesque span across the Tiber illuminated by a string of amber lights.

"Isabel, wait!" Kash grabbed her arm and tried to get her to stop, but Isabel shook her off and kept walking. "Come on. God damn it!" She had to take long strides to match Isabel's rapid acceleration.

They were off the bridge and headed toward the hotel when Isabel stopped and spun around, her eyes glinting fire. She was breathing heavily from her retreat, and so was Kash, from trying to catch her. "What the hell do you want from me?"

People were pushing past and around them. Kash spotted a narrow alley ahead, dimly lit and unpopulated, so she grabbed Isabel's arm and propelled her roughly toward it.

There they faced each other down like two boxers halfway through a bout, guard firmly in place, adrenaline pumping. Waiting to see who would get in the next punch.

"I want…" Kash began, but the words died when she gazed into Isabel's eyes. She had mistaken the fire she saw there for anger, but she could see now it wasn't fury at all, but a combination of frustration and desire. It snapped the last fragile restraint holding her back.

As she pushed Isabel up against the ancient brickwork that formed the walls of the narrow passageway, her mind went hazy.

Isabel gave a startled cry, but didn't object or resist when Kash grabbed both of her wrists and pinned them firmly to the wall above her head with one hand while she roughly cupped Isabel's sex with the other.

"You know what I want," Kash said, her voice low and husky as she pressed their bodies together. Her mouth descended on Isabel's neck.

Isabel's irate exasperation faded and her pulse quickened under the abrupt change in Kash. *Here? Now?*

Her first experience with Kash had been jarring enough. *But this?* Isabel had never been the adventurous type sexually. Sex for her took place in a bed, involved a half dozen positions at most, and rarely lasted an hour. It was gentle, mostly predictable, and always an act between two people in private.

Her naïveté in this regard certainly never prepared her for how immensely a rough and restrained quickie in a public alleyway in Rome where anyone might happen upon them could excite her.

Kash's warm breath on her neck and the hot, wet caresses of her tongue sent Isabel's heartbeat into overdrive, but the press of Kash's hand between her legs threatened to buckle her knees. Regardless of whether anyone might see them, she wished desperately they didn't have any constrictions of clothing between them.

Assaulted by a cavalcade of sensations—the rough brick against her hands, the blare of car horns in the near distance, the musky scent of Kash's perfume, the furious drumming of her heart against the walls of her chest—she felt more completely and fully *alive* than she could ever remember.

When Kash spread her legs apart with a firmly insistent thigh and began to fumble for the clasp of her jeans, Isabel gasped in anticipation, her body poised and eager for the deliverance of Kash's hand.

Nothing about this situation seemed familiar; she ached to return the almost frantic bites and nips that were sending her higher and higher, wanted to pull Kash even tighter to her, though that seemed impossible given the current crush of their bodies, and the fact that she could do neither was driving her mad. Suspended in a delirium of need, she surrendered fully to Kash's control.

"Kash...please..." It was hard to speak, hard to breathe, hard to reason. A sound escaped her, a whimper of desperation. "*Please.*"

Entirely focused on the throbbing urgency for release, Isabel didn't hear or feel the tug at her shirt, nor did she immediately register the soothing rush of air against the heated flesh of her chest and stomach. But Kash's hungry mouth on her breast and the tug of teeth on her oversensitized nipple brought her to full awareness that she was exposed to the night.

The loud bang of a window being thrown open, very close by, warned her that someone might be watching, and she was shocked to discover that the possibility only heightened her arousal.

"Take me. Now. *Please.* Fuck me." She pled loud enough to be overheard, which surprised her as well. Kash had unleashed a part of her she hadn't known existed, a wanton and unfettered Isabel—*no, Isa*—that felt, that wanted, that *craved* much more powerfully than the old one ever dared.

Kash's answer, from deep in the back of her throat, sounded more animal than human.

"*Please!*" Isabel cried, afraid she would burst apart in the waiting. "*Please!*"

Kash's hand, when it finally found her, was every bit as gentle at that first touch of discovery as her mouth was rough on Isabel's breast, and the contrast startled her. Cool fingertips skimmed slowly down along her stomach, raising goose bumps, then slipped beneath the silk of her panties and paused there briefly, as if to drive her to the very brink of herself.

She rocked her hips forward and noisily exhaled the breath she had been holding when Kash's hand descended into the swollen and ready folds of her sex.

"So wet for me," Kash whispered breathily in awe, and Isabel could feel her own fluid as Kash's hand spread the evidence of her immense arousal over her clit in maddeningly light passes. "Just like the last time. You get so wet for me, it makes me crazy."

"Jesus!" she panted. "*More,* Kash. *More!*" She bucked her hips and strained against the restraint on her wrists, but Kash only pinned her down harder, until the rough brick began to scrape the back of her hands. And still, where she wanted it most, the touch was unbearably light and indirect.

Her pleas became nonverbal—groans and sighs and thrusts of her pelvis—until all at once Kash impaled her, slipping into her wetness and filling her completely, almost lifting her off her feet. At the same moment, Kash's thumb centered on her clit and held there, the strokes short and swift and torturously firm. She exploded, then, in the sudden rush of sensations from within and without, her orgasm so strong and powerful her body pulsed with it.

She collapsed against Kash, struggling to catch her breath, her rapid heartbeat drumming in her ears and her clit throbbing. Her wrists were suddenly her own again, and she wrapped her arms around Kash's neck, grateful for the support, her legs trembling, her body boneless.

Slowly she regained herself and realized that the body she was clinging to was only stiffly tolerating her embrace. Kash's eyes revealed nothing. As before, once the deed was done, Kash became cold and distant, as though unaffected by what had just happened.

"You...uh...you'd better..." As Kash extricated herself from

Isabel's arms, she indicated, with a tilt of her head, her open blouse, before turning back toward where they had come from.

Glancing down, Isabel saw her exposed breasts, nipples still rosy and prominent. Her pants were open, too, her panties pushed down far enough to allow a glimpse of honey blond hair.

By the time she had redressed, Kash had already taken two steps toward the main thoroughfare.

What did you expect? she asked herself as she followed Kash back into the horde of people. Whatever she had expected, it was certainly not this. Even more than the first time with Kash, this experience had left her feeling completely content yet profoundly unsatisfied.

During the short walk back to the hotel, Isabel prayed that Kash would invite her to her suite. Despite what Kash had told her about herself, she ached to make Kash feel what she had felt. But with each passing step, she grew more convinced that their encounter in the alley was their last. Kash was more distant now than ever—not speaking, not paying much attention to her at all.

You got exactly what you asked for, she told herself. *The way she made you feel, you have nothing to complain about.* But instead of feeling sated, she realized all the more that she had needs long hidden and still unfulfilled that she never even knew existed.

Chapter Fifteen

Though Kash masturbated vigorously, then drank a considerable amount of vodka, she still craved Isabel and was guilty about how things had transpired. Both developments unsettled her. She had never felt guilty in her dealings with women and never fucked someone but still been attracted to them.

And most alarming of all—she had begun to want Isabel to touch *her*.

She could still feel Isabel's hand on her arm and hear her sweet, wistful tone. And damn it, with Isabel walking beside her, if she hadn't begun to experience Rome's romanticism.

That's why they had ended up quick and dirty in an alley, and not back at her suite.

Isabel had made her wish for things she believed herself incapable of, imagine possibilities she knew could never be. She felt pulled in a direction totally against her nature.

And the more sweet and romantic Isabel had become, the worse Kash's frustration had grown, until finally she had reacted in the only way she knew. She couldn't listen to Isabel anymore, because she was letting herself get carried away. And so she had *taken* her, yet again, in the way that she always *took* women, to demonstrate to herself that nothing had really changed and to prove to Isabel that no woman had a right to shake up her world and everything in it.

A part of her knew, even as she fucked Isabel again, that any and every experience with Isabel was different, but she couldn't stop herself. She was desperate to set her world back on its axis, and Isabel's excitement had swept her away.

In retrospect, however, she was sorry for the way she had acted. Isabel deserved more and better. *I should have made it nice for her, like I planned. Tender. Private. She deserved that.* Kash felt ashamed she could not control herself, but Isabel made her *feel,* and feel too much.

She knew Isabel would regret what had happened. So she drank, and paced, and drank some more, and wondered how in the world she could manage another two weeks with Isabel without going mad. It was two in the morning when she settled onto her balcony with the last of the vodka, hoping that she could sleep or find something to distract her from thinking about touching Isabel.

Though the hotel's famed swimming pool was dark and long closed to guests, pool lights made it a tranquil oasis of blue, so she noticed immediately that a lone swimmer had slipped past the gate and was doing laps.

It was Isabel. *Oh, fuck. Some days, you shouldn't get out of bed.*

❖

Lap upon lap upon lap, and still she couldn't get Kash out of her mind. Once they returned to the hotel, Isabel had tried to sleep, but the memory of how Kash had made her feel was still too fresh. No matter how much she wanted to put the experience in its proper place—*a one-night stand, that's all. I knew that going in*—her heart and mind and body wanted more.

She scarcely recognized herself. *Talk about makeover. What an understatement.* She was changing far more than her hair, makeup, and wardrobe. She would never have believed she would even *wish* for a solitary sexual interlude with someone, let alone remember two quick and casual assignations—one of them in public, no less—with such relish and longing.

How is it possible at nearly thirty to discover facets of myself that I never knew existed? This sudden voracious appetite for the kind of passion that Kash had unleashed in her felt almost primal.

Where did all this come from? How have I gone so long thinking I was one way, believing I was comfortable in my own skin, only to find I've been—what? Deluding myself? That's what it felt like. She'd thought she was relatively happy with her life and the way she lived it, had never noticed that her sexual activity with women was both scarce and too predictable.

I've always viewed sex outside of a relationship as completely undesirable and thought that those who participate in it should be chastised and criticized. I believed that if I got to know someone before I slept with them I would somehow be more mature or noble. She wondered why she thought this way. Her parents and rather conservative upbringing probably had a lot to do with it, as did the fact that none of her lovers had really challenged or encouraged her to be any other way.

And when women I might be interested in looked past me to someone prettier, that philosophy made being rejected a lot easier. How many times had she tried to console herself when that happened by telling herself, *Well, she's not the type of woman I'd want, anyway, if she's ready to jump into bed with someone based entirely on their appearance.*

Rather hypocritical of me, considering how totally I've embraced Isa and am doing everything I can to use the right makeup and clothes to get Kash's attention.

Oh, she could see the potential problems of adopting a *totally* no-strings-attached, casual-sex-only lifestyle. Avoiding emotional attachments entirely, as Kash apparently did, held no appeal for her. She still needed to connect in some way with someone she was interested in. But she'd been wrong not to let sex be a spontaneous bit of fun and not to allow herself to know how exciting it could be, and how liberating, to put on a provocative dress and allow it to work some magic. *Naughty can be awfully nice, that's for sure.*

Even as she wondered why no other woman had ever brought out this passionate side of her, she wondered what she would do with this new, sexually charged persona once she and Kash resumed their normal lives. She knew it was not so much a matter of the where, and when, and how that had given birth to Isa as the *who* involved. *You're going to have to let her go. How will you cope when it happens? Will Isa fade back into the woodwork, never to be seen again? Can she?*

She didn't want to relinquish this new sexy side, but she knew that physical excitement alone couldn't bring her happiness. *Kash is proof of that. She has all the sex she wants, it appears, but has that made her happy?*

The fact that Kash had triggered these changes puzzled her as much as the existence of this hidden side of her. *Why her?* Kash certainly wasn't the type of woman she was usually drawn to. In fact, the polar opposite. She could be rude, and abrupt, and way too full of herself. A woman who obviously ran from relationships—*hell, not only relationships, but from a polite evening out together as a precursor to sex. Just slam, bam, thank you, ma'am, and here I am thinking she's something special?*

Kash had said hardly two words to her on the way back to the hotel. And once there, she had muttered only a polite good night as they got on the elevator, to make sure Isabel knew their evening was over.

Damn infuriating woman. Isabel swam another lap, automatically shifting from breaststroke to backstroke. *One minute we're walking arm in arm along the Tiber, heading to a nice dinner, and the next she's being a jerk.*

But she couldn't stay angry with her. Not with the memory of how Kash had turned her on and made her feel so fresh in body and mind. *Amazing. Like I suddenly walked out of a black-and-white photo into blazing Technicolor.* And though the issue of sex was now center stage with Kash, she knew a lot more was going on between them, at least for her. She'd begun to develop feelings for Kash, real feelings, though apparently she had nowhere to go with them. She certainly didn't dare admit them to Kash.

No, if I'm to have any chance of spending any more quality time with her, I have to keep things light and casual.

Countless laps had failed to calm the singing in her blood, so she emerged from the pool and padded over to the sunken hot tub, slipping into the shadowed recesses of the heated water with a groan. She floated, head back against the polished stone side, but she couldn't relax. The memory of Kash's hand was still too vivid. Glancing around and listening intently, she assured herself no one else was about.

Her body was too stirred up and the pulsating jets of the hot tub were too inviting. She faced the nearest one and braced her hands on the rim of the tub. Spreading her legs, she arched her back and leaned forward so the force of the water was directed at her clit. *Ahhhh.*

❖

*Oh, Christ. She's not...*Kash strained through blurry eyes to see the figure in the shadowy depths of the hot tub. Certain enough of what she was seeing to risk walking on wobbly legs, she stumbled into the suite to finally relinquish her death grip on her glass of vodka and retrieve her camera and longest telephoto lens.

The lens brought Isabel into vivid clarity as she stripped off her suit. *Damn, that's hot.* Her hands were shaking so from the alcohol and her rapidly beating heart that the body she was watching slipped out of view briefly as Isabel threw her head back in ecstasy. Kash cursed under her breath to miss even a millisecond of the show.

Straining to regain the image in her viewfinder, she saw the naked expanse of Isabel's chest reappear, breasts uplifted, as she positioned her body to maximize the effect of the jets. Kash couldn't risk a flash and so was grateful for enough ambient light from the pool for her camera to capture the image. *Click. Click.*

Isabel's mouth was open, and her body was rocking hard now against the sides of the tub. *Click. Click.* Kash ached to hear the sounds she was making as she approached orgasm. *Fuck, yes.* What she would have given for a bit more light. *Click.*

With her left hand still gripping her long lens, she lost interest in taking pictures with her right. Her fingertips were still a bit cool from the ice when she slipped them into her trousers, but her fuzzy brain allowed the shock more readily than if she'd been sober.

Take your time, Isabel, she urged silently, as she stroked herself. *Take your time.*

❖

When they all converged on the airport the next day for their flight to Cairo, Kash wanted to indulge her fascination with Isabel and *watch* her unabashedly, but she couldn't bring herself to. She felt guilty about how she'd surreptitiously watched her in the tub and used the experience to get herself off. She missed the detachment her camera afforded her.

In addition, Isabel wasn't acting as though she regretted what had happened, as she had expected. No, Isabel was her usual perky, happy self. All smiles, greeting Kash with genuine warmth and discreetly not referencing their liaison or expressing any expectations. *Classy.* Yet her direct eye contact and warm tone made it clear that she had very much enjoyed what had transpired in the alley.

Kash's heart fluttered, but she kept her expression neutral and tried not to think about the invitation in those deep blue eyes and of all the things she'd imagined doing with Isabel while she watched her climax in the hot tub. Isabel was making her want things out of her reach, like romance, and love, and trust, and really connecting with someone.

Their flight didn't board for forty minutes, so relatively few people had gathered at the gate. She sat across and down a bit from Isabel, near enough to be polite and get a good view of her, but far enough away not to have to make conversation. They were near a large window and sunlight was streaming in, so she put on her sunglasses, grateful for the opportunity to conceal where her attention lay.

It's your birthday coming up, that's all. You're going through some midlife thing, the drama queen worrying she's going to end up alone. Though that concern was somewhat valid, it really wasn't why she couldn't stop obsessing about Isabel. *There's something about her. She makes me want to give her more…treat her differently…even be a better person.*

The way Isabel routinely opened doors for strangers or offered an assisting elbow to the frail or unsteady impressed Kash. The friendly, interested tone she used in her interactions with ticket vendors, salespeople, wait staff, and the like also appealed to her. Most of the populace looked right through such people, barely acknowledging their presence. But Isabel engaged almost everyone she met, even briefly, in a way that always left them smiling.

You're real, that's what you are. A genuinely sweet and selfless individual. And a wickedly sexy one. That's a potent combination. And why do you have to be so luscious in whatever you wear? Isabel had on an off-white linen suit from her new wardrobe, with a beige V-necked shell beneath. She was chic, and sexy, and extremely hard to resist.

Am I capable of monogamy? No woman had made her wonder such things. *No. Stop thinking crazy. You have nothing to offer a woman like Isabel, so don't encourage any further involvement. You'll only hurt her.*

❖

"Here's your cappuccino." Gillian's voice brought Isabel out of her musings. She wanted so much to watch Kash, but those sunglasses made it impossible to tell when she was looking her way, and she didn't want to be caught rudely staring. She took the paper cup, and Gillian sank into the empty seat beside her.

"Thanks. Where's your friend?" Isabel had been more than a little surprised that she hadn't seen or heard from Gillian until she'd shown up at the airport, still with Ambra, the sizzling Italian woman she had danced away with at the club three nights earlier.

"Making some phone calls." Gillian crossed her legs.

"So she's coming to Cairo?" Gillian sometimes carried a one-night stand into a few days, or a week, but rarely continued one into another continent. "This one something special?"

Gillian shrugged, a new dreamy, faraway quality in her eyes.

"Well, not that anything's going to come of it," Gillian admitted. "But she's something else, that's for sure. *The* most charming woman I have ever met. Bar none. She is *so* damn irresistible." Gillian was clearly smitten. "Formal manners, and all attentive and romantic. And *so* hot in bed."

"And she must be taken with you, too, to come with us."

Gillian grinned. "Well, we have been pretty much inseparable since we met. But enough about me. So when did you two finally get together?"

Isabel blushed, remembering the night before. She had to smile.

"Oho! I see it was great, too." Gillian punched her playfully on the thigh. "But…if so, then why is she sitting over there?"

"It's not been…what I expected," Isabel confided in a low voice. "Fantastic," she hastened to add. "I mean…*unbelievably* exciting. I only wish it could be…more."

Gillian gave her a resigned smile. "Well, Izzy, these kinds of things…it's all about having some fun and not dreaming for anything beyond what it is, *whatever* it is. Or *was*."

"I know that," Isabel said. "But…don't you ever want more? Haven't you ever met someone that you don't want to let go of?"

"Sure I have," Gillian admitted. "A few times, I've felt a spark of something besides 'wanna fuck?' So when that happens, if you're lucky, maybe you both decide you want to see each other again." She glanced down the length of the terminal, but her new girlfriend wasn't in sight. "I'm sure going to be sorry to say good-bye to Ambra." A long sigh followed, then she gave Isabel a frown of commiseration. "But I knew going into it with her, like you did with Kash, that this was only going to be an affair. I mean, look at how *they* live…and then at us. We want different things. We lead completely different lives."

Can't argue with that. She nodded her agreement.

"You have to be content with having whatever it is you have together," Gillian concluded. "As long as it lasts. Maybe it's not all you want. Maybe not by a long shot." She stared off down the terminal again, seeking Ambra. "But sometimes it's still truly wonderful and memorable. Maybe only a brief instant in time, but if it lives often enough in your head because of how incredible it made you feel…if it becomes one of your most frequent and fond memories…then it's certainly worth the bittersweet disappointment that it couldn't be more. No?"

"I've always worried about you a little," Isabel said, taking Gillian's hand. "You're always so flippant about your nights out and kind of laugh them off anytime I suggest you might want to think about actually dating someone. I thought you might be averse to having a real relationship. But I see now you're certainly open to it if it happens."

She glanced over at Kash. From the tilt of her head, she appeared to be watching the agent behind the counter, who was busy checking in passengers; but with those dark glasses on, Kash could be staring right at her. *I wish you'd take those things off.* "And I have to admit," she said, returning her attention to Gillian, "I'm glad you talked me into loosening up and being open to new things. My time with Kash, however brief, will certainly become a fond and frequent memory, that's for sure." Isabel could feel her skin get hot again as her mind flashed back to the alley.

"I'm glad you had a good time. And hey, if it's any consolation, I think she really likes you. She couldn't take her eyes off you at the club while we were dancing. And other times, too. I mean, she really watches you." At Isabel's surprised gasp she added, "And by the way, I essentially *threw* myself at her and she turned me down, basically saying sex was a bad idea, considering the circumstances."

Isabel glanced over at Kash again. She hadn't moved and was still infuriatingly unreadable.

"You'll pardon my saying so," Gillian went on, "but all of that didn't deter her when it came to *you*, and perhaps that says something. Is it going to be awkward being around her for the rest of the trip?"

"No, no," Isabel answered immediately because she certainly

had no problem being around Kash, even if nothing further happened. Any chance to be near her a while longer was a blessing. And it didn't seem as though it would be awkward at all for Kash. *Polite, but distant, and acting completely unaffected. If she was interested in me, it was apparently only until she could get in my pants a time or two.* "It'll be fine."

"I wonder what's keeping Ambra," Gillian said, her eyes riveted on the growing crowd.

"Really gone on her, aren't you?"

Gillian grinned. "This one is hard to resist. The accent, the body, the manners. I've invited her to visit—not that I think she will. But who knows, right? You're the one who's always telling me anything is possible."

"Whoa! What am I hearing? You mean to tell me you're *finally* connecting with your inner romantic? 'Bout damn time!" She rubbed Gillian affectionately on the back. "I hope she takes you up on it, Gill, if she's something special. I really hope she does." Glancing over at Kash again, she noticed that the sky was now overcast, noticeably darkening the gate area, but Kash made no move to remove her sunglasses.

The gate agent announced that pre-boarding for their flight was now underway for travelers with children and special needs. Gillian glanced at her watch. "Jeez, I hope she hasn't changed her mind or gotten hung up. Not much time before we leave."

"She have a cell phone?"

"I don't think I have time to track down a phone card." Gillian frowned when the gate agent announced general boarding for all passengers. "Hey, you two go ahead. I'm going to wait until final boarding."

"You sure?" Isabel glanced over at Kash, who was on her feet, carry-on bag over her shoulder and boarding pass and passport in hand. Facing her. Waiting for her. Like she had been listening in the whole time.

"Yeah," Gillian urged. "Go. I'm right behind you."

Kash waited for Isabel to precede her toward the gangway, not out of any sense of decorum, but so she could selfishly stare at Isabel's ass and catch a whiff of her perfume.

The embarking passengers bunched up at the entrance to the plane, putting Kash and Isabel in close proximity. When they were stopped briefly at the door Isabel half turned, giving Kash, a handsbreadth behind, an unobstructed view of the cleavage revealed by her V-necked shell.

Watching the rise and fall of Isabel's breasts was delicious torture, especially when she caught a glimpse of lacy white bra.

"What seat do you have?" Isabel asked.

Kash lost herself again in the deep blue of those inviting eyes. Not trusting her voice, she held up her boarding pass.

"One row behind and across the aisle," Isabel said. "If you want some company during the flight, let me know and maybe we can get one of our seatmates to switch. Gillian's arranged to be next to her new friend."

Kash nodded and tried her hardest not to stare at Isabel's chest.

The line started moving again, and when they got to Isabel's row she turned sideways to let Kash through to the seat beyond. Their breasts brushed briefly as Kash passed, and when they did, their eyes made contact. Isabel smiled that imperfectly perfect smile and Kash melted, and without thinking she grinned back. She quickly tried to correct her lapse in judgment by averting her eyes and assuming a neutral expression, but the damage had been done. When she slipped into her seat and stole a glance, Isabel smiled at her with a knowing expression that said, *Busted but good. You can't stop thinking about last night either, can you?*

Gillian and her Italian friend made it on board right before the doors were closed and settled in several rows ahead of them.

Kash didn't attempt to change her seat or talk to Isabel during the more than three-hour flight, and remained distant as they retrieved their gear and rendezvoused with their Egyptian driver—an enthusiastic but solemn young man named Nazim. The car he drove was badly dented front and back and was barely large enough to contain all five of them. Isabel ended up squished between Kash and Gillian in the back. Ambra shared the front seat with all their carry-on bags.

The difference in their surroundings as they negotiated the chaotic, forty-minute ride to the hotel was jarring. They were definitely in another continent and culture.

She had never seen anything like the slum they passed on the highway and its desperate poverty. The scent of urine and trash hung pungent in the air, and only the lines of tattered laundry scattered among the ramshackle structures, and the occasional gaunt occupant staring out of a window, convinced her that people did indeed call such wretched and filthy structures home.

Most native women on the street were dressed modestly, despite the summer heat, their bodies fully covered and veils concealing all but their faces. Street vendors crowded the curbs, hunched beneath umbrellas and makeshift awnings, their wares displayed on blankets and tarps.

Sand coated every street and building, monument and living soul. The slightest breeze or any passing vehicle stirred it up, sometimes creating mini-sandstorms in the streets that would briefly obscure their vision. Garish billboards with bright colors and broad Arabic captions advertised movies and soda pop.

"Have you been here before?" Ambra asked Kash.

Kash nodded. "Many times."

"Do you know the hotel?" Gillian chimed in.

"Yes. The Nile Hilton. Right by the river, so great balcony views again. You can see the pyramids in the distance." There was a long pause. "And it has a nice pool."

Isabel glanced at Kash, who was staring out the window with what could best be described as a rather guilty grin on her face. It took Isabel several seconds to link the pool mention…and balcony views…to her self-pleasuring session in the hot tub. *Nah. No way. A coincidence. That's all.*

But the mere possibility that Kash had been watching sent her pulse racing. *Yet another surprise. I'd certainly never have considered myself an exhibitionist.*

"Well, you'll get your own bed and balcony again," Gillian told Isabel. "Ambra's going to get a room and I'll be staying with her."

"Very busy now," their driver interrupted, as he beeped his horn and swerved around a donkey-drawn cart overflowing with papers and trash. "No rooms."

Ambra turned to Gillian in dismay, then the driver. "No rooms at the Hilton? Are you sure?"

"All tourist hotels," Nazim clarified. "Americans. Japanese. Europeans. All here now. All full."

"*Merda,*" Ambra said. Creases appeared in her forehead as she frowned at Gillian. "And now?"

Isabel glanced Kash's way, but Kash was gazing out the window.

"I guess we'll cross that bridge when we come to it," Gillian said uncertainly as she gave Isabel a help-me-out-here-can-you.

Nazim cursed and laid on the horn as he jerked the car violently to the left to prevent a collision. As Isabel was thrown into Kash's side, she wondered why Egypt apparently didn't embrace the notion of marking lanes in the road.

Kash had surprisingly fast reflexes. She managed to partially catch Isabel; they ended up with Isabel's head on her shoulder and Kash's arm around her in a half-embrace.

"Sorry," Isabel muttered, pushing herself off Kash as the car corrected. They had only brief contact, but her skin tingled from the sudden warm press of their bodies.

"No problem." Kash wondered whether Isabel could feel, during their brief contact, how hard and fast her heart was beating.

Before they knew it, they were at the Hilton. While Nazim attended to their bags, they headed into the lobby. The concierge intercepted them before they made it halfway to the front desk.

"Miss Kash! How splendid for you to stay with us." He was a rather short but Omar Sharif–handsome older gentleman with a well-trimmed mustache and an elegant splash of gray at his temples. His charcoal suit fit him perfectly. "I am Rasui. Welcome to the Hilton. May I show you and your party to your suites?"

Kash extended her hand and they shook. "Pleased to meet you, Rasui. And that would be lovely, but I should first alert you that we have an extra person and wonder if you can provide us another suite?"

When Rasui's smile faltered slightly, Gillian added, "Doesn't have to be a suite. Any room will do."

The concierge did not immediately reject the request as impossible, but Kash knew he was well trained to mentally exhaust all possibilities—however remote—before daring to deny a celebrity any request. His expression and stiff body language told her the driver knew what he was talking about.

"I cannot immediately provide you with another room, I am very sorry to say," he said at last, his tone effusively apologetic. "Of course, if there are any cancellations…but I am afraid the entire hotel is booked for the length of your stay with us. We certainly can provide an additional bed in either of your suites."

"Great," Gillian muttered under her breath. Then louder, "Izzy? Do you mind?"

"No. No, of course not," Isabel replied.

Kash didn't volunteer anything.

❖

Well, that was certainly rude. Kash surveyed the sitting area of her suite and spacious bedroom beyond. She could easily have offered this room to Isabel and kept the bedroom for herself. It would have been the polite thing to do. Putting the three of them in the smaller suite would give Gillian and Ambra no privacy at all.

But it was impossible to share a confined space like this with Isabel right now. Seeing her in whatever she wore—or didn't wear—to sleep in. Crossing paths as they came or went from the shower. *Nope. No way.* Already she couldn't get Isabel out of her mind. If they were to be cooped up together, anything could happen.

Chapter Sixteen

At seven the next morning, Kash spotted the envelope that had been slipped under her door. Her first thought—no, *hope*, if she was honest—was that it was a note from Isabel. She didn't even really care what it said; nearly anything would do, because she had been up half the night, missing her. Wanting so much to be with her, but fearing it, too.

It would have been much worse, though, if she had stayed here. At best, you'd have been just as awake and unable to pace through the whole suite. And to even think about the temptation of her on the other side of an unlocked door all the while, dressed in…? Speculation about what Isabel slept in had consumed a good portion of her waking thoughts the night before. She had conjured up the whole gamut of possibilities, but kept returning to the image of a silk teddy in black or red. Probably not at all what Isabel really wore to bed—she seemed more the tank-top-and-pajama-bottoms type—but Kash's imagination wouldn't forsake the teddy.

The envelope contained not a missive from Isabel, however, but a note from their Egyptian driver, who was supposed to pick her up at ten to scout locations.

> *Miss Kash,*
> *Weather advisory has been issued for strong winds beginning tonight. Major sandstorms tomorrow. Please advise.*
> *Nazim*

This was certainly an unwelcome development. Sandstorms could shut down everything—all travel—and keep people indoors, often for several hours or a day or more.

A call to the concierge's desk confirmed the forecast. She carried a cup of coffee out onto the balcony to consider the possibilities. The sky was clear and cloudless, with no sign of the trouble to come. The best thing to do, she decided, was to take advantage of the decent weather while it lasted.

Nazim answered on the first ring. She discussed a number of possibilities with him, told him what equipment she'd need, and set up a tentative itinerary for the day that would commence at eight thirty.

Then she called Isabel. She took several deep breaths before she dialed her room. Isabel picked up the phone almost immediately and sounded wide-awake.

"Yes? Hello?"

Kash felt her insides clench at the sound of Isabel's voice. *Oh, this is bad. This is so bad.* "Isabel, it's Kash."

"Oh! Hi." In two words, Kash heard Isabel's clear delight at the unexpected call.

"I know we were supposed to do our shoot tomorrow, but a bad sandstorm's forecast." She tried to keep her voice even. Professional. "I'd like to reschedule for today. Can you be ready in an hour?"

"Sure. Of course." Isabel's sparkling exuberance made it difficult for Kash to remain unaffected.

"Good. Wear something comfortable. I'll drop by your suite and pick out a few outfits for you for today, and we'll go from there."

"I'll be ready."

And ready she certainly was. When Isabel answered her door, she was wearing a pair of sexy, low-cut jeans and another button-down shirt. The shirt was lavender this time, but styled very much like the one she had worn in the alley.

They stared at each other for a very long and awkward moment. Kash couldn't believe how time had slowed. Had it really been less than forty-eight hours since she had touched Isabel? Kissed those lips? It seemed infinitely longer. Far *too* long. And even more jarring, she realized she had known her less than two weeks. How quickly Isabel had become such a fixture in her thoughts. *And she'll as quickly leave my life. Don't forget that.*

Finally, Isabel broke the tension. "Come on in." She stepped aside and allowed Kash into the sitting room, where selections from her new designer wardrobe lay on the couch and single bed. "They're not up yet," she added in a low voice, indicating Gillian and Ambra with a tilt of her head toward the closed door to the bedroom. "Late night."

Kash's mind filled with the image of Isabel, awake, listening to the sounds of sex emanating from the other room, and once again she felt like a heel for not volunteering to share her suite. "We'll be quick," she replied in an equally subdued tone, crossing to the bed to begin selecting Isabel's wardrobe for the day. She picked out four outfits and had them packed into a garment bag and ready to go in a couple of minutes.

The uncomfortable strain between them continued during a silent elevator ride down to the lobby, where Nazim was waiting. During their drive to their first stop, Isabel tried a couple of times to initiate polite conversation, but when Kash barely responded, she gave up and concentrated on the scenery.

They did the requisite shots at the pyramids, including a few of Isabel on one of the many camels for hire, then moved to the nearby Sphinx for a few more photos. Through it all, Kash spoke only when necessary, giving instructions to Nazim or altering Isabel's pose with small corrections—"Tilt your chin up slightly," or "Turn a bit more this way."

By now, Isabel was beginning to get a pretty good sense of how to pose and what expressions Kash seemed to favor, so she tried flirty and fierce, seductive and sexy, and all of the other attitudes that Kash had directed her to feign. Inside, though, she was beginning to seethe, even though she had to admit that Kash *was* really starkly beautiful against the endless desert backdrop, her brown hair a nice contrast to her lightweight khaki trousers and safari-style shirt.

Though the shutter kept clicking away, Kash's expression never changed. Not even when Isabel tried deliberately provocative poses. *Cold, hard Kash. Yup. For sure you've heard that before, if you treat all the women you screw the way you're treating me.*

She tried to keep telling herself she had no reason to be annoyed. *I got precisely what I asked for. And it was great.* It was really beginning to rankle her, though, to have Kash be so damn…well, unnecessarily *remote*. Every now and then she wanted to *shake* her. *How can what*

*happened in that alley have been an experience I can't forget, and one
you don't wish to acknowledge ever happened?*

When they stopped for lunch Nazim took advantage of their
reticence to initiate conversation. He peppered Kash with questions
about photography, celebrities she'd met, and her travels, while Isabel
and Kash tried unsuccessfully not to constantly look at each other.

Their third shoot of the day was on a rented felucca, one of the
ubiquitous native sailboats that plied the Nile. Kash expected disaster
any second. All the ingredients were there: a slightly tippy boat, lots of
water, expensive photographic equipment, and a very sexy and slightly
accident-prone distraction. But somehow they escaped the experience
unscathed and moved on to their final location, a village on the Nile
about an hour's drive from Cairo.

As they walked about and mingled with the natives, Kash shot
a variety of candids. Young children in clean but well-worn clothes
ran alongside them, curious and smiling. Old men stared with serious
expressions from the doorways of homes built of mud bricks and
straw.

"One more stop, and then we're done." Kash led them back toward
Nazim's battered car. "We'll do some shots out in the desert. The light
is really wonderful."

They drove until Kash found the perfect backdrop for the lowering
sun: a vast desert landscape, with the village far in the distance. No one
else was within sight as Nazim parked at the edge of the road.

"Do you want me in another outfit?" Isabel knew what was coming,
and she thought that if anything might get a reaction out of Kash today,
this would be it. She would push aside her annoyance and make one
more effort to see if she could coerce Kash into something more.

"Yes, please."

As expected, Kash handed her the final ensemble. When Isabel
had seen Kash select it that morning, she had almost objected. She'd
been afraid of wearing it out in public because she thought it far too
immodest for their surroundings, too likely to cause ill will. So she
was greatly relieved Kash had reserved it for a location where no one
would see her. Nazim and Kash turned their backs while she quickly
changed.

A pale yellow minidress in a very sheer fabric, it showed off as
many sexy body parts as possible while still allowing the wearer to

avoid arrest for indecent exposure. At least in the West. Here it could certainly get her into trouble.

Ordinarily, this type of garment would have made her extremely self-conscious, but Nazim had been nothing but respectful and polite. And Isa was in her bloodstream now and was enjoying too much the newly discovered thrill of taking risks, being daring, and oozing sexuality. "Okay, I'm ready," she told them, once she had made certain her breasts were covered by the thin panels of material.

Nazim's pupils widened and his whole body stiffened. After a moment, he looked away, out over the desert, and kept his eyes averted, his only outward signs that he might find Isabel's appearance disturbing.

Kash, on the other hand, had quite the opposite reaction. Her gaze was fixed on Isabel.

"How do you want me?" Isabel's tone was all innuendo.

Over easy. Kash took a deep breath before speaking. It was difficult not to outwardly display how excited she was getting. "I want you to blend with the environment. Make it one with you. I want you to show how being here makes you feel."

Isabel wet her lips and struck a sexy, powerful pose, face-on to the camera, her gaze smoldering and lustful, as if saying, *I'm going to show you how I feel being with you, instead, Kash.*

Kash focused as she zoomed in with a long lens from fifteen feet away. Her heart was already beating fast because of the dress, but it accelerated rapidly when she brought Isabel's eyes into close-up view.

It was as though they were face-to-face. Isabel's eyes said *I know you want me. I want you, too.*

If they really had been standing close together, Kash would have kissed her. Instead, she depressed the shutter and enjoyed the painful twitch low in her abdomen. *Click. Click. Click.* It was doubtful these shots would appear in the magazine, but Kash would refer to them often.

She started to sweat, though the sun was rapidly descending toward the horizon, and she chalked her reaction up to the heat emanating from Isabel. *Click. Click.*

The next pose Isabel chose was sensually playful, presenting her backside to the camera and looking over her shoulder with a come-hither suggestiveness. *Click. Click. Click. Damn, she's got a nice ass.*

Kash zoomed in on her eyes again. Now they said *You want to fuck me, don't you?*

Her hands started to tremble, so she gripped her camera tight to keep Isabel from seeing. *Click. Click.*

Now Isabel got down on her hands and knees and struck a pose more *Penthouse* than *Sophisticated Women.* Kash did not correct her mistake. *Click. Click. Click. Click. Click.* Another, even more provocative, pose. *Click. Click.* The sweat really poured off Kash now, running down her back in a thick trickle along her spine. Hot weather always made her a little horny anyway, but Isabel was making her insides twist in the agony of acute arousal.

Kash heard a muffled cough from behind her and glanced around. Nazim had put some distance between them and had his back to them. He obviously didn't want to witness what was going on.

She watched him for a few seconds, and when she turned back around she discovered that Isabel had changed positions again. She was on her feet, and this pose was clearly not intended for the camera. *Now, who can be expected to be able to resist that?* Not thinking, she stepped away from her tripod to get an unobstructed view in the flesh, instead of through a viewfinder.

Isabel wasn't really *posing* at all. She was…casually *waiting.* Expectant. The invitation in her eyes, even at this distance, unmistakable. Now they said *Let's go somewhere, huh? Enough of this, already.*

Damn. Kash couldn't stop staring. A heavy bead of sweat ran between her breasts, over her stomach, and down to the apex of her thighs. It felt like a tongue, Isabel's tongue, tracing a path to her clit.

"Isabel, I need you to…" *let me take off your clothes.* Kash coughed, clearing her throat. "Uh…*do* something. Pose. We're not finished yet." With great reluctance, she returned to her tripod and focused on the image in her viewfinder. Isabel hadn't moved.

Kash looked around the camera at her. "Isabel?"

"Tell me, Kash," Isabel said, her tone honey-thick and seductive. "Why are you acting as though we're not hot for each other when it's so obvious that we are?"

Kash's mouth went dry. It was hard to swallow and she wished for the distance that her camera provided. She felt open and vulnerable, certain that Isabel could see, despite her best efforts, how excited she was.

"I've told you, Isabel, we had what we had, and it's over. I'm here to take pictures of you, not to satisfy your needs. Can we get back to work now?" The words were difficult to say because she didn't feel them, but she was so far out of her comfort zone—crazy with desire and yet terrified, too—that she just wanted to get Isabel to stop looking at her that way. And fast.

"Bullshit, Kash." Isabel shook her head and sighed. "We could have such a great time together during the next few days, but you're bent on denying this…this chemistry between us. Not only denying it, but acting completely…well, beyond *cool*…almost to the point of being *rude*. Why?"

She sought a suitable answer, but she felt like she was standing in quicksand. None of her pat and practiced responses, which she used when a woman wanted *more*, would work with Isabel.

There had been a trickle of breeze now and then, but suddenly a hot gust of wind blew through, stirring up the sand and pelting them with it, stinging exposed flesh and making them all turn their faces away. When the long, sustained blow of several seconds was over, they spat out sand and brushed it off their arms, faces, necks. It was in their ears and embedded at the edge of their eyes, and it had made its way into every loose article of clothing.

"That was horrible!" Isabel reached under her dress to brush the sand from her breasts, a sight that Kash couldn't ignore, so she didn't immediately remember her camera.

"Christ!" At least all her other equipment was still in her bags. But the Hasselblad she was holding would be a bitch to clean, and the lens was probably ruined.

She heard a grinding noise behind her and pivoted. Nazim was trying unsuccessfully to start the car, which had been pointed grill-first in the direction the wind had blown in from. *Oh, fuck.*

Another, shorter gust of wind blew across them, and she and Isabel cowered while Nazim tried once again.

"Get in!" Kash yelled to Isabel once the breeze died down. She quickly unscrewed her camera and collapsed the tripod, and made it to the vehicle a few steps behind Isabel. They both scrambled into the back.

It was easy to translate Nazim's short outbursts as curses. They grew louder as the car's labored efforts to start got quieter. Another strong gust of wind stirred the sand and obscured their view for several seconds. Neither of them spoke until Nazim slammed both palms against the steering wheel, so hard the little car shook. He cursed again in Arabic, then took a deep, calming breath and faced them. "I will walk for help back to the village," he said. "You stay here."

"We should all go," Kash said, and Isabel opened her mouth to agree.

He held up his hand. "Please. These storms can get bad very fast. It is better if you are here safe. We may get separated, and I can move faster alone." He partially unwrapped the cotton cloth turban on his head so that part of it could cover his face. He was indeed much more suitably attired to deal with hiking back to the village—covered head to ankle in the traditional long loose shirt, or galabiya, and matching trousers. "I have dealt with this many times before. I will be back as soon as I can."

"All right," Kash conceded, and Nazim got out of the car and started off toward the village at a brisk pace. He hadn't gone twenty steps before another blast of wind obscured him temporarily from view. When he reappeared, he was a good bit farther away, slowed but not stalled by the sand, walking in the middle of the pavement.

"I should change," Isabel said.

"Yes. Right," Kash agreed, glancing over to find Isabel's dress open in a way that allowed her a clear view of cleavage and a lot of breast. *No bra.* She pulled the keys from the ignition to get Isabel's bag from the trunk. Nazim was making good time, but the village was quite a distance, and she could see mini-sandstorms springing up in the vast desert around them.

She opened the door nearest Isabel and handed her the bag but stayed outside the car, watching Nazim. Imagining Isabel inside, getting naked, was making her feel restless and out of control. A sandstorm began in the distance and gained strength as it barreled toward her, obliterating the sun and painting the sky yellow. She watched it until it got close, then dove into the driver's seat right before it reached them. She knew Isabel hadn't had time to fully change.

Kash was able to resist the urge to turn around, but though she knew better, she couldn't keep from glancing in the rearview mirror. It allowed her only a view of Isabel's face; those deep blue eyes were watching her intently. And from her expression, Kash knew that Isabel was nude.

Neither of them moved, or even blinked. In the stillness that followed, Kash became aware of how fast she was breathing. Isabel was, too.

She gripped the steering wheel so hard her forearms ached.

Isabel leaned forward against Kash's seat while maintaining eye contact in the mirror. Kash could faintly feel her warm breath against the back of her neck. *Oh, don't do that. That's just cruel.*

Another powerful gust outside obliterated their surroundings and shook the car, reminding them of their isolation.

All Kash could see in the rearview were Isabel's eyes…the pupils dark with arousal, the expression in them unforgiving need.

This can't be happening. She watched in horror as Isabel leaned forward even farther, until her lips were against Kash's ear. Isabel paused there, her breathing fast and uneven. Then she licked the back of Kash's ear, and Kash almost went through the roof.

She stiffened, feeling that lick right between her legs, and squirmed in her seat, unconsciously trying to create some friction where she needed it most. When Isabel licked her again, totally against her will she relaxed into the wet caress, the throbbing between her legs growing painfully insistent.

Isabel's tongue immediately accepted the offering and traced a slow, sensual path along Kash's neck to her jawline. Kash could feel warm, rapid exhalations against her cheek as Isabel's mouth sought hers.

She ached to put her hand between her legs, to say *fuck it* to all the voices in her head telling her this was a bad idea. She was at a crossroads and had only seconds to decide what to do before Isabel's mouth claimed hers. She knew that if it did, she would be lost, swept headlong toward an unknown destination.

Her terror overcame her lust, and she pulled away. "Get dressed," she said hoarsely. "Nazim should be back soon." Grateful for a lull in the wind, she got out of the car, her heart beating furiously. She was so turned on she could think of nothing but how badly she needed to come and how frustrated she was that she could apparently do nothing about it. She was angry at herself, too, for being so out of control and unable to cope with what was happening to her.

❖

Isabel pulled on her jeans, her eyes on Kash all the while, trying to gauge what was going on with her. She couldn't stop what seemed to be happening between them. Her body simply craved Kash's in a way she felt completely helpless to fight.

A part of her was beginning to feel foolish since Kash had spurned her so often. But she knew in her heart, from the expression in Kash's eyes and how Kash had kissed her, that there was definite heat between them. *The more you feel for her, the worse it gets. But how much longer are you going to keep throwing yourself at her?*

Kash stayed outside whenever possible, and when the wind forced her back into the car, she stayed in the passenger front seat, eyes ahead, and made no further conversation.

Isabel, frustrated at being rejected yet again, had nearly decided to make no further moves on Kash. But she changed her mind about the time that Kash returned to the car for the third time. By then, she understood.

Clearly, Kash wasn't aware she was even humming, let alone that the tunes she chose obviously reflected some of what was going on in her head. The first time she got in the car she was humming Louis Armstrong's "A Kiss to Build a Dream On."

When she came back the second time, she had changed to another old standard—Ella Fitzgerald's "Something's Gotta Give."

The third song Isabel considered definitive evidence that Kash was much more affected than she let on. It was a Foreigner tune from the '80s—"I Want to Know What Love Is."

Isabel was content to say nothing as Kash came and went, grateful to have these little glimpses into the enigmatic woman and what was really going on beneath her distant exterior. They also gave her an insight into Kash's musical tastes, which were apparently quite varied. She had never heard Kash burn through so many tunes in such a short period of time before and wondered whether the fast pace was relevant to her stress or anxiety, or something else Kash was feeling.

By the time help arrived, Isabel had also heard snippets of the Fine Young Cannibals' "She Drives Me Crazy" and Boyz II Men's "I'll Make Love to You," as well as bits of two tunes she couldn't identify. Oh, how she wanted to identify those mystery songs. So bad she could taste it. So bad she wanted to ask Kash each time what exactly she was humming, but she knew such questions would make her instantly self-conscious and all too aware of what she was doing.

It was after nightfall before Nazim returned with another man in an old wreck of a car with a makeshift cloth bib tied in front of the grill to keep the sand out. They piled in with their bags and set off toward the village. "The road to Cairo is closed," Nazim informed them. "We will have to stay in the village. This man knows somewhere we can go."

Kash had frankly been surprised that Nazim had managed to find a car in the village to come get them. She knew the place was too small to have any kind of hotel or other accommodation for outsiders.

"Thank you for your help," Kash said to the driver, a slight man of perhaps thirty, with dark eyes and stained teeth. When Nazim repeated in Arabic what she had said, the man smiled and nodded.

They had to stop five times on the way back to the village because of the blowing sand, sometimes for several minutes. The situation was definitely getting worse. The driver took them to a small squat home made of mud brick, a short distance away from the area they had explored on foot. He said something in Arabic to them, which translated as "Welcome to my home. May I ask you please to take your shoes off before entering?"

"His home," Isabel exclaimed as she bent down to remove her sandals. "Gosh, that's wonderfully generous."

Though humble, the three-room dwelling was clean and well kept. There were Persian rugs everywhere and low tables, with pillows to sit on. They met the man's wife, who was wearing what Kash was certain were her best garments, and were shown their room—a small chamber with a mattress not much bigger than a single bed. It was, no doubt, the couple's own bed, freshly made up for their guests.

"We can't take their bed," Kash protested to Nazim. Her objection had little to do with imposing on their hosts and everything to do with the prospect of sharing that little bed with Isabel. Though the occupants spoke no English, Kash's tone showed that she was displeased, which drew immediate frowns from both of them.

"It is an insult to them to refuse their hospitality," Nazim said gently.

"Then we mustn't refuse." Isabel, standing beside Kash, placed a hand on her arm. "We mustn't."

Kash knew she was right. They couldn't decline the offer or the couple would lose face, so she said to the homeowner, "We are very grateful for your generous offer."

Nazim translated, and the couple beamed. The man gave a small bow.

The woman began speaking rapidly to Nazim, who nodded. "She has been cooking for us and hopes that we have brought big appetites."

"Yes. You bet." Kash was indeed hungry, but she was also grateful for anything that would delay lying down next to Isabel.

CHAPTER SEVENTEEN

How long are you going to keep avoiding this?"
Kash knew the confrontation was coming. She had seen it in Isabel's eyes throughout the long evening as they ate the tempting array of dishes and lingered over strong coffee while lounging on the oversized pillows. Their hosts, initially quite reserved, relaxed as the visit progressed and deluged them with questions about their lives, their jobs, and their families. Isabel answered with candor and unexpected humor. Kash, on the other hand, volunteered very little about herself, except for the general information that had been well documented by the media.

She and Isabel had said almost nothing to each other, but Isabel had positioned herself across from Kash and looked at her often with a definite I-have-plans-for-you-later directness that kept Kash on edge.

And now, they were alone together in an eight-foot by ten-foot room, dimly lit by a few small candles.

"Let it go, Isabel." Kash walked over to the only window and stood before it, staring out, her back to Isabel. It was very warm with the window closed, and there was no view; the swirling sand obscured any lights that might have been visible from neighboring homes. Her blood was racing but she worked to appear unaffected, by trying to have a relaxed posture and putting her hand in her pocket. *Go to sleep, Isabel. Lie down and go to sleep and don't tempt me anymore.*

Isabel was disheartened by Kash's answer, but it wasn't long before her spirits lifted. *There she goes again.* Isabel had to strain to even hear the tune, let alone identify it. She crept a few steps closer, so she could make out what Kash was humming this time.

"The Nearness of You."

It gave her courage. She quietly crossed to Kash, took a deep breath, and slipped her arms around Kash's waist from behind. The humming stopped.

Kash straightened, and every nerve and muscle in her body tensed, but she didn't pull away. Isabel took this reaction as tacit encouragement and pressed against Kash's back. They were close enough in height that she could rest her head on Kash's shoulder.

Softly, Isabel started singing the song that Kash had been humming. She had a beautiful rich alto, and she sang with meaning. As she did, she traced lightly over Kash's stomach with her fingertips, and it wasn't long before Kash began to relax against her.

"Come to bed," Isabel whispered.

"Nothing more is going to happen between us," Kash said unsteadily. "You go ahead, and I'll be there soon."

"Stop denying this, will you?" Isabel loosened her hold on Kash and pivoted her until they faced each other. Before Kash could respond, Isabel slipped one hand behind her neck, pulled their faces together, and kissed her.

Isabel's lips were feather soft as they glanced over Kash's, and as they did, Isabel trembled, a shudder of poised anticipation. A heartbeat later, her mouth laid claim to Kash's, firm and insistent. Her tongue demanded entry, wetly caressing Kash's lips, pushing in, and Kash's mind fogged as she surrendered to the rush of feeling pouring through her. When Isabel kissed her, it was as though her whole body was being kissed.

With her lips, and teeth, and tongue, she returned Isabel's passion, and the kiss grew so heated she didn't immediately realize that Isabel had managed to unfasten her trousers and unzip her fly.

She became aware of it when Isabel's fingertips slipped between her shirt and pants and touched the naked skin of her stomach. She closed her own hand firmly around Isabel's wrist. "No, Isabel. I told you."

"Yes. You told me," Isabel agreed. Kash's stomach muscles had gone suddenly rigid beneath her hand, but she didn't withdraw it and was encouraged when Kash allowed it to remain. "But you also said the way you usually are with women didn't feel right with me. So let it be different, Kash. Let me touch you." She gave Kash several slow, wet kisses on her neck. She wasn't ordinarily comfortable with taking the initiative sexually, but she knew that she had to with Kash. "You can deny it all you like, but I can tell from the things you say to me with your eyes, from the way your body moves against mine, and especially from the way you kiss me, that you want me to, very much. Am I wrong?"

Kash didn't respond verbally, but she took her hand away from Isabel's wrist. When she did, Isabel began moving her fingertips lightly over Kash's abdomen, tracing circuitous paths that moved lower with each rotation. The muscles beneath her hand began to relax. "Do you like that? Feel good?"

Her mouth was still nuzzling Kash's neck, so she felt more than saw Kash's nod of assent. "I crave it, Kash. Touching you. Exciting you the way you excite me."

"You do, Isabel." Kash's voice was strained. Her hands, which were now on Isabel's ass, gripped tighter but didn't move. Isabel knew that she must be struggling with what was happening.

"Please let it happen, Kash. I want to so very much. So much." She punctuated every other word with more kisses and gentle bites on Kash's neck. *Let me make love to you.* She couldn't say the words aloud for fear of chasing Kash away, but she felt the truth of them in her heart. No matter how improbable or impossible, she was falling in love, falling fast and hard, and this was definitely *making love* for her, not just sex.

Kash's heart was pounding and her mouth was parched. It was warm in the room with the window closed, and perspiration trickled down her chest, between her breasts, as though chasing Isabel's hand to push it lower, toward the swollen, ready ache between her legs. But she couldn't ask for it. She was doing her best merely to allow it.

She roughly massaged Isabel's ass as she took a half step back so that she could use the wall behind her for support. Her head spun as she leaned back against the cool brick and closed her eyes, and her legs felt rubbery as she spread them to allow Isabel greater access. This was as much encouragement as she could manage.

Isabel's hand detoured from its sweetly torturous exploration of her lower abdomen and slipped to the waistband of her trousers to pull them down and off, exposing her overheated skin to the air.

"Jesus, Kash, that is so hot."

She opened her eyes hazily to find Isabel staring at her black string bikinis with a lustful expression. Kash got harder, and her need for release intensified unbearably. *Please touch me, Isabel. Please. I'll die if you don't.*

As if answering her unspoken plea, Isabel slipped her hands beneath the slim waistband of the thong and smoothed it over her thighs and off. Kash's clit grew harder still, and she bit her lower lip to keep from voicing her desire.

Isabel slowly straightened to stand again before her and on the way ran her hands up Kash's ankles, calves, and thighs, palms spread to explore, getting her used to the feel of a woman's touch on her body again after so damn long. *So damn long. Was I waiting for you, Isabel? It sure feels as though I was. With you, it's almost...easy.*

She closed her eyes when Isabel touched her stomach again, moving upward, this time to unfasten the buttons on her shirt. Without looking, she put her hands around Isabel, who stopped her, gently placing them instead at her sides, palms flat against the wall.

Kash gritted her teeth at the surrender of control but allowed it for, surprisingly, it only increased the pulse between her legs. "Isabel." It came out more growl than word, but had the desired effect. At once, her shirt was open and Isabel's mouth was on her breast. *Oh, fuck, yes.* She spread her legs farther and braced for deliverance.

Isabel built her slowly, and every blessed bit of it, from that first maddeningly light touch of her fingers to the driving thrusts that shattered her, were somehow worth the long wait, the self-imposed exile of sexual solitude her life had become. When she finally came, she was weak and gasping, and sank to her knees, scraping her back against the rough brick.

"You okay?" Isabel gently inquired from somewhere close. But she couldn't move, couldn't speak. Dared not even open her eyes, afraid that Isabel could see how vulnerable she had let herself become. Kash felt raw, and exposed, and suddenly afraid that she had let things go much too far.

With Isabel, she had felt out of control almost from the start. *All along, I've been trying to tell myself that Isabel couldn't handle sex with me without complications and expectations. But it's not her at all. It's me. Somehow I knew that if I let her touch me, I'd be lost.*

Now what? What have I done? I let her in, all the way in, when I'm going to have to say good-bye to her in a little more than a week. Kash began to realize and accept how truly important Isabel had become.

"Isabel," she said when she could find her voice. "It's late. Why don't you get ready to go to sleep?" She indicated the bed with a tilt of her head, feeling too vulnerable to be able to meet Isabel's eyes.

"Kash?"

She could hear the concern in Isabel's quiet inquiry, but had no ability to do anything about it at the moment. "Please, Isabel."

"All right, Kash." Kash heard a soft sigh, then the soft footfalls of her retreat toward the bed, the sounds of her undressing, and the quiet stillness after Isabel had slipped beneath the covers.

Only then did she redress and extinguish all the candles but one faint one, near the head of the bed. She stood over Isabel, who was watching her with the same uncertainty and confusion that she was feeling to her core. Much as she wanted to give Isabel some reassurances that somehow, something had just changed between them, she could not. She'd stepped in some kind of quicksand, and she couldn't bring herself to succumb to it. "Sleep. Sweet dreams."

"Are you going to join me?" It was more plea than question.

"Isabel, I…I'm not very comfortable sharing a bed with you," Kash admitted. "Especially one that size. I sleep alone, except when I drift off unintentionally."

"I'll be very respectful, Kash," Isabel said. "I mean, I'll try not to touch you, if you don't want me to. But it *is* a small bed, and I might accidentally put an arm over you or curl up next to you while we sleep. Can't help it."

Kash felt her skin get hotter with the prospect of Isabel lazily cozying up behind her, half-asleep. *That would certainly wake me up in a hurry. Would I be able to stop myself from touching her, getting even more irrevocably lost in her embrace? I'm not certain I would.* "Thanks for the warning. Please don't take it personally if you wake up and I'm curled up on a pillow on the floor."

"Oh. Okay. I'll try not to," Isabel replied. She was hurt, though she clearly tried to hide it.

You try so hard to please and encourage me, though I've treated you pretty shabbily at times, pushing you away again and again. I can't hurt you anymore. And I can't let you hurt me. Kash sat on the edge of the bed. "I…I'm not in a familiar place right now, Isabel. I need a little time alone."

"I didn't mean to make you uncomfortable, Kash. Or in any way increase the distance you already want to put between us. But you…make me feel *so much*. And I wanted…still *want*…to share that experience. As much as I can, as long as I'm able. I've…I've come to care a lot about you."

Isabel's voice was low and somehow extraordinarily soothing, as though by just listening to her, Kash could heal the fractures that all the women who had used her had inflicted.

"I don't regret what happened, Isabel. Not for a moment. I wanted very much for you to touch me." However brief their time together was to be, Kash wanted Isabel to know that she, too, had impressed her, deeply. She owed her that much. "You're an extraordinary woman, and I've come to care a great deal about you, too."

Isabel smiled, and Kash's heart melted. She would miss that lopsided smile, so much. Along with so many other things. "Sleep now. It's very late. I'm going to stay up a while." *And try to figure out how the hell I'm going to manage without you in my life.*

Chapter Eighteen

Kash yawned and massaged the crook in her neck she'd gotten from nodding off, something she thought impossible given her posture and current mental and emotional state. She sat beneath the window, back against the wall and legs stretched out in front of her. The sandstorm was blowing in earnest, and the steady drumming of the tiny grains against the glass had lulled her, like the soothing cadence of a wire brush on cymbals in a good piece of jazz.

Knowing Isabel was across the room, half naked in bed, was driving her mad. *What have you done to me, Isabel, that suddenly so much of my whole life seems...wrong? How can I go back to Manhattan and act as if all of this never happened?* She rubbed her eyes and tried to see her watch. Another half hour until dawn.

The sandstorm seems appropriate, somehow. All Isabel, a combination of such tiny things that you don't feel threatened at first... you don't see it coming, but all of a sudden, the world as you know it is gone, and you have no idea which way is up. In the scant two weeks since they'd first met, those simple traits that made up Isabel—her sweet and open honesty, perky optimism, dogged and sexy determination—had combined to obscure Kash's vision of where her future lay.

All she knew for sure was that her old routine didn't fit so well anymore. She didn't think she could get much further satisfaction out of drinking the night away alone and going to the right parties and screwing models now and then. *And taking bullshit pictures because it's easy and gives you plenty of women to fuck.*

That thought led her to the answer as to what to do next. She would try to regain the passion she once had for what she did. Bury herself in her work. Photography was the one thing that might be enough to get her mind off Isabel and her life headed in a positive new direction.

As soon as Kash heard people up and about in the outer room, she slipped out of the bedroom and away from Isabel.

❖

Isabel knew immediately that Kash had never joined her in bed. The other side of the thin covering was unwrinkled, the pillow untouched. She frowned in disappointment. *I bet she got no sleep at all.* It had taken her a long while to doze off, her mind too preoccupied with trying to think of something she might say or do to get Kash to let her guard down and open herself up to the possibility that something real—something deep—might develop between them.

Kash's admission that she had come to care for her, too, had been a welcome surprise. But she didn't allow herself to take it as encouragement for the future. And that was what she wanted with Kash. She knew that now. A future. Or at the very least, more time. Time for Kash to learn to trust again. Time for the two of them to get to know each other better. Time to see if something more than a brief affair might come from their undeniable mutual attraction and growing connection.

She thought back to what Kash had told her about her previous relationships. Though Kash had avoided any kind of emotional commitment for some time, she was certainly capable of love. She had once loved, and loved deeply—she had just been terribly hurt and was too afraid of it happening again to open herself up.

Well, we still have ten days left. And things seem to be moving in a positive direction. She let me touch her and opened up to me a little.

One thing was certain. They wouldn't be going anywhere anytime soon. Her watch said it was eight in the morning, but she could scarcely tell it from the way the sandstorm had blotted out the sun. Dressing quickly, she joined the others and found them clustered tightly together on pillows in the outer room, focused on Kash's laptop.

All of them looked up at Isabel when she came in and hailed her with good mornings and smiles, but only Kash held her eyes. Nazim and their Egyptian hosts immediately returned their attention to whatever Kash was showing them.

"Evidently I'm missing something pretty fascinating," Isabel observed as she moved to a place behind Kash where she could also see the screen.

"Oh, yes, truly magnificent," Nazim answered without taking his eyes from the computer, which currently displayed a full-screen photo, black and white. It was an adolescent boy in the Khan al-Khalili bazaar in Cairo, stoking coals for a glassblower. He was rail thin and his shirt was stained and dark with sweat, but his eyes held no anger or depression with his wretched lot in life, only placid acceptance.

After a few seconds, the screen pixilated into another photo, brilliant with color this time. An elderly Asian woman with a flowery dress was weaving a basket of green fronds in a lush tropical paradise. Once again Kash had captured her at the precise instant where her expression told the story of her life. The satisfied smile on her face said she had been doing this forever, and she kept at it because she liked to, not because she had to.

"Lovely," Isabel commented. "Where was it taken?"

"Thailand," Kash said.

The third was an Indian elephant-keeper, caught smiling as his charge rubbed his back with her trunk. The fourth, a dour Russian guard with severely bloodshot eyes and a mustache caked with ice.

There were many more like them, and all had captured their subjects in a way that conveyed much more than simple photos usually did.

"Are these published in a book or something?" Isabel had always respected Kash's talent as a photographer; she thought her reputation well deserved. Her celebrity portraits also captured their subjects in an authentic and insightfully unique way. But while the star shots nearly always had some element of unexpected humor, these portraits painted a moving snapshot of the common man, caught at work. Isabel thought it was remarkable how well Kash was able to convey whether the subjects enjoyed or despised their labors.

"No. These are some photos from my travels, many years ago."

"You have a fine talent, Kash," Nazim remarked, and their Egyptian host and his wife echoed his enthusiasm.

As she studied the photos, Isabel sensed that Kash had probably spent some time getting to know her subjects, to ensure that whatever pose and expression she chose to represent them reflected their true nature, just as her celebrity shots did. And this realization made her relax quite a lot about how she would be portrayed in *Sophisticated Women*. Although she still abhorred the media attention that her appearance on the cover would likely generate, at least she felt confident that the cover would not be something she would dislike. *Kash will show me only in a positive way, I'm sure.*

"You should let people see these," she urged as Kash exited her photo program. Their hosts were now in the kitchen preparing breakfast, and Nazim was helping out, so they had a few minutes out of earshot. They were lounging side by side on pillows, Kash seated, her laptop on a low table in front of her, and Isabel lying on her side, propped up on one elbow. "They're extraordinary."

Kash faced her. She was used to people complimenting her photographs. But usually her popular advertisements or sexy model shots drew the attention. "Most people like the other stuff I do."

"Oh, I think you do all types of photography well, Kash," Isabel said. "You have a wonderful eye. But I like these best. These…well, these are *art*. They *say* something. They make you *think*." She blushed, suddenly embarrassed. "Oh, sorry. I don't mean to imply that your magazine covers and other stuff aren't important."

Kash smiled. "I know what you mean, Isabel. No offense taken. In fact, I'm happy you appreciate what I was trying for with these."

"So…if that was what you were trying for, why haven't you put them out there?"

Kash considered her answer. "Those were all shot before I got famous. I took three months for myself and traveled the world. I always intended them to be part of something larger, but I got sidetracked from that idea not long after I got back."

"Sidetracked?"

"Got my first magazine cover," Kash supplied. "And things kind of took off for me quickly after that. I mean, I got deluged with offers, and then I met Lainie."

Isabel nodded. "It's a shame you didn't pursue that project. These photographs could open some minds."

Kash started to say she had, in fact, been thinking about picking up that long-delayed project, which was why she'd dug out the photos in the first place. But a sudden change in Isabel's expression stopped her.

Isabel had happened to glance at Kash's laptop. When she did, she sat up abruptly and a quick succession of reactions crossed her face—confusion, then recognition, then horror.

By the time Kash glanced back at the computer, the picture displayed was of a smiling Isabel at the Eiffel Tower.

That's obviously not what she's upset about. As she quickly closed the lid of the laptop, Kash berated herself for not remembering her screen saver. She'd set it to randomly display her growing folder of contest/trip photos, so it was filled with shots of Isabel. Among them were the ones she'd taken with her telephoto lens of Isabel climaxing in the hot tub. That had to have been what she had seen. *Damn.*

"What the hell was that?" Isabel asked, so loud that Nazim poked his head through the doorway from the kitchen.

"Is everything all right?"

"Yes, fine." Kash waved him off, and he took the hint and returned to what he'd been doing.

"I asked you a question, Kash." Isabel kept her voice down, but she made no attempt to hide her outrage. She knew precisely what she had seen, though she had only glimpsed the picture. Among others, Kash had secretly photographed her with a telephoto lens as she masturbated, capturing her with vivid clarity right as she climaxed.

Kash wouldn't meet her eyes. "I apologize, Isabel. And I'll delete those photos. I promise you. I shouldn't have taken them."

"That's an understatement. Talk about invasion of privacy! Why did you?"

Kash shrugged and shifted uneasily on the pillow. "I'd had a lot to drink."

The apology and explanation didn't help. "That's no excuse. What you did was unbelievably callous. And unimaginably indiscreet—having them on your laptop like that where anyone could see them! What were you going to do with these? Do you take pictures of the women you've fucked to keep as trophies?"

"No, Isabel, of course not. No one would have seen them. No one."

Isabel got to her feet. "That doesn't carry a lot of weight with me, Kash. You totally disrespected me and disregarded my feelings."

"You have every right to be angry."

"No shit. You know, Kash, you're not one to talk about how women have used and taken advantage of you. You need to look in a mirror. How have you been treating me?"

When Kash stared down at her feet and didn't answer, Isabel left her alone to consider what she had said. She needed some time as well. This was a new side of Kash, and she didn't like it one bit. She couldn't remember when she'd been this angry.

CHAPTER NINETEEN

Kash suffered all day, feeling more claustrophobic by the minute trapped in that house with Isabel's silent fury and her own guilt. They spoke little, Isabel spending her time with their Egyptian hosts while Kash pretended to be absorbed with her laptop. Finally, in the late afternoon, the sandstorm abated, and not long after, Nazim reappeared after a long absence, saying he and a local had managed to clean enough sand from their car's engine for it to run again. They were able to negotiate around or through the drifts on the road back to Cairo, and they reached their hotel as the sun was setting.

"Nazim, I probably won't need you until we leave for the airport on Friday," she told him as he stopped to let them out. "Please make yourself available to Isabel until then, and take her wherever she wants to go. I'll contact you if my plans change."

"Certainly, Kash."

Isabel exited the vehicle and sped into the hotel without further acknowledging Kash.

I don't blame you. Not one bit. It was a shitty thing to do. And I'd been treating you badly even before that. Isabel's disappointment and rage made Kash's heart clench. She hated hurting her. Hated it. *But maybe it's for the best. You're much better off without me. And now you know it. Yes, it's best for both of us.*

Even as she thought the words, she knew they were a lie. For her, anyway. She could never believe she was better off without Isabel. But to believe that there might be any future together? That was still too terrifying to really contemplate.

Rasui, the concierge, intercepted her before she reached the elevators. "Miss Kash! Have you seen your messages?"

"Messages?"

"Yes. You received several urgent telephone calls last night and this morning. The messages are in your suite."

"Thank you for the heads-up."

More than a dozen slips had been pushed under her door. Eight were from news organizations, one was from her assistant Ramona, three were from Miranda, and two were from Stella England, the hottest young actress in Hollywood and the current favorite cover girl of tabloids around the world. All asked her to call them as soon as possible. Miranda, because she had phoned three times, got the first call.

"It's Kash. What's going on?" she asked as soon as the publisher came on the line.

"Kash! Where the hell have you been? Did Stella England get in touch with you?"

Kash fingered the message slips with Stella's name on them. One call had come in the previous afternoon, the other this morning. "I have two calls here from her, yes. But I haven't returned them yet. I just got in. What's this all about, Miranda?"

"Stella's publicist issued a press release last night. She's getting married tomorrow, somewhere in Europe, but she won't say to whom or where or anything."

"I didn't even know she was seeing anyone," Kash mused aloud.

"No one did. No one has a clue who he is. Here's the catch, Kash. She says she'll only let *you* photograph this secret wedding."

"Me? Did she say why?" Kash knew the reason. She had shared a memorable night with the actress not six months ago, but she doubted Stella would have shared that information.

"Not really. Only that she trusted you would do a great job, without being intrusive."

"So that's why I have all these messages from the networks." Kash flipped through the rest of the slips.

"Only the first of many, I'm sure. You haven't gotten more than that only because most of them don't know how to reach you. I know you have to do this, Kash…but since you *are* leaving a job you're doing for me, how about you give *Sophisticated Women* first crack at the photos, if Stella agrees? We can still get one on next month's cover."

Kash fell silent, her mind racing. Of course she had to do this; it would be a big coup professionally, and the rights to the photos would be worth a lot of money.

It was also the perfect opportunity to get away from Isabel for a while and get her shit together. *And maybe not for just a while. Maybe this is my opportunity to make a clean, quick break. Better and easier that way. And with Isabel feeling like she does about me right now, she probably won't be disappointed to see me leave.*

"Kash?" Miranda repeated. "Kash? You there?"

"I'm here. Miranda, we may be able to work something out. Here's what I have in mind…"

❖

Isabel returned to an empty suite as well. Gillian had left a message saying she and Ambra were out sightseeing, so Isabel showered and changed, intending to head out, too. But she hung around the suite a while, pacing, still furious with Kash, unable to get the photos she'd seen on the laptop out of her mind. When she discovered that the knock at her door belonged to the object of her musings, she started to launch into her again—until she noticed Kash's carry-on bag at her feet.

"Hey," Kash said.

"Going somewhere, I see."

"Yes," Kash confirmed. "I know you're still angry. And you have every reason to be. But I'd like to talk to you a few minutes. May I come in?"

"All right." She stepped to the side to admit Kash, who dropped her bag just inside the door, then proceeded into the sitting area.

"Stella England's getting married," Kash said as she settled onto one end of the couch. "Tomorrow morning, on one of the Greek islands. She's giving me an exclusive on photos of the ceremony."

"Stella England?" Isabel repeated. "Who's she marrying?"

Kash didn't answer immediately. That little tidbit was worth a lot of money, and she knew that Stella trusted her not to do anything that might tip off the press before she was ready. But she also knew she could trust Isabel. "You can't tell anyone, and I mean *anyone*, even Gillian."

"I won't."

"Frankly, I can't believe she's kept it a secret this long. She's marrying Joshua Greenbriar."

"Joshua Greenbriar? The director? Isn't he like…what, thirty years older than she is?"

"Something like that. And you know what? I don't think it's a big publicity gimmick. She sounded like she sincerely loves the guy."

"Well, then, more power to her, I say. I'm all for following your heart, wherever it leads you." As upset and angry with Kash as Isabel was, she didn't welcome the news Kash was leaving. Taking the hot-tub photos of her was extremely insensitive, but Kash had been apologetic, and Isabel wanted to believe her regret was sincere. She just needed time to calm down and forgive Kash. And she wanted Kash to think hard about what she had done. *So maybe a little time apart isn't so bad. It will give us both time to get over things. But it will also be time taken away from our precious nine days left together.*

"Somehow I knew you'd feel that way," Kash replied. *Ever the romantic, Isabel. Love knows no boundaries and all that. I hope you never change. The world would do a lot better with more pie-eyed optimists, like you, and fewer cynics, like me.*

"So how long will you be gone? Will you get back before we leave for the Bahamas?"

"That's the thing…" Kash began, avoiding her eyes.

The pause that followed was so long that Isabel filled in the blanks herself. "You're not…coming back?"

"The happy couple is going to drop out of sight for a while for the honeymoon, so the media frenzy will center around me, I'm afraid," Kash confirmed. "The only guests will be family, and they won't be talking. So I'll be busy for several days afterward, doing interviews and figuring out who gets what photos."

"You won't be able to make it to the Bahamas at all?" *I'm never going to see you again, am I?* The realization felt like a punch to the stomach.

"No, I'm afraid not. As you know, Miranda is sending a correspondent to meet you in Nassau to interview you about the trip. I've asked her to book a local photographer to tag along, so we'll have pictures of every stop for the layout."

Isabel frowned. "I don't care about the magazine, Kash. I keep telling you that. But I hate it that you're apparently telling me we won't ever see each other again. I may be pissed as hell at you at the moment, but I…I'm not ready to say good-bye."

I know exactly how you feel. Although she had firmly resolved to deliver the news and then leave, all nice and clean and tidy, Kash couldn't do it. She knew what she *should* do, but her mind and heart and body wanted nothing more than to take Isabel in her arms, beg her forgiveness, and tell her that good-bye was a word she never wanted uttered between them. *Jesus, will you listen to yourself? Pretty powerful stuff you have there, Isabel, if your romanticism can even rub off on me.*

She forced herself to her feet. "Ready or not, as they say. I have a plane to catch."

Isabel rose, too, and they faced each other without speaking for several seconds before Kash stepped to Isabel to kiss her good-bye. She knew Isabel might likely push her away, but she had to take the chance. She couldn't resist one more press of lips before they parted.

Tentatively, Kash brushed her mouth over Isabel's and felt her heart swell in her chest, the grief of loss already acute.

Isabel pulled back, but only a few inches. And her voice, when she spoke, was as gentle as Kash's mouth had been. "I'm still angry with you."

"I know." Kash kissed her again, and when Isabel responded by running her tongue along the contours of Kash's mouth, then nipping at Kash's lower lip, Kash's control dissolved. She opened her mouth and met Isabel's tongue with her own, deepening the kiss as she pulled their bodies tight together.

Isabel slid her hands around her neck, and they remained locked together, pouring all of their long-held passion into that kiss, until they had to break apart to breathe, bodies shaking crazily, hearts hammering in sync.

"I'm still angry with you," Isabel repeated as she clung to her, breathing heavily against her neck. "But you know I'll forgive you."

"I won't forget you." The most unexpected thing of all, in this whole alien world that she'd been inhabiting since Isabel had entered her life, were the tears Kash fought. She considered tears a weakness, so they gave her the courage she needed to gently extricate herself from Isabel's embrace. No one, not even Isabel, would see her cry.

She picked up her bag and left before Isabel could say any more, and she never looked back. Not once. She didn't have to. Isabel's face would be vividly imprinted on her mind forever, every bit as much as the taste of her lips.

Chapter Twenty

Anything yet?" It was the third time Gillian had called. She was nearly as anxious as Isabel to see the October issue of *Sophisticated Women*.

"No. Nothing. The mail finally came, and it wasn't there. But UPS doesn't usually get around this way for another hour or two, so that's still possible. Don't know about FedEx or any of the other delivery services."

"I wish you'd asked Miranda how she was sending it," Gillian complained.

"I didn't talk to her. I just got an e-mail saying she was sending me an advance copy. She didn't say how."

"What are you wearing to this thing next week? And do you think Kash will be there?"

"One of my new cocktail dresses, not sure which yet. And I have no idea. You know I haven't heard from her." *Not one damn word in two and a half months. Not one. Like you don't even owe me the common courtesy of an explanation why. I guess you didn't hear a thing I said.*

"Oops, customer. Gotta run. Call you about dinner later."

"Okay, Gill." Isabel hung up and stared at her computer terminal. It was displaying pictures of Kash in a slide show—some that she and Gillian had taken, and others she'd gotten off the Internet. *Such a masochist you've become. You need a new screen saver. And you need to get out more.* Isabel was almost as angry with herself as she was with Kash.

The fact that Kash hadn't called or written since Cairo should have been ample reason to let her go and move on, never mind the hot-tub photos and her cold distance after their sexual encounters. *Just more evidence I meant nothing to her. She's a player, and that's all she'll ever be,* she reminded herself. *She won't allow herself to get emotionally involved.*

But try as she might to push Kash from her mind, she'd been unable to. She'd glimpsed the vulnerable woman inside that cold exterior, and her heart believed that something very real and deep and *mutual* had been developing between them. Nothing, not even Kash's silence since Cairo, had been able to quash that belief.

Where are you, Kash? Why haven't you called? Could I have been so very wrong about you? Isabel had been searching online nearly every day for some hint of what Kash was up to, but had found nothing at all about her in the news or tabloids after all the hoopla about the wedding photos had died down.

Her only foreseeable opportunity to see her again would be at the bash next week that Miranda had invited her to. A party at a chic Manhattan restaurant to celebrate the release of the issue with her picture on the cover.

I still wish I knew what that phone call was all about. Miranda had called her not long after they'd gotten home from the Bahamas, ostensibly to welcome her back from the trip. They'd had a nice chat, and at Miranda's urging, she had shared a few stories about some of the things she'd seen and experienced, careful to avoid anything she didn't want to end up in the magazine.

Miranda had been saying good-bye when she threw one last question at Isabel as though it was an afterthought.

"Say, Isabel, I won't be offended if you answer this the way I think you will. But Kash mentioned that you didn't want to be on the cover. She said you didn't want this whole magazine thing at all. Is that right?"

"Gosh, Miranda. I wish she hadn't told you that. I don't want to seem ungrateful for all the wonderful things that winning your contest has done for me."

"So it is true," Miranda said, her warm tone conveying that she was perfectly okay with the admission.

"Yes. It is. I have no desire to be famous. But I know you've promoted this and invested a lot of money in it and everything. Kash explained."

"Isabel, I'm going to fax you a waiver to sign," Miranda said. *"It essentially will say you're okay with us not living up to our promise to put you exclusively on the cover and make you the subject of our feature article. I'll try to scale back our coverage, if possible. No promises. But this waiver ensures you can't come at me later and complain you didn't get everything you won. Okay?"*

"Sure. Send it over. I'd appreciate anything you could do. That would be great!"

"No promises," Miranda repeated.

She had faxed it to Isabel that day, and Isabel had returned it, signed, within the hour.

Maybe it won't be so bad. She dreaded the media attention she would likely get when the magazine hit newsstands. Her mind flashed back to the rude, probing questions the tabloid reporters had shouted at Kash during the kickoff press conference. And worst of all had been her nightmare of a fall. But despite her anger and better judgment, she knew she'd suffer it all again for the chance to see Kash. Because no amount of time, or distance, or return to her normal routine had changed how much she thought about Kash. Day and night. Waking and dreaming. Even Kash's silence couldn't deter her.

She hadn't known precisely when it had happened, the moment her fascination with Kash had gone from lust to love. But it had. Probably fairly early on, she decided. Maybe when Kash had first opened up to her about her past and how she'd been hurt. Or perhaps when Kash had awakened Isa. *Not that she's been out much since.* The new sexual side that she'd discovered in Europe had totally disappeared. She enjoyed the attention she got with her new look, new clothes, and more confident attitude. But she'd had no real interest in dating other women since she'd been home. She was still longing for Kash.

Gillian called her a hopeless romantic, and she'd certainly realized the truth in that statement. *Once you fall in love, it's for keeps, hopeless or not.* Meeting Kash had made that fact all too agonizingly clear.

She was being utterly ridiculous, she knew, to go on mooning over her this way. Kash probably hadn't thought about her for two minutes. If she had, she'd have called. *Then why did she say that? She could have just said good-bye. But no. Her last words to me had to be those.*

"I won't forget you."

And I can't forget you, either, Kash.

Her doorbell startled her so much she jumped. Her heart was thudding at a pretty good clip, but its speed increased exponentially when she opened the large express envelope that the UPS driver had brought.

She wasn't on the cover at all.

Kash was.

A beautiful, relaxed, and carefree-looking Kash, smiling at the camera in some kind of breezy tropical setting. Her skin was dark from the sun, and she wore a white linen short-sleeved shirt. *Nice. Very nice.*

The cover caption read IT'S KASH WHO GOT THE MAKEOVER, NOT OUR CONTEST WINNER!

Below it, Miranda had attached a large Post-it note on which she'd written

> *Hello, Isabel!*
> *Read page 6 first,*
> *then flip to page 23.*
> *– Miranda*

The first reference was to Miranda's Letter from the Publisher page. It had a photograph of her at her desk, with Kash standing behind her. Her missive read:

Dear Readers,

This month's issue was supposed to feature Isabel Sterling—the winner of our Make Your Dreams Come True contest—as our cover girl, along with an in-depth interview of her and a pictorial spread of the fabulous dream vacation and makeover she won.

You'll still find the scoop on Isabel's trip inside (see page 23), but the greatest impact of this adventure was not on the contest winner, but on Kash, who was supposed to be along only to take some pictures and have some fun.

Kash happens to be a friend of mine, which is why she agreed to photograph Isabel's experience in the first place. But no amount of threats or pleas or cajoling has ever before been enough to convince her to sit down for an interview with *Sophisticated Women*, let alone agree to be on the cover.

So I was rather surprised, to say the least, when she volunteered for both. Kash says it is all a matter of timing—and that now she has something to say. When you read her story, which follows Isabel's, I think you'll agree.

Miranda

Isabel flipped to page 23 and found a two-page collage of images taken of her during her trip. Most were the formal photos she expected, but Kash had included candids as well, including two with Gillian. She was a little shocked at how well they'd turned out. She'd never considered herself particularly photogenic before, but...*I have to admit, I look pretty hot in these.* The photo spread was followed by transcripted portions of the interview that the reporter from *Sophisticated Women* had conducted with her in Nassau.

All in all, she was happy with it—the article was tasteful, not too invasive. She flipped the next page and came to Kash's story, written in her own words.

I have to be honest and say that when it came time to leave on my assignment for *Sophisticated Women*, I tried to get out of it. It had been several months since I had promised my friend Miranda (in a moment of weakness) to accompany the winner of the Make Your Dreams Come True contest on her trip and photograph her for the magazine. And although the idea of dropping in on Paris, Rome, Cairo and the Bahamas for a while was attractive, I was concerned about being so long and so far away from my office.

But Miranda kept me to my promise, though neither of us had any idea at the time that my attachment to this project would result in anything more than a brief detour from the clientele and business I had been building for two decades. She hoped that her contest and makeover might prove to be a thrilling adventure—and a new start, perhaps—for some lucky reader. Instead, it would be my life that got the makeover.

I guess I should start at the beginning, shouldn't I? Well, I didn't quite believe Isabel Sterling when she first told me that she had no interest in her promised appearance in this magazine and chance to be its cover girl. I knew by then that she hadn't entered herself in the contest [*Editor's note—see Isabel's story on page 23*], but let's say that it had been my experience that few women would refuse the chance for their fifteen minutes of fame.

I also had trouble believing that any woman might not welcome the makeover that came with the prize, though Isabel insisted she was content with the way she was.

But then I got to know her, and guess what? She was right. Though she ended up pleasantly thrilled with the new look that Clifton gave her, Isabel certainly didn't need any kind of beautification project, that's for sure. She is a remarkable woman just as she is, inside and out. The kind of woman, in my mind, we should all aspire to be.

I'm sure you know the type. The salt-of-the-earth, sweet and caring kind of woman who's the first to bring you soup when you're sick. Or volunteer to listen if you're having a rough time of it. But who also isn't afraid to tell you straight-out when you're making a fool of yourself or taking the wrong course, if she feels that knowledge will help you. And most of all, she's the optimist we all need in our lives—someone who will rush to assure us that everything will be all right, that it's never to late to realize our dreams, that we're never too old to change.

Nope, it wasn't Isabel who needed the big makeover—though the contest win couldn't have gone to a nicer and more deserving individual. As it happens, it was my life that needed a little shaking up, and Isabel helped me realize that.

Isabel's eyes were so moist that she could hardly see the words on the page. She blinked hard and swiped at her tears with the back of her hand before she continued to read.

Long ago, when I first started taking pictures, I intended for each and every photograph to say something meaningful. I wanted my body of work to be something that I could reflect on as having artfully reflected my point of view, while at the same time perhaps opened a few minds, changed a few opinions or broadened a few perspectives.

But somewhere along the line, I got waylaid, as so many do—by money, and fame, and the ever-present invitation to the next A-list party full of the rich, and powerful, and beautiful.

And still I had the gall to be annoyed when some tabloid or other chronicled my misadventures with alcohol and women for all the world to witness.

Well, you won't be seeing as much of me in the celebrity rags, I'm happy to report. It's time for me to step out of the public eye, get my act together and start taking some responsibility for my actions. Besides, I'm too busy with a project I've been putting off for too many years— the chance to take the kind of photographs I'm most passionate about, in anticipation of a one-woman show in New York sometime early next year. You'll see a few examples of what I'm talking about on the next page.

Isabel flipped ahead and found several of the photographs she'd seen on Kash's laptop, along with some additional portraits done in the same vein. *Good for you, Kash. Good for you.* She flipped back to continue reading the final paragraphs of Kash's story.

Here in a nutshell are a few of the lessons I took from Isabel Sterling. I pass them along for you to consider.

Follow your heart wherever it leads you, take risks to pursue your dreams, keep a sense of humor in all things, and never let anyone convince you that something is impossible.

Kash

Isabel ran her fingers lightly over the words on the page. *Oh, Kash. Why couldn't you have said any of this to me?* Then she noticed the addendum from Miranda at the bottom of the page, and her heart sank.

Editor's note: When last contacted, Kash was somewhere in the Himalayas, on her way to photograph sherpas at the base of Mount Everest.

For a moment, Isabel considered skipping the *Sophisticated Women* party, since Kash apparently wasn't going to be there after all. But Miranda had sent tickets to both her and Gillian, and Gillian was really looking forward to it. Besides, in light of Kash's article, perhaps Miranda might be willing to put her in touch with Kash.

Chapter Twenty-one

Come *on*, already, Isabel! I swear to God, if you aren't ready to go in two minutes I'm leaving without you." Gillian was decked out in one of Isabel's designer dresses, an avant-garde evening gown the color of eggplant cut so high on one side that Isabel didn't dare wear it herself, for fear of exposing more than she wanted to at an event where photographers were sure to be present.

"Don't get your britches in a wad," Isabel responded good-naturedly as she emerged from the bathroom of their suite and joined her friend in the sitting room. "What do you think?" She pivoted so Gillian could get the full effect and was gratified to hear her low whistle of approval.

"*Hot*, Izzy, and I do mean sizzling. Damn shame Kash won't be there."

"Thanks, Gill." Isabel took one last look at herself in the large wall mirror, still somewhat unaccustomed to the sight of herself all dolled up in a designer exclusive that was worth more than she made in a month. It was a cocktail dress in a smoky blue-gray, the color of a stormy sky, with a shimmery underlayer that caught the light as she moved, directing one's eyes to the nicely rounded curves of her hips, ass, and breasts. *Not bad, if I do say so myself.*

Miranda had conveniently booked them a suite at the Four Seasons. Since the magazine's soirée was to take place at the hotel's famed restaurant, L'Atelier de Joël Robuchon, they merely had to take the elevator down forty-nine floors to join the party.

When they stepped off the elevator, Gillian screamed, "Oh my

God! Ambra," and rushed into the arms of her Italian girlfriend, who appeared to be waiting for them.

"Ambra?" Isabel repeated as she crossed to them. Ambra had an *I've got a secret* expression on her face. "What are you doing here?"

"Yeah!" Gillian pulled back from their embrace to address Ambra. "What's going on? Your e-mail this morning said you were in Naples."

"She's here to keep Gillian company so I could have you all to myself. I'd hate to have to beg your forgiveness in front of an audience." Kash's voice, from directly behind her, was such a surprise that Isabel was afraid she might faint.

She whirled around unsteadily, and her breath caught when she saw a smiling Kash looking tanned, fit, and irresistibly dashing in a black suit and starched white shirt—her own classically elegant version of a tux.

"What? How?" she stuttered.

"There's no magazine party," Kash explained. "All a ruse, I'm afraid, to get you here."

"A ruse," Isabel repeated in a daze. *Is this really happening? Can you really be here?*

"Yup." Kash turned to Gillian and Ambra. "You have reservations in the restaurant in Gillian's name. Please order whatever you like and have a fun evening, on me. I know you'll forgive me if we don't join you?"

Gillian let go of Ambra long enough to plant a kiss on Kash's cheek. "I apparently underestimated you, Kash, I'm happy to say. Be good to her. And thanks." She whispered in Isabel's ear, "Pretty soon you're going to have even me believing that dreams can come true. I'm so happy for you, Izzy. And *details*! I expect *details*."

"Don't hold your breath," Isabel replied with a smile as Gillian reached for Ambra and they headed off toward the restaurant, arm in arm.

They were in the lobby of one of the most popular hotels in Manhattan, but Isabel felt suddenly as though she and Kash were the only two people on the planet.

"So you planned all this…" *God, you're so scrumptious. No woman should look so good. How can I be as angry with you as I should be, when you're so irresistible?* "…just to ask me to forgive you?"

"Well, I have a lot to apologize for," Kash replied, gazing into her eyes with a new, vulnerable directness that warmed Isabel. "And I was kind of hoping that if you accept my apology, we might also…talk. Really talk. About *us*. And how we feel about each other."

"Talk?" Isabel repeated dumbly. "Talking's good."

"And if the talking goes well," Kash added cheekily, "maybe we can throw in some touching, too?"

The way Kash said the word *touching*…slowly, with meaning, as her eyes caught Isabel's with unguarded yearning…made Isabel feel as though Kash was already undressing her.

"I…I think that can be arranged," Isabel replied, trying not to stammer. *You're supposed to be mad at her*, she reminded herself.

"Although…with you in that dress, I'm going to be hard-pressed to do the talking before the touching. You're stunning, Isabel."

She could feel her cheeks warm under the compliment. "I still can't believe you're here."

"Better get used to it," Kash replied softly, her cocky façade dissolving as she closed the distance and took Isabel in her arms. "God, how I've missed you," she whispered as they clung to each other.

"Me, too, Kash," Isabel whispered back. She thrilled at the press of their bodies against each other and wondered whether Kash could feel how her heart was fluttering wildly. "I've been damn angry with you, yes. But I never stopped missing you. Wanting you. So much. I thought I'd never see you again."

"Pretty relieved you're happy to see me," Kash said. "I sure did everything I could to push you away."

"Yes, you did. I hope you've smartened up."

Kash heard her name called and glanced up to see a cluster of Japanese tourists watching them curiously. "Say…Isabel? You mind if we continue this in private?"

Isabel turned to see what Kash was looking at, just as one of the gawkers snapped a photo, blinding her with the flash. "Sounds like a plan."

Kash took her hand and led her to a private elevator, and soon they were headed up.

"I hope you don't mind," Kash said, shifting her weight from foot to foot. Rehearsing this meeting a dozen times had failed to calm her nerves. "I imagined the best-case scenario and arranged to have dinner for us in my suite."

"Your suite?" Isabel asked. "You're staying here?"

Kash laughed. "Two floors above you. This still hasn't quite sunk in, has it?"

"No. It's like a dream." Isabel sighed as she looped an arm through Kash's. "You make it kind of tough to stay furious with you."

"I sure hope so."

The elevator stopped on the fifty-first floor and Kash led her to one of the hotel's two presidential suites, a fifteen-hundred-square-foot plush accommodation that boasted original oil paintings, a full marble bathroom, gas fireplace, library, and floor-to-ceiling windows, with a spectacular view of Central Park and downtown Manhattan.

The dining table was set with the finest linen and china, champagne was chilling in an ice bucket, and fresh flowers adorned nearly every available surface.

"Is this all right?" Kash asked uncertainly. She stuck her hands in her pockets so Isabel wouldn't see how badly she was shaking. *How you throw me off balance when I look at you. And here I thought it was impossible for me to feel nervous around a woman.*

"It's wonderful," Isabel said, taking it all in as she glided into the room. They stood for a long moment, fifteen feet apart, staring at each other, not moving, before she spoke again. "Or I should say…it's wonderful if it's the start of something, Kash, and not just your guilt talking. Or a classier way to get me into bed, only to pull away from me again without explanation."

"I deserve that. And more." Kash ran her hand through her hair. "Isabel, I've been a fool, behaving badly from start to finish. I should've called, sent flowers, written. *Something.* I know. But I was afraid. Afraid you wouldn't forgive me. Afraid you'd moved on. And I needed to make some changes first. I wanted to make sure I was capable of being the kind of woman you deserve."

"And now?"

"Now I'm willing to do whatever it takes to be a part of your life. As much as you'll let me," Kash said. "I've changed, Isabel. I'm still changing. And it's all very much for the better, thanks to you."

"I believe that's true. Sure, in part, because I want to believe it," Isabel said. "But I also read the article. It really touched me."

"The one thing I couldn't say in the article," Kash said, taking one tentative step toward Isabel, "is how much I love you. But I really wanted to say that in person anyway."

Isabel closed her eyes and let the words sink in. *She loves me.*

She felt the hurt and disappointment of the last several weeks begin to fade.

"Isabel?"

When she opened her eyes again, Kash was watching her with such fearfully anxious anticipation that she knew things would be all right. *She really does love me.*

She forgave Kash fully and let go of the rest of her anger. "Well, I guess you're damn lucky, then, that the feeling is quite mutual."

"Mutual?" Kash's face relaxed and a relieved grin turned up the corners of her mouth. She still had her hands firmly in her pockets, as though she didn't know what to do with them.

"Very. I love you, too, Kash."

The grin got bigger and Kash bounced up and down on the balls of her feet. "Great. That's great!" It was kind of adorable, actually, Isabel thought, the way this worldly playgirl had been suddenly reduced to acting like a schoolgirl with her first crush.

"You really look hot, by the way," Isabel said. Kash had never appeared more...*movie-star dashing* seemed the right description. Her tanned skin against the white shirt, the flattering cut of her suit, the light brown highlights in her hair from her time in the sun.

Kash's expression gained an aw-shucks kind of Cary Grant debonair that fit right in with her tuxedoed elegance. "Uh...hungry?" she asked, running a hand through her hair. "They'll send up the food as soon as I make a call."

Eating was actually the very last thing on Kash's mind. Her stomach was in knots—*she loves me!*—and all she could think about was how badly she needed to touch Isabel. All that soft, fair, delectable skin, just out of reach, aching to be kissed and caressed. She was nervous and excited and terrified in a way she had never imagined she could be. Though she thought she had experienced almost everything possible about sex, this felt entirely different. *As it should be. This time I will really be making love.*

She had imagined it many times in the past weeks. Hoped for it. Prayed that her stupidity hadn't killed any opportunity for a future with Isabel. *Remember. Slow. Tender.* But she wanted to tear that dress off Isabel. *I've wanted you for so long. And since you, I've wanted no other.*

And now what? She was on unsteady ground, already so aroused she was ready to blow, but Isabel's needs and wants were what had become most important to her, which was a rarity. *I so want to please you, Isabel.*

Isabel swallowed hard. The way Kash was looking at her—like her dress was transparent. *Hungry, all right, but certainly not for what room service has to offer. So why are you holding back?*

She thought she knew the answer. *You're waiting for me, aren't you?* "Don't tell me you're really thinking about food at a time like this." She smiled encouragingly as she walked slowly toward Kash and was relieved to see her breathing visibly increase as she neared.

Oh, Isabel. What you do to me. Who can resist that? Who? "All I can think about is how much I want you." Kash pulled Isabel to her as soon as she got within reach and kissed her, hard. Fiercely. She splayed one hand across Isabel's bare back, and her heart soared at the first touch of warm skin beneath her fingertips. She let the other hand descend to Isabel's ass and fondled it firmly as her tongue filled Isabel's mouth.

Isabel surrendered eagerly, instantly molding her body to Kash's and wrapping her arms around Kash's neck. She sucked lightly on Kash's tongue and moaned, long, a needy sound from the back of her throat.

*Oh, Christ, Isabel. When you do that…*Kash felt many of her resolutions to herself slip away as she kissed Isabel. Trying to prolong this moment felt close to impossible. She knew she was already wet; hell, she'd denied herself for so long that by the time today dawned she was so profoundly horny in anticipation she had barely managed to keep from getting herself off.

Isabel's tongue sought its own opportunity for exploration, and she allowed it, granting Isabel access to the warmth of her mouth. Their tongues stroked—deep, wet, slow exchanges. Isabel nipped her lower lip and she responded with an answering bite, proprietary. Their mouths conveyed what words could not about how long and how much they had wanted and waited for this.

Their lips parted, but just barely. They remained locked together, every possible inch of their bodies that could touch pressed against the corresponding body part of the other—thigh, pelvis, stomach, breasts. Even their foreheads still touched. Both of them were breathing hard, but they were reluctant to disengage even the slightest bit.

"God, Isabel…so much…" Kash felt as though every muscle in her body was tight as a bowstring. She was poised, and ready, instinct urging *take her, just take her to the bed and throw her down on it. Enough already!*

But another inner voice was battling for dominance now, the one born during their time apart. The one that had spent endless days contemplating what her life would be like with, and without, Isabel. She wanted to do everything right, and she had vowed to herself to make it an evening Isabel would remember well. *The best.* "Tell me what you want," she managed, though her throat was so tight her request came out funny, in kind of a breathy exhalation.

"I want what you want, Kash." Isabel squeezed her tighter and kissed her cheek wetly before she moved her mouth to Kash's ear. "I want your hands on me. And your mouth." She sucked on Kash's earlobe, and Kash's clit felt every movement of her mouth.

"I want us to get these damn clothes off so I can feel you against me," she continued in a provocative purr. "And on top of me and, most of all, inside me. Filling me up and making me come."

Kash whimpered and gripped Isabel's ass tighter.

"So if you don't get me in a bed in about ten seconds I'm going to have to take control of the situation and drag you there myself." Isabel barely got the words out before Kash was propelling her, with firm hands on her waist, directly to the suite's king-sized bed.

When they stood beside it, Kash loosened her grip and put her hands lightly on Isabel's shoulders, pausing as her fingers slipped beneath the straps of her dress until Isabel met her eyes. Only then, when she saw the clear desire there, the need as demanding as her own, did she pull the straps down and expose Isabel's breasts.

She sucked in a breath at her first glimpse of those soft swells, the ivory skin, the nipples pink and erect. They were round and high, and a bit larger than her own, and she had begun the task of choosing which to taste first...when she became aware that Isabel had a hand on the clasp of her trousers. From long habit alone, she reached down to stop her.

"Please, Kash. I need to feel how wet I make you." Isabel continued as though unimpeded—for although Kash's hand remained wrapped around her forearm, it was a loose and unenthusiastic restraint.

By the time Isabel had the clasp unfastened and the zipper down, Kash had withdrawn her hand completely. She could deny Isabel nothing. For the first time in a very long while, she wanted to touch someone so badly that it would drive her mad if she didn't. And she couldn't deny herself, either. She wanted and needed Isabel's touch.

When Isabel loosened the buttons low on her shirt and lightly grazed her abdomen, the heavy thudding of her heart in her chest almost overwhelmed her. She found it hard to breathe. "Christ, Isabel."

"All right?" Isabel put her mouth on Kash's neck as her hand widened its caress of Kash's lower abdomen.

"Yes. Very." It was hard to speak. "But…not yet. As soon as you touch me, I'll…I won't last long."

"Sure, Kash." Isabel's gentle exploration detoured around Kash's waist, sensitizing the skin it passed over. Her tongue traced Kash's jawline just as lightly. "Why don't you finish taking my dress off? That will delay things a bit."

"Not necessarily," Kash confessed, smiling, and she could feel Isabel's satisfied chuckle as a low vibration against her neck. "But yes. Please."

Isabel turned to allow Kash access to the snap on her dress, low on her back.

As Kash unfastened it with trembling hands and let the dress fall to the floor, she kissed Isabel between her shoulder blades. Isabel hummed her approval, stepped out of the dress, and faced Kash, wearing only her heels and brief silk panties, a shade lighter than her dress.

CHAPTER TWENTY-TWO

You are…a feast for the eyes, Isabel." Kash drank in the well-proportioned curves and planes of Isabel's body, letting her eyes linger on the wonderful subtle shadows created by breasts, hip bones, navel, and the V of her legs, taking mental photographs of the unique landscape she had hours ahead to explore. She could feel herself getting wetter by the minute, and she imagined how Isabel would find her when she finally touched her there.

The anticipation was excruciating. She was dizzy with desire, dancing on the precipice of pain.

"I'm glad you think so. Now it's your turn." Isabel stepped close again and reached up to unbutton the remaining buttons on Kash's shirt. She brushed her fingertips into the crevice between Kash's breasts and popped the first button. "I really love your body." The second button went. Her touch was perfect torture in its teasing indirectness. "I only got a glimpse that first day in your studio. When you changed your shirt?" The third button went, and the shirt fell open, revealing Kash's white lace bra, stark against her tanned body. "So beautiful," Isabel said, reverent, adoring.

Isabel slipped Kash's suit coat and shirt off and reached for the front hook of Kash's bra. When it, too, was undone, she stared openly and admiringly at Kash's breasts and licked her lips. *What a magnificent body.* "I'm going to taste every inch of you tonight," she promised. Isa was back, with a vengeance, and she wanted to play.

She placed a palm on Kash's chest, between her breasts, and gently pushed her to sit on the edge of the bed. "Tell me, Kash…do you like to…watch?" Reaching down, she removed one of her heels while she waited for Kash's answer. She moved slowly, provocatively, then tossed the shoe casually aside.

Kash smiled and nodded.

"Thought so." Isabel peeled off her other shoe and did the same. Next, she put one hand on each hip and slipped her fingers beneath her panties, ready to peel them off. But she paused, enjoying the way Kash was eyeing her. A muscle in Kash's jaw jumped as she waited for her to remove that final barrier to an unobstructed view. "I like it when you watch. Of course, as long as you're not taking pictures that you shouldn't…" She couldn't help the one reminder of the hot-tub photos, but her remark carried only a hint of reproach.

"Never again. I'm *so* sorry, Isabel." Her voice was sincere.

"Apology accepted. I might have a way you can make it up to me," Isabel said teasingly.

Kash's eyes were fixed on her panties. "Anything. Anything at all. Now, please take them off. *Please*. Take them off now and come here." *Or I'll have to rip them off you. Really, I will.*

At the urgency in Kash's voice, Isabel took mercy, or perhaps she, too, could simply wait no longer. She slid the panties quickly down her thighs and off and stood naked before Kash, her legs slightly apart. Her cheeks were flushed, and Kash could see she was breathing fast. But her eyes showed the depth of her desire and it was that—the undisguised hunger, the unrelenting need every bit as intense as her own—that made her clit begin to throb as Isabel started toward her.

Kash caught her scent just before they touched, a mixture of perfume and arousal that sent her blood roaring through her veins, the noise in her head from it deafening. She put her hands on Isabel's hips and held her there at arm's length for a few moments to appreciate both her breasts—which were roughly at eye level from where she was sitting—and also, so close, the fine silky hairs at the apex of Isabel's legs. Her mouth watered. *God, I need to taste you. So bad, so fucking bad I'll die if I don't.*

Isabel's hands were in her hair, fierce against her scalp. Kash knew Isabel was desperate, too, like she was. It was too much. *Too much.* It was driving her crazy. *Enough.*

She spun Isabel around and put her hands purposefully on Isabel's ass, caressing her firmly, thrilling at the soft skin and the eager response of Isabel's body, pressing back into her touch. She teased her with a glancing fingertip up the inside of her thigh and heard Isabel moan as she spread her legs, inviting more.

Yes, Isabel. Soon. I can see. I know.

Kash smoothed her hands over Isabel's back, then stood and wrapped her arms around Isabel's waist, reversing their positions until Isabel faced the bed. She could tell how turned on Isabel was by her rapid breathing, and she had no thought, no reason now, no need but the primal need to taste Isabel's desire, to discover for herself the effect she was having on the woman who had captured her heart.

She pressed forward into Isabel, her nipples so hard and sensitized they sent a wave of pleasure through her with each brush against that lightly freckled back. Pushing more insistently, she curved her body to Isabel's until Isabel was bent over the bed, supporting her weight on her outstretched hands.

Isabel's legs were trembling in anticipation and her scent hung thick in the air, a heady siren's call. Kash shifted, kissing her way down Isabel's body, her hands making a path along her back, hips, and legs, as she reached her knees.

Ignoring her own clit's demand for attention, she gently urged Isabel's legs farther apart, fingertips tracing through the soft triangle of hair as she savored the sight and smell of this moment, one she had imagined often during their time apart.

But never in those daydreams had she come close to how she felt now that the real thing was at hand. *So wet. All for me. Only for me.*

Her tongue stroked the length of Isabel's sex, tasting her, exploring and memorizing how her body responded. She delighted in the way Isabel moaned and moved and sighed.

But all too soon, Isabel stopped her—pulling away unexpectedly, panting for air, until she was sitting on the edge of the bed. Her pupils were so dilated the irises were thin bands of blue. "Not...not yet." Her voice was gravel thick and unsteady. "Not yet."

"Fuck, Isabel," she groaned. "You taste so good. *So* hard to stop..." Kash made fists of her hands to keep from giving in to the driving urgency to regain control. She wanted to make Isabel come right then, and the denial of that desire, even briefly, both frustrated and exhilarated her.

"Soon," Isabel promised as she threaded one hand through Kash's hair. "It's…it's so much…" she said breathily. "So intense. I just want it to last."

"Isabel…" Kash stood and tried to force her racing heart to slow, but it was a useless endeavor. She was beyond the point of no return, well beyond, in the danger zone, in fact—at risk of imminent spontaneous combustion, she was certain.

There was nothing else to do. She took Isabel's hand and placed it atop the open zipper of her trousers. "Take them off."

Isabel's hands were immediately on her hips, pushing her pants down and away, leaving her in a black thong.

"Oh, God, I do love that, Kash." Isabel ran her hands over Kash's muscular thighs to her ass, fingertips following the erotic frame of the string.

Kash shuddered involuntarily and pressed her legs together, feeling a sudden surge in the moisture between them. The pressure for release was so acute she worried she would come at the first glancing touch of Isabel's mouth, but she could stand no further delay. "Off," she pleaded in a hoarse croak.

Isabel removed the final barrier between them and slipped off the bed to kneel in front of her as Kash spread her legs. She could feel warm exhalations on her stomach as she took Isabel's head in her hands and urged her forward.

Isabel's arms encircled her thighs, trapping her, as that wonderful mouth slowly descended. The throbbing in her clit intensified with each puff of breath, stroke of tongue, and nip of teeth, until the sensation was beyond unbearable.

More forcefully, she led Isabel's face where she needed it, her fists in Isabel's hair, the anticipation dreadful, her body singing out for deliverance.

And when it came, finally, that sweep of tongue across her clit, the sweetest of caresses across the very core of her, her whole being cried out with the joy of it. She felt almost airborne for an instant, lifted out of her body, until the next stroke brought her crashing back to earth, every cell in agony for *more*. She needed so much more. But she couldn't find words to ask.

She pressed harder against the back of Isabel's head as she pushed her pelvis forward, a slow, easy rhythm against Isabel's mouth. Isabel grasped her ass, fondled her, matched the rhythm of her thrusts, and soon her tongue was also laving her, firmly in sync. Her touch was exquisite, torturously exquisite, and she gave herself over to it, let it build and take her with it, higher and higher, until she could bear no more.

Sounds escaped her—a grunt, a whimper, a wail of anguish—and then Isabel took her, pushed three fingers into her and drove her forward, then sucked her hard and shattered her, sent her into a maelstrom of feeling that tore through her and blew her apart, and left her raw and gasping in its wake.

Collapsing on her back on the bed, she opened her arms and Isabel slipped into them, coming to rest half atop Kash, head nestled into the crook of her shoulder and one leg casually across her thigh.

"Christ, Isabel, you wasted me on the first go," she griped good-naturedly, still pondering how easy it had been to let go completely with Isabel, easier than she'd imagined it would be. But then, really nothing to do with Isabel had been what she had expected, from their first meeting until this moment.

And thank God for that. Somehow, Isabel had slipped past all of Kash's cynicism and carefully built defenses and had gotten her to trust again and, perhaps even more importantly, to dream again. She had shown her there was more to life than the enviable-looking but ultimately unsatisfying indulgent lifestyle she had fallen into.

In recent weeks, Kash had allowed herself to imagine the possibilities, and she had been somewhat surprised to find herself getting so excited about the prospect of sharing simple things with Isabel—things that ordinary people took for granted: Coffee in the morning. A summer sunset at the beach. Most of all, she had wondered how it might feel to wake up with Isabel in her arms, perhaps as they were right now. The position was unfamiliar, but wonderfully so. *Yup. I can get used to this. As easy as falling off a log.*

Isabel's mouth against her neck, first warm breaths, now wet kisses, renewed the throbbing in her groin before it had barely subsided, assisted by the circles that Isabel's fingertips were tracing on her stomach and abdomen.

"Well, maybe I'm not quite wasted *yet*." She caught Isabel's hand with her own and rolled them over until she was lying on top, one leg between Isabel's thighs, resting her weight on her elbows. And then she was kissing her with every bit of the wellspring of feeling that Isabel had stirred in her.

Isabel kissed her soundly back, writhing beneath her, her nails raking Kash's back to leave little half-moon crescents in her ass as she urged Kash's thigh more firmly against her sex. She moaned into their enjoined mouths, and the unexpected ferocity of her passion loosened an answering response in Kash.

Kash shifted until she was lying between Isabel's legs. "I have to be inside you." Her words came out more demand than request, but Isabel's face was nothing but certain and eager enthusiasm.

"Yes, you do." Isabel tilted her hips and opened her legs farther to allow Kash better access. "I'm so ready for you."

Kash shifted to one side, to run her hand down the length of Isabel's body, from cheek to neck to breast—where she paused, to relish the weight of it in her palm and to tease the nipple with a fingernail—then firmly down ribs, stomach, abdomen, to the soft hair below. As she rediscovered the abundant wetness she knew was there, she found Isabel's other breast. It was like coming home.

Isabel cried out, a breathy "Oh!" of pleasure, and arched her body off the bed as Kash brushed over her clit. "Oh, Kash. I need you so bad. Please!"

"I'm right here." She grazed Isabel's nipple with her teeth more firmly as she let her fingers play across Isabel's sex, then eased into her.

Isabel was open, and ready, and accepted her with an upward thrust of her hips. "Mmm, yes, so nice."

Kash worked her up with slow and steady penetrations, varying the depth, enjoying the way Isabel's body responded—welcoming her with a rocking of her hips, urging her on with a satisfied moan of delight.

She had touched so many women that she knew what to do, and where, and when, with almost clinical accuracy—able to read even the most subtle signs and then adjust her technique to ensure maximum gratification. Kash kept Isabel on the brink until she begged for mercy, then sent her crashing over and nearly came again herself at the joy of feeling those hard, quick spasms around her hand.

Isabel relaxed, spent and panting for breath, but clutching Kash to herself as the aftertremors of her climax subsided. "I...I so wish I could tell you how you make me feel. Like no one. Like never."

"I'm glad." Kash gently kissed the thin sheen of perspiration on Isabel's neck, then licked her way slowly to Isabel's ear. She couldn't remember when she'd ever felt this totally and absolutely content. "That works for me, too," she whispered. "Like no one. Like never."

"You...you mean that?" The uncertainty in Isabel's voice, so unexpected at this moment, shook Kash from her sated semistupor.

She pushed herself up on her elbows to look down at Isabel. "Of course!" She let her tone add, *How can you ask that?* and *Don't be ridiculous!*

Isabel appeared both relieved and chagrined. "I know that you've had a lot of...*experiences* with women...to put it mildly." She smiled and rolled her eyes, and Kash chuckled.

Isabel continued, more seriously. "And I know that usually...well, that it's not usually like this. I'm glad it's...that it's *good* different, and not *weird* different. If that makes sense."

"Not just good different. *Great* different," Kash agreed, kissing Isabel lightly on the lips, amazed and grateful for her sensitivity. "Of course, *you* may not think so when you wake up with me crowding you because I'm not used to sleeping with someone—"

"Never," Isabel promised, hugging her tightly. "I want you to know, Kash, that...that you can be yourself with me, too. I mean...not that you *aren't*. But if you..." Her cheeks colored, and Kash thought her sudden shyness absolutely adorable. "What I mean to say, is...that I don't want you to feel as though you have to...to rein in your passionate nature with me."

"So you think I'm reining in, do you?" Kash teased before she claimed Isabel's mouth in another scorching kiss. She shifted her weight until they were once again groin to groin, positioned so even the slightest rocking of their bodies would create a pleasant friction for them both.

But just as she started that fire again, she felt Isabel stiffen slightly beneath her and pull her mouth away, obviously intent on making her point. Kash raised up on her elbows again and looked at Isabel curiously.

"When you kiss me like that, you make it hard to think, let alone complete a sentence." And it was true that Isabel's expression right then could best be described as besotted.

"And that's bad?" Kash asked, kissing her again. She very much liked putting that look on Isabel's face.

"Mmm, great," Isabel sighed, long moments later when they needed to breathe. "What was I saying?"

"Something about passion," Kash answered, nuzzling her neck with little bites.

"Oh yeah." Isabel wrapped her arms tighter around Kash. "I guess what I meant to say, was…I *like* it when you…you know, take control. When you made me come in that alley, in Rome…God, it was *so* exciting." She was shy again, her voice a whisper. "Not that I'm saying I want to run out and have sex in public every other week…but I do want to encourage your more…spontaneous and forceful impulses."

"Exciting, huh?" Kash asked, thrusting her hips forward and glorying in Isabel's answering gasp of pleasure. "I was afraid you'd regret it, later. The way it happened."

"*Oh,* no." Isabel shook her head purposefully, then repeated their earlier reference with a smile. "Different for me, yes, I'll admit. But *great* different." She bucked her hips, giving Kash a jolt of pleasure-pain on her sensitive clit.

Kash had imagined doing a lot of things with Isabel, and *to* Isabel, and the affirmation that there would be no barriers to their pleasure immediately made her think about which to choose first. "I'm glad to hear that, Isabel. Very glad. You know I'd never hurt you."

"Of course," Isabel answered at once, gazing deep into her eyes. "I trust you, Kash, with all my heart. I have from the start, though I'm not sure why. More instinct, I guess, than anything else." She caressed Kash's back with the lightest of touches. "Loving you took only slightly longer."

She said it so casually that Kash answered the same way, though the intensity of the look between them belied the insignificance of the exchange. She wasn't used to talking about love. "For me, too. I think I fell in love with you long before I dared to admit it to myself."

"I was so afraid I'd never see you again." Isabel remembered how bleak her future had seemed without Kash in it. "I knew I'd made an impression on you when I saw the article—which was incredibly sweet and wonderful, by the way—but it said you were on the other side of the world."

"I was," Kash confirmed. "But you're certainly worth interrupting my trip for."

Isabel tried not to show the sudden ache inside of her that the words evoked. "That sounds like you'll be leaving again."

"Well, of course," Kash said offhandedly. "You *are* the one who convinced me to pursue this photo project of mine, so that shouldn't surprise you."

"Oh, I'm not surprised." Isabel tried to smile, but she had to force her show of cheer. "It's wonderful that you're doing this, Kash. I know it's been a dream of yours for a long time." Though it was the truth, Isabel didn't at all relish the idea of being separated from Kash again, for who knew how long. But apparently what she wanted and what Kash wanted, weren't compatible.

"I'm not in any hurry, though," Kash added casually, running a finger along Isabel's chin. "I can wait until you can get away, too."

Say what? Isabel pushed Kash off her and raised up on her side and narrowed her eyes to look over at her as Kash began to laugh. "What did you say? As soon as I can get away?"

"Well, of course. I'm not planning to go anywhere without you," Kash said. She wrapped her arm around Isabel's waist and pulled her back against her body, but this time with Isabel lying half atop her. "Think the cakes and swimmers and Gillian can get along without you for a few months while we travel and figure things out? I told you I wanted to talk about *us*. I mean, you *said* there were a lot of places you always dreamed of seeing. We can start right at number one, wherever you like. As long as I have my cameras and you, I'm golden."

Isabel was beaming. "Oh, Kash. It sounds wonderful. But…but I can't. I can't let you—"

"Hush." Kash pulled Isabel tight and silenced her objections with a long kiss. By the time she ended it Isabel had a dreamy expression, swollen lips, and badly mussed hair. "Don't let something irrelevant like money keep us from being together. I'm loaded. Let's enjoy it, huh?"

Isabel bit the inside of her lip and nodded, her eyes shining.

"So…does that mean you're okay with coming with me?" Kash's heart soared.

"Coming with you? Oh, yes. I like the sound of that," Isabel said very provocatively as she raised up on all fours and slowly turned her body one hundred eighty degrees above Kash, until they were positioned so they could taste each other. "I want to come with you, Kash. Wherever. Whenever. However possible. Starting right now."

About the Author

Kim Baldwin has been a writer for three decades, following up a twenty-year hitch in network news with a much more satisfying turn penning lesbian fiction. She has published five novels with Bold Strokes Books: the intrigue/romances *Flight Risk* and *Hunter's Pursuit* (a finalist for a Golden Crown Literary Society Award in 2005) and the romances *Force of Nature*, *Whitewater Rendezvous* (a finalist for a GCLS Award in 2007), and *Focus of Desire*. She has also contributed short stories to four BSB anthologies: The Lambda Literary Award–winning Erotic *Interludes 2: Stolen Moments*, *Erotic Interludes 3: Lessons in Love*, IPPY and GCLS Award–winning *Erotic Interludes 4: Extreme Passions*, and *Erotic Interludes 5: Road Games*. She lives in the north woods of Michigan.

Visit her Web site at www.kimbaldwin.com.

Books Available From Bold Strokes Books

House of Clouds by KI Thompson. A sweeping saga of an impassioned romance between a Northern spy and a Southern sympathizer, set amidst the upheaval of a nation under siege. (978-1-933110-94-3)

Winds of Fortune by Radclyffe. Provincetown local Deo Camara agrees to rehab Dr. Bonita Burgoyne's historic home, but she never said anything about mending her heart. (978-1-933110-93-6)

Focus of Desire by Kim Baldwin. Isabel Sterling is surprised when she wins a photography contest, but no more than photographer Natasha Kashnikova. Their promo tour becomes a ticket to romance. (978-1-933110-92-9)

Blind Leap by Diane and Jacob Anderson-Minshall. A Golden Gate Bridge suicide becomes suspect when a filmmaker's camera shows a different story. Yoshi Yakamota and the Blind Eye Detective Agency uncover evidence that could be worth killing for. (978-1-933110-91-2)

Wall of Silence, 2nd ed. by Gabrielle Goldsby. Life takes a dangerous turn when jaded police detective Foster Everett meets Riley Medeiros, a woman who isn't afraid to discover the truth no matter the cost. (978-1-933110-90-5)

Mistress of the Runes by Andrews & Austin. Passion ignites between two women with ties to ancient secrets, contemporary mysteries, and a shared quest for the meaning of life. (978-1-933110-89-9)

Sheridan's Fate by Gun Brooke. A dynamic, erotic romance between physiotherapist Lark Mitchell and businesswoman Sheridan Ward set in the scorching hot days and humid, steamy nights of San Antonio. (978-1-933110-88-2)

Vulture's Kiss by Justine Saracen. Archeologist Valerie Foret, heir to a terrifying task, returns in a powerful desert adventure set in Egypt and Jerusalem. (978-1-933110-87-5)

Rising Storm by JLee Meyer. The sequel to *First Instinct* takes our heroines on a dangerous journey instead of the honeymoon they'd planned. (978-1-933110-86-8)

Not Single Enough by Grace Lennox. A funny, sexy modern romance about two lonely women who bond over the unexpected and fall in love along the way. (978-1-933110-85-1)

Such a Pretty Face by Gabrielle Goldsby. A sexy, sometimes humorous, sometimes biting contemporary romance that gently exposes the damage to heart and soul when we fail to look beneath the surface for what truly matters. (978-1-933110-84-4)

Second Season by Ali Vali. A romance set in New Orleans amidst betrayal, Hurricane Katrina, and the new beginnings hardship and heartbreak sometimes make possible. (978-1-933110-83-7)

Hearts Aflame by Ronica Black. A poignant, erotic romance between a hard-driving businesswoman and a solitary vet. Packed with adventure and set in the harsh beauty of the Arizona countryside. (978-1-933110-82-0)

Red Light by JD Glass. Tori forges her path as an EMT in the New York City 911 system while discovering what matters most to herself and the woman she loves. (978-1-933110-81-3)

Honor Under Siege by Radclyffe. Secret Service agent Cameron Roberts struggles to protect her lover while searching for a traitor who just may be another woman with a claim on her heart. (978-1-933110-80-6)

Dark Valentine by Jennifer Fulton. Danger and desire fuel a high-stakes cat-and-mouse game when an attorney and an endangered witness team up to thwart a killer. (978-1-933110-79-0)

Sequestered Hearts by Erin Dutton. A popular artist suddenly goes into seclusion, a reluctant reporter wants to know why, and a heart locked away yearns to be set free. (978-1-933110-78-3)

Erotic Interludes 5: Road Games, ed. by Radclyffe and Stacia Seaman. Adventure, "sport," and sex on the road—hot stories of travel adventures and games of seduction. (978-1-933110-77-6)

The Spanish Pearl by Catherine Friend. On a trip to Spain, Kate Vincent is accidentally transported back in time—an epic saga spiced with humor, lust, and danger. (978-1-933110-76-9)

Lady Knight by L-J Baker. Loyalty and honor clash with love and ambition in a medieval world of magic when female knight Riannon meets Lady Eleanor. (978-1-933110-75-2)

Dark Dreamer by Jennifer Fulton. Best-selling horror author Rowe Devlin falls under the spell of psychic Phoebe Temple. A Dark Vista romance. (978-1-933110-74-5)

Come and Get Me by Julie Cannon. Elliott Foster isn't used to pursuing women, but alluring attorney Lauren Collier makes her change her mind. (978-1-933110-73-8)

Blind Curves by Diane and Jacob Anderson-Minshall. Private eye Yoshi Yakamota comes to the aid of her ex-lover Velvet Erickson in the first Blind Eye mystery. (978-1-933110-72-1)

The Devil Unleashed by Ali Vali. As the heat of violence rises, so does the passion. A Casey Clan crime saga. (1-933110-61-9)

Dynasty of Rogues by Jane Fletcher. It's hate at first sight for Ranger Riki Sadiq and her new patrol corporal, Tanya Coppelli—except for their undeniable attraction. (978-1-933110-71-4)

Running With the Wind by Nell Stark. Sailing instructor Corrie Marsten has signed off on love until she meets Quinn Davies—one woman she can't ignore. (978-1-933110-70-7)

More Than Paradise by Jennifer Fulton. Two women battle danger, risk all, and find in each other an unexpected ally and an unforgettable love. (978-1-933110-69-1)

Flight Risk by Kim Baldwin. For Blayne Keller, being in the wrong place at the wrong time just might turn out to be the best thing that ever happened to her. (978-1-933110-68-4)

Rebel's Quest: Supreme Constellations Book Two by Gun Brooke. On a world torn by war, two women discover a love that defies all boundaries. (978-1-933110-67-7)

Punk and Zen by JD Glass. Angst, sex, love, rock. Trace, Candace, Francesca…Samantha. Losing control—and finding the truth within. BSB Victory Editions. (1-933110-66-X)

When Dreams Tremble by Radclyffe. Two women whose lives turned out far differently than they'd once imagined discover that sometimes the shape of the future can only be found in the past. (1-933110-64-3)

Stellium in Scorpio by Andrews & Austin. The passionate reunion of two powerful women on the glitzy Las Vegas Strip, where everything is an illusion and love is a gamble. (1-933110-65-1)

Burning Dreams by Susan Smith. The chronicle of the challenges faced by a young drag king and an older woman who share a love "outside the bounds." (1-933110-62-7)

Fresh Tracks by Georgia Beers. Seven women, seven days. A lot can happen when old friends, lovers, and a new girl in town get together in the mountains. (1-933110-63-5)

Too Close to Touch by Georgia Beers. Kylie O'Brien believes in true love and is willing to wait for it. It doesn't matter one damn bit that Gretchen, her new and off-limits boss, has a voice as rich and smooth as melted chocolate. It absolutely doesn't… (1-933110-47-3)

The Empress and the Acolyte by Jane Fletcher. Jemeryl and Tevi fight to protect the very fabric of their world…time. Lyremouth Chronicles Book Three. (1-933110-60-0)

First Instinct by JLee Meyer. When high-stakes security fraud leads to murder, one woman flees for her life while another risks her heart to protect her. (1-933110-59-7)

Erotic Interludes 4: Extreme Passions, ed. by Radclyffe and Stacia Seaman. Thirty of today's hottest erotica writers set the pages aflame with love, lust, and steamy liaisons. (1-933110-58-9)

Broken Wings by L-J Baker. When Rye Woods, a fairy, meets the beautiful dryad Flora Withe, her libido, as squashed and hidden as her wings, reawakens along with her heart. (1-933110-55-4)

Whitewater Rendezvous by Kim Baldwin. Two women on a wilderness kayak adventure—Chaz Herrick, a laid-back outdoorswoman, and Megan Maxwell, a workaholic news executive—discover that true love may be nothing at all like they imagined. (1-933110-38-4)

Unexpected Ties by Gina L. Dartt. With death before dessert, Kate Shannon and Nikki Harris are swept up in another tale of danger and romance. (1-933110-56-2)

Tristaine Rises by Cate Culpepper. Brenna, Jesstin, and the Amazons of Tristaine face their greatest challenge for survival. (1-933110-50-3)

Force of Nature by Kim Baldwin. From tornados to forest fires, the forces of nature conspire to bring Gable McCoy and Erin Richards close to danger, and closer to each other. (1-933110-23-6)

Passion's Bright Fury by Radclyffe. When a trauma surgeon and a filmmaker become reluctant allies on the battleground between life and death, passion strikes without warning. (1-933110-54-6)

Sleep of Reason by Rose Beecham. Nothing is as it seems when Detective Jude Devine finds herself caught up in a small-town soap opera. And her rocky relationship with forensic pathologist Dr. Mercy Westmoreland just got a lot harder. (1-933110-53-8)

Grave Silence by Rose Beecham. Detective Jude Devine's investigation of a series of ritual murders is complicated by her torrid affair with the golden girl of Southwestern forensic pathology, Dr. Mercy Westmoreland. (1-933110-25-2)

Carly's Sound by Ali Vali. Poppy Valente and Julia Johnson form a bond of friendship that lays the foundation for something more, until Poppy's past comes back to haunt her—literally. A poignant romance about love and renewal. (1-933110-45-7)

Of Drag Kings and the Wheel of Fate by Susan Smith. A blind date in a drag club leads to an unlikely romance. (1-933110-51-1)

Sweet Creek by Lee Lynch. A celebration of the enduring nature of love, friendship, and community in the quirky, heart-warming lesbian community of Waterfall Falls. (1-933110-29-5)

Hunter's Pursuit by Kim Baldwin. A raging blizzard, a mountain hideaway, and a killer-for-hire set a scene for disaster—or desire—when Katarzyna Demetrious rescues a beautiful stranger. (1-933110-09-0)

Sword of the Guardian by Merry Shannon. Princess Shasta's bold new bodyguard has a secret that could change both of their lives. *He* is actually a *she*. A passionate romance filled with courtly intrigue, chivalry, and devotion. (1-933110-36-8)

100th Generation by Justine Saracen. Ancient curses, modern-day villains, and a most intriguing woman who keeps appearing when least expected lead archeologist Valerie Foret on the adventure of her life. (1-933110-48-1)

The Traitor and the Chalice by Jane Fletcher. Tevi and Jemeryl risk all in the race to uncover a traitor. The Lyremouth Chronicles Book Two. (1-933110-43-0)

Punk Like Me by JD Glass. Twenty-one-year-old Nina writes lyrics and plays guitar in the rock band Adam's Rib, and she doesn't always play by the rules. And oh yeah—she has a way with the girls. (1-933110-40-6)

Forever Found by JLee Meyer. Can time, tragedy, and shattered trust destroy a love that seemed destined? When chance reunites two childhood friends separated by tragedy, the past resurfaces to determine the shape of their future. (1-933110-37-6)

The Devil Inside by Ali Vali. Derby Cain Casey, head of a New Orleans crime organization, runs the family business with guts and grit, and no one crosses her. No one, that is, until Emma Verde claims her heart and turns her world upside down. (1-933110-30-9)

Erotic Interludes 3: Lessons in Love, ed. by Radclyffe and Stacia Seaman. Sign on for a class in love…the best lesbian erotica writers take us to "school." (1-9331100-39-2)

Turn Back Time by Radclyffe. Pearce Rifkin and Wynter Thompson have nothing in common but a shared passion for surgery. They clash at every opportunity, especially when matters of the heart are suddenly at stake. (1-933110-34-1)

Promising Hearts by Radclyffe. Dr. Vance Phelps lost everything in the War Between the States and arrives in New Hope, Montana, with no hope of happiness and no desire for anything except forgetting—until she meets Mae, a frontier madam. (1-933110-44-9)

Innocent Hearts by Radclyffe. In a wild and unforgiving land, two women learn about love, passion, and the wonders of the heart. (1-933110-21-X)

Justice Served by Radclyffe. Lieutenant Rebecca Frye and her lover, Dr. Catherine Rawlings, embark on a deadly game of hide-and-seek with an underworld kingpin who traffics in human souls. (1-933110-15-5)

Justice in the Shadows by Radclyffe. In a shadow world of secrets and lies, Detective Sergeant Rebecca Frye and her lover, Dr. Catherine Rawlings, join forces in the elusive search for justice. (1-933110-03-1)

A Matter of Trust by Radclyffe. JT Sloan is a cybersleuth who doesn't like attachments. Michael Lassiter is leaving her husband, and she needs Sloan's expertise to safeguard her company. It should just be business—but it turns into much more. (1-933110-33-3)

Storms of Change by Radclyffe. In the continuing saga of the Provincetown Tales, duty and love are at odds as Reese and Tory face their greatest challenge. (1-933110-57-0)

Distant Shores, Silent Thunder by Radclyffe. Dr. Tory King—along with the women who love her—is forced to examine the boundaries of love, friendship, and the ties that transcend time. (1-933110-08-2)

Beyond the Breakwater by Radclyffe. One Provincetown summer, three women learn the true meaning of love, friendship, and family. (1-933110-06-6)

Safe Harbor by Radclyffe. A mysterious newcomer, a reclusive doctor, and a troubled gay teenager learn about love, friendship, and trust during one tumultuous summer in Provincetown. (1-933110-13-9)

shadowland by Radclyffe. In a world on the far edge of desire, two women are drawn together by power, passion, and dark pleasures. An erotic romance. (1-933110-11-2)

Love's Masquerade by Radclyffe. Plunged into the indistinguishable realms of fiction, fantasy, and hidden desires, Auden Frost is forced to question all she believes about the nature of love. (1-933110-14-7)

Honor Reclaimed by Radclyffe. In the aftermath of 9/11, Secret Service Agent Cameron Roberts and Blair Powell close ranks with a trusted few to find the would-be assassins who nearly claimed Blair's life. (1-933110-18-X)

Honor Guards by Radclyffe. In a wild flight for their lives, the president's daughter and those who are sworn to protect her wage a desperate struggle for survival. (1-933110-01-5)

Love & Honor by Radclyffe. The president's daughter and her lover are faced with difficult choices as they battle a tangled web of Washington intrigue for…love and honor. (1-933110-10-4)

Honor Bound by Radclyffe. Secret Service Agent Cameron Roberts and Blair Powell face political intrigue, a clandestine threat to Blair's safety, and the seemingly irreconcilable personal differences that force them ever farther apart. (1-933110-20-1)

Above All, Honor by Radclyffe. Secret Service Agent Cameron Roberts fights her desire for the one woman she can't have—Blair Powell, the daughter of the president of the United States. (1-933110-04-X)